ORPHAN'S RITE

Orphan's Rite

M. WARREN ASKINS

Orphan's Rite
M. Warren Askins

Second Edition: 2025

ISBN: 978-1-7341200-7-3 (paperback 2nd edition)
ISBN: 979-8-6930639-2-1 (paperback 1st edition)
ISBN: 978-1-7341200-1-1 (e-book)

Books by M. Warren Askins

Through the Thorns
Ian
The Dead Men are Dying Saga
Beyond the Spire of Navarene
Martyr for Cowards
Orphan's Rite
Ghosts of Halodwyth

For Mikey

Author's Note

For those who have yet to read the works within the *Dead Men are Dying* Universe, here is a very short list to help make this book more accessible.

Laif – An elf, in the nearest traditional sense. You know, tall, slender immortals with pointy ears.

Knotwithstadt – A forest village whose inhabitants were massacred by the Church for not adhering to a strict, new edict that harshly restricted reproduction.

Divine Marks – Humans are sometimes born with a mark (typically adorning the side of the neck) that imbues the bearer with powerful abilities. For instance, a child born with the Warrior's mark will have heightened reflexes and extraordinary strength, as well as a myriad of other gifts pertaining to warfare.

THE ORPHAN

"**C**are to repeat that?" the shopkeep requested, placing his hands on the counter and leaning forward to better hear the laif girl. She had rushed in alone a few minutes prior, setting the bell above the door tinkling wildly, and her meanderings through the three aisles filled with curios had eventually led her to the counter. She had mumbled to him as she tucked her chin into the sizable scarf wrapped around her neck. Her hands were empty and the shopkeep wagered that she didn't have any money to spend, however her eyes held an intensity that she was attempting to express. She mumbled what seemed to be the same phrase again, but frustratingly at the same volume and timbre as before.

"Where are your parents, sweetling?" the man asked with a tinge of concern. The child's only response was to narrow her eyes and critically scan his face. The older man appeared friendly, his round face perfectly shaped for the graying moustache perched atop his upper lip. A wooden plate of game hen and potatoes sat next to the man's elbow, the steam long gone from the meal and most of the bones were picked clean, though it was not entirely apparent as to whether he had finished with the meal yet. A thin coat of coagulated gravy was swirled around the plate where the man had used his spoon to try and snag the three remaining lumps of potato, but had been interrupted when she had entered.

"Listen, you have got to speak up. I can't help you if I can't understand you," the man said, waiting for some sort of intelligent response, working his jaw impatiently. "If you're looking to get warm, feel free to stand over by the stove, but once that's done if you aren't aiming to make a purchase, I'd be grateful if you scuttled off elsewhere." The laif girl appeared completely focused on his half eaten dinner and was not paying attention to him in the least. The shopkeep had developed a keen sense for detecting a grift after several experiences with scoundrels in the past, and while this girl did not have that type of air, it was possible she was involved in a scheme using her as some kind of distraction.

"If you don't tell me what it is that you want..." he trailed off as he noticed a pair of Church guardsmen passing by his front windows, intently tracking footprints in the recently fallen snow.

Much like most of the populace, the man was not heavily in favor of the Church at the moment, especially after that unreasonable edict and the ensuing slaughter at Knotwithstadt. And the way the Church was treating all the orphans from that brutal business, the ones that sur-vived...*Orphans!* The shopkeep hurriedly turned back to the girl, but she was not where he had last seen her.

One of the guards peered into the window and the shopkeep met his gaze with a reassuring nod, hoping to indicate "good morning" not "please enter." Apparently nodding etiquette was not a learned skill amongst current law enforcement, as the guard immediately pressed inside under the tinkling bell.

"Lots of junk in here," the guard sneered, passing a shelf and gingerly lifting a stuffed gremlin with a monocle on its eye and a lantern in its hand.

"Well, it's a curio shop, friend," the clerk replied po-litely, absentmindedly reaching for his dinner plate, which like the girl, was not where he last saw it.

"Curio?" the guard queried, placing the gremlin onto the counter.

"Curiosity shop," the clerk stated. "Knick-knacks and nonsense. Some things of great value to some and utterly worthless to others," he elaborated as the bell tinkled again, ushering in the second guard. "For instance, this jeweled blade." The man reached below the counter and produced a dagger with what appeared to be a crude de-piction of a bumblebee as its scabbard.

He held it out to the guard who glanced at it with less than mild amusement. "Looks splendid," the guard said dryly. His face seemed perpetually locked in a sneer as he surveyed the items beyond the counter while his companion was lurking around the aisles, lifting pots and rummaging through chests.

"We seem to have lost a mutt from our kennels," the guard began. "Have you seen one sniffing around this..." he paused, raising an eyebrow to look at the ogre head mounted on the wall with a lit smoking pipe protruding from its mouth. A tendril of smoke swirled from the bowl and the guard wrinkled his face and shook his head. "This," he continued, waving a hand, "Whatever you called this foul store."

"A curiosity shop."

"Yes, well, the mongrel's prints appear to lead to your doorstep," the guard said. He lifted his hand waist high. "The creature stands about this tall with a scarf wrapped nearly up to its pointy ears. More than likely looks like any other pathetic stray."

"Oh, well," the shopkeep murmured uncomfortably, scratching the back of his neck, "you two are the first customers to darken my doorway all afternoon. And to be perfectly honest, we don't allow animals into the shop, so I would be grateful..."

"Don't," The guard cut him off. "Do not waste our time. This particular whelp bit the hand that fed it, and anyone suspected of harboring such a creature will answer to the Arbiter." The man watched his words register as the clerk suddenly became tense and nervous. "I didn't catch your name?" the guard continued, his sneer growing more pronounced.

"Neil," the shopkeep replied apprehensively, tucking the dagger away. He chose his next words carefully, knowing that a lie could land him in front of the Judge. "I haven't entertained any strays, mutts, or whelps all day."

"You won't mind if we take a peek then?" the guard queried, obviously dissatisfied with the response. "We'll need to check your stock room as well." He flicked the gremlin's nose and stared nastily at the keeper. Neil opened his hands in surrender and nodded his head with a forced smile.

"Good," the guard said, hastily skirting the counter and making for the back room. The other guard had finally wound her way to the last aisle and was standing before the multitudes of books in front of the window. Neil was unsure as to whether she was admiring the expansive collection of manuscripts or if she was peering outside, monitoring for a possible escape.

He took a few strides toward her and followed her gaze down the row of books.

"They're all originals," he said proudly, tapping a dusty shelf. "Every last one of them. Each one is absolutely priceless." He rubbed his fingertips together, working the grime off.

"I do enjoy a good tale," she murmured with reverence, her eyes sweeping side to side. "Perhaps I will venture back here on another day."

Neil gave her a nod and walked back to the counter. "I hear that we are to be receiving a sheriff soon?" he asked at length, attempting to fill the silence.

He heard an exasperated groan in reply, and he took that as a sign to continue. "It has been generations since this district has had any formal law. I don't believe even my great grandfather would be able to recall the last one."

"It is utter foolishness," the female guard grumbled with disdain, holding a leather-bound tome and thumbing through the pages. "The Church has been overseeing the enforcement of laws for ages and has been doing a pretty decent job of it, if you ask me." She regarded the pages of the tome for a few more seconds before slamming the bindings shut with a satisfying thud, sending a cloud of dust upward and tainting the air where the sunlight poured in.

"I was pondering what it will mean for people such as yourself and your accomplice back there," Neil said, gesturing to the back stockroom, the door left ajar.

"It means some dipshit is going to serve a term as *sheriff*, and apparently nothing much else will change for us," she scoffed, approaching the clerk. "Instead of the Church giving orders we will be taking our orders from her. Well, those of us who decide to remain as guards at least."

"Oh, is service voluntary? I mean— " his words were cut short by a shriek from behind. The clerk and guard briefly locked eyes, then both wheeled around to face the stockroom. Standing at the threshold was the sneering guard, a chunk of the laif girl's hair clenched in his fist, painfully hoisting her up on tiptoes. The female guard pushed past the shopkeep and began clapping her hands in delight.

"Looky what I found!" the male guard crowed, his sneer evolving into a wicked grin. "Seems like our evening hunt has been cut short, Briel," he remarked while roughly shaking his quarry. Tears trickled down the girl's face as she sucked in air through her clenched teeth while half-heartedly swinging both fists at the man's groin. One fist nearly connected causing the guard to yank up and violently twist the locks of hair in his grip, forcing out another shriek from the child.

"She was back there in a corner eating table scraps like the wretched little mutt that she is." The guard fixed a hard gaze on Neil, tossing the dinner plate in his direction. "So it was chicken and potatoes on the menu tonight, eh? You can lie to me all you want, you bloody clown, but try and pull that with the Judge and see what happens," he threatened. "I'll be sure to make a special notation for you in my report," the guard finished with a wink, the words tinged with malice.

Neil raised his hands in submission. "Listen, listen," he said, trying to avoid the girl's desperate stare. "She came in only five minutes before you did. I don't even know her name. I thought she was cold and offered her warmth by my stove. That's all! I swear! We don't need to involve

Amyr in this!" he pleaded anxiously, taking a step toward the guard. "Let's be reasonable here."

"Get back to your shop," Briel stated, placing a hand on the man's chest. "This no longer concerns you."

"I just..." the clerk began, unsure of what to say. "Alright," he acquiesced, sending the girl an apologetic shrug before turning back to his duties.

Neil heard the sneering guard order the horses brought around. In short order, the rear door to the loading docks creaked open amidst a myriad of whimpering and begging. Briel brushed past him on her way out and Neil firmly closed the stock room door, effectively muting the pitiful sounds. His emotions were a confusing cloud of guilt and fear that entered his lungs, pervading his soul, causing him to endure a spell of panicked suffocation. The tinkling bell indicated that Briel had left the building, but he hardly took notice as he gripped his chest. His eyes were drawn to the yellow and black rings on the ridiculous bumblebee dagger tucked on a shelf below the counter.

The man was unsure how long he stood there debating if he should become the violent man that he never had been nor wanted to be. The horses passed the front windows as he stood locked in indecision, and the group would be long gone if he waited much longer.

"Just hold out a few more minutes, old man," he whispered to himself. "You're no hero." He could not dispel the image of the helpless laif struggling against the iron grip of that cruel guard. Deep in thought, he pounded his fist on his thigh, hardly noticing when he snatched up the blade and whirled to the back door.

What are you doing, you fool? His good sense tried to hold him back as he hurried through the stock room. He had not noticed the slick patch of gravy on the floor and suddenly his world was sailing upward. As soon as the back of his skull bounced off the floor, he spiraled into unconsciousness.

HOW LONG? NEIL SAT UP SLOWLY and raised a hand to touch the back of his head, immediately regretting the decision once his fingertip grazed an elevated lump that caused his teeth to rattle in a shiver of agony. He looked around through bleary eyes, the meager light dribbling through the windows indicating that he had been out cold for at least an hour, if not longer. With a few curses and loud groans, the man gradually reached a standing position.

"Just how hard did you crack your noodle, old man?" he muttered to himself, walking to the exit. Neil could hear voices very clearly coming from behind the store, but questioned his senses. The back alley was not a popular place for folk to meet and typically was silent at this time of the day. As he cautiously approached, it became clear that he was not imagining things. There was definitely more than one voice, and as he congratulated himself on not losing his mind, he heaved the dock door open.

To his surprise, the walls were illuminated by flickering torchlight revealing a startling scene. A man pressing a kerchief over his mouth drew the curio clerk's attention to what appeared to be a dead body slumped against the wall. The street beyond the dock was congested with onlookers and busybodies peering over a handful of Church guards in varying stages of investigation.

One guardsman held his torch aloft while vomiting at the base of the dock staircase, just below Neil's feet. Once the man was finished with the last dry heave, he looked up and bashfully apologized before getting back to the matter at hand. "Did you see anything suspicious tonight, friend?" the guard inquired, wiping his mouth with the back of his vambrace.

All Neil could think to reply was that he had just awoken from a nap, which was not altogether false. After being threatened with judgment earlier, he was not too keen on discussing the details of his day with those who enforced the law.

"Ah," the guard replied, bobbing his head in what appeared to be an exaggerated nod, but then his shoulders heaved and he doubled over renewing the disposal of his most recent meal. Neil gave the man a reassuring pat on the back as he tiptoed past to gain a closer look at the scene. He was still a bit unsteady from his fall, and he stumbled on the cobbles, drawing the attention of several surrounding guards.

"Careful, friend," one guard cautioned, suddenly appearing with a gentle hand to the clerk's chest, urging him back. "I'm not too sure you want to see this."

Neil thumbed toward the shop as he began his reply, "This is my..." he stopped abruptly when he recognized the face of the corpse propped up like a discarded doll. *Briel.* Two symmetrical weeping wounds were apparent on her azure tunic, exactly an inch from each armpit, right below her spaulders. Painful, but likely not lethal. A moment later Neil identified the killing strike. A third equal sized puncture bisected the bridge of the guard's nose, between the eyes. Judging by the stains on the brick facade, she had been standing upright when the weapon had perforated her skull. The eye could easily trace a triangle with the wounds, the locations placed methodically and executed with swift precision.

The guard removed his hand, realizing that it was too late to prevent the shopkeep from witnessing the disturbing mess. "It appears that one was killed by a surgeon," the guard said with a shrug, indicating Briel. "And that one," he paused, rubbing his sternum, clearly uncomfortable, "looks to have been set upon by a pack of faewolves," he finished, tilting his head toward the opposite wall.

Neil gasped and slapped a hand over his mouth when his gaze fell upon the other corpse.

In the fluttering torchlight he recognized the sneer-faced guard now crumpled in a heap. What remained of his head jutted at an awkward angle from the rest of his body. His jaw had been completely torn off and the rest of his face was an exposed crimson skull. The unblinking eyes had been left intact and were somehow completely untarnished by blood, creating a particularly disturbing contrast. It was not possible to even discern which limbs were attached, and which had been simply collected and piled atop the corpse.

~ 2 ~

THE ORACLE

Six weeks, Winter thought as she trudged down the stone steps that led to the crude makeshift holding cells. *Six more weeks, then I will be in charge of this...*

"Hear ya are, my lady," the gaoler said gallantly, handing her what appeared to be a crumpled wad of cogs. As he pressed the lump into her hands, she realized with disdain that they were in actuality the cell keys.

This catastrophe, she concluded in her head, dangling the clutch of mismatched metals. "My deepest thanks, uh," Winter trailed off, noticing the gaoler was much more handsome than the gatekeepers that she usually ran across during her career as a royal guard. Well, to be fair, she had only been a simple guard for a mere three months before she had been promoted, rising through the ranks faster than anyone else in recent known history.

"Kirk," the gaoler finished her sentence, bashfully looking down and kicking a loose pebble.

"Yes, Kirk. Uh, thank you," she coughed and nodded, fumbling with the keys, trying to loosen them for use.

Kirk reached out and she yielded the rattling mess to him. "Here. It's this one with the wooden crown," he said, displaying the key after masterfully releasing it from the grip of its determined mates. "You have to jiggle it real good at first. The lock sometimes gets all frozen when it's cold outside."

Winter accepted the keys from Kirk with a smile and strode to the heavy iron door. Thrusting the key into the mechanism, she rattled it around as instructed until she could feel it bypass the internal obstructions. With much less persuasion than she had expected, there was a satisfying click and she wrenched the shaft ninety degrees, sending the door swinging free.

"I greased the hinges this morning," Kirk revealed as she walked into the room. He took a tentative step toward her.

"That's tremendous," she replied as she firmly closed the door. "Thank you again, Kirk." If the gaoler was unsure whether the soon-to-be sheriff would want an escort through the small dungeon, the resounding thud of the door closing issued an unmistakable response.

After only three steps inside the basement of the old barracks, used to house particular "persons of interest," Winter realized that she still held the cumbersome metal wreath of keys. She plunged the wooden crowned key back into the lock and left it hanging like a poorly calculated caltrop. She had no doubt that embarrassing messes like this were merely the fringe of the forest that she

would be navigating once she donned the mantle of sheriff.

Six more weeks until this is all your problem, she reminded herself, grimly watching a rat scale a wall before it disappeared into some dank oblivion. The Church was not overly keen on maintenance when it came to places that the public was not openly privy to, which was not something she could really blame them for. The organization had its hands quite full, spinning a lot of plates at once, so she reasoned that it was quite easy to allow some areas to fall into disrepair. Unfortunately, the enforcement of law had trickled through a convoluted stream of idiots for centuries now, and the dereliction had become habitual, almost hereditary in a sense. Whenever an official was feeling the faint knocking of a headache over an issue, they would simply ferry the problem to the Arbiter and congratulate themselves on "a job well done." She expected it to be the most trying of struggles, to be sure, but she felt that she had been born for the job.

This was just one of the many jails scattered throughout the realm, and in addition to being haphazardly located, each was poorly maintained. She made a mental note that she would either need to allocate funds or repurpose a large enough building to create a centralized dungeon.

After removing a torch mounted on a sconce, she began to walk the single corridor. Twenty-six cells stretched the width of the basement, most of them vacant, but for some reason "the illustrious warden" Lloyd Inglebart, in his infinite wisdom, had decided that it would be a swell idea to place the sole witness in the farthest reaches of cell number twenty-six.

A toothy grin and a pair of bloodshot eyes leered at her from cell ten, offering services that Winter had no desire to have serviced. When she turned her face to him, casting light on the scar adorning the right side of her visage, the filthy fellow visibly recoiled at the sight.

"Nevermind," he muttered as he backed into the recesses of his cell. She was accustomed to that type of response, but for some reason this particular encounter irked her.

Kirk didn't seem to mind, she mused. *He's a rare one.* If she were not to be his superior in the coming months, she would have given some serious thought to asking him out for a pint.

How much further does this disgusting den go? The long hall was dimly lit by a handful of torches that seemed to float in the inky pools surrounding them, offering meager light and even less warmth. She was, however, grateful for the cold weather that permeated from the outer walls, which aided in dampening the various unpleasant aromas wafting from the inhabited cells.

As she passed the twentieth cell, her mind began to focus on the task at hand...the task that she decided to undertake out of sheer boredom. It was not every day you hear news that two of the church's finest guards had been completely eviscerated in an alley during the night. And these were not the first deaths. Oh, no, there had been a string of Church guard murders over the past several weeks. Adding to the intrigue of these homicides, there was actually a witness to the latest blood bath; the first and only witness concerning any of these murders. Unfortunately, the man was a known drifter whose speech patterns were exceedingly difficult to translate into plain, understandable words. *Just gets better and better.*

After the interrogators had given up out of pure frustration, smashing their heads against the walls trying to gleam some sort of meaning from the verbal hieroglyphics spewing from the drunken sod's lips, they had tossed him into the furthest cell to rot until he decided to start making sense.

Winter batted at a cluster of moths that congregated around her torch as she peered into cell twenty-six, quickly realizing just why Inglebart had decided to place the witness in this particular pen. The damp walls were weeping punishingly cold water along the bases, seeping across the floor. In defense of this, the prisoner had cleverly placed his wooden sleeping pallet on its side against the opposite set of bars, and was now perched atop it like a mangy cat on a fence.

His eyes darted to the flickering light then shot up to her face, fixing her with a surveying gaze. Winter was the first to look away, taking in the expertly formed and shaped bars. It was the only representation of skill or precision within this decaying titan of a building. She wondered for a moment whether it was true that the cells had been fused together by squeezing a gremlin over the metal joints, forcing the creature to join the steel by spewing its magical spittle over them.

"Are you here to inquire about the pocket dimensions?" the voice interrupted Winter's thoughts, and she looked up to see the man still sitting on his pallet. Now that he held her attention, he continued, "the magistrate's soup makes my skin sizzle. It gets bunched up and tight...constricting! Yes, yes, much like the coils of a baker's twizzled loaves."

"Oh, come on..." Winter sighed. All hopes for a decent conversation were dashed. She had been warned that it was impossible to speak with the man, and right out of the gates this was proving to be true. *Might as well give it a try.* "What's your name?" she asked, not expecting much.

Though his eyes appeared lucid, the words that tumbled out seemed to be irrational nonsense. "If it were up to me, I'd send them all sailing," he said, folding his arms and nodding emphatically.

"I see, I see," Winter responded, wondering if she should cut to the chase for the sake of brevity. "Well, I'll just call you "Rudder" then. Sound good?" The man tilted his head at the proposed name and muttered a few indecipherable phrases, tucking his chin into a bushy beard that rappelled to his sternum.

"So, Rudder," she continued, inching closer to the cell and spreading torchlight over the swampy living conditions. "What did you see last night? The men in blue that brought you here told me that you saw two people get killed by some—"

"RIGHT MESS OF IT I TELL YOU!" Rudder blurted, kicking his heels against the pallet's frame.

"Yes!" Winter pointed at him, mirroring the excitement at a half measure. "Yes! I was told it was a right mess!"

"RIGHT MESS! RIGHT MESS! RIGHT MESS!" Rudder loudly repeated the words over and over, spit flowed onto his beard as he worked himself up into a frothing mess. After a few more repetitions, his body suddenly seemed to deflate and he locked eyes with Winter once more. "It was a proper job by a werewolf. He was a gentleman with that sabre though," he said. "But I wasn't the only one watching!" The man pointed a gnarled finger to the sky, casting a wink at Winter before pounding the back of his skull against the steel bars at his back. "RIGHT MESS! RIGHT MESS! RIGHT MESS!" he screamed, the annoying mantra beginning again, each "mess" concluding with ear-piercing sibilance.

Winter waited patiently, watching the man rock back and forth on his makeshift edifice. She felt that Rudder's momentary lapse into semi-rational speech offered a bit of insight. Perhaps she could steer him in a more *stable* direction. Though she dearly hoped that the phrase "right mess" was in reference to the bloody murder and not a statement about his current chamber pot situation.

She waited for the split second between words and shouted, "Rudder!" effectively breaking his concentration. In response, he bared a toothy grin in her direction, displaying oddly impeccable dental hygiene.

"Can you tell me more about the werewolf and the gentleman?" Winter asked, pinpointing the only specific identities he had mentioned.

Rudder scratched his head. "Wrong mess?" he queried.

This is heading nowhere. Winter swiped at another moth and lowered the torch. "No, the same mess," she insisted. She felt like she was paddling in the middle of an ocean at this point, merely guessing toward the semblance of a connection. "The right mess," she said, raising her hands defensively. "Please don't shout at me anymore. But you said something about a gentleman and a werewolf. I would like you to tell me more about them. Are they friends of yours?" she asked with complete sincerity.

"No. He is no friend of anybody," Rudder responded, tugging at his lower lip. "Family recipes are quite dull but they're acceptable with the proper company," he concluded in a helpful tone.

"So was the gentleman there at all?"

"The gentleman was there at first! Then he burrowed into a fuzzy tree. POP!" he shouted, the sudden shrill outburst not startling Winter in the least. A momentary tremor of disappointment flashed over Rudder's face, but was then dispelled as fast as it had arrived. "But the watcher on the wall was watcher-ing," he pointed to the sky again with the same crooked finger.

"A fuzzy tree, you said?" Winter inquired, playing along. "Was it the beard of an ancient guest perhaps? Did it tickle the squirrel's underbelly as it climbed up the great tree-man?" She adopted the tone of one speaking to a child, hoping to coax more details before another bout of shrieking ensued.

Rudder shook his head, utterly perplexed. "What?" He regarded the woman beyond the bars, wrinkling his weatherworn features into tight creases.

"The fuzzy tree, Rudder. You said there was a fuzzy tree and I am just wondering what sort of tree it is."

"One that has nuts but doesn't produce any. Set loose from the killing fields...a savage dog without a leash."

We may be getting somewhere.

Rudder continued. "It would be a grave mistake to carelessly spill the windowpanes onto the sandy beaches. They would get into everything...and everyone."

"Not true!" Winter scoffed, wagging a finger at him. "The crabs would pick them up and use them as forks for their dinner parties."

A soft giggle grew to a chortling laugh. "Crabs *are* dinner at the parties!" Rudder responded playfully. He scooched a few inches toward her on his pallet, excitedly giggling while somehow maintaining balance.

Another prisoner laughed from somewhere in the teen numbered cells.

"She's funny!" Rudder bellowed, pointing at Winter's face.

"Aye!" the prisoner agreed, shouting over the damp quiet of the basement.

"Alright, alright," said Winter gently, attempting to guide the conversation back toward reality. "What about the werewolves? Are they invited as well?"

"Crabs are always crabs. No matter what the moon tells them."

Winter guessed that Rudder was alluding to the faery tale misconception that werewolves exclusively appeared during a full moon. It was utterly false, but she decided to continue to focus on the two details that seemed to create headway. "Was there a moon out last night? When the gentleman and the werewolf were out taking a stroll?"

Rudder's laughter came to an abrupt conclusion. "A blood moon."

"Oh, I see."

"It was a tight bundle, keeping her warm, just under the frosty tips of her ears," Rudder added calmly.

"Yes, her ears can get quite cold on a winter night," Winter agreed.

"A laif without a mother. Without her lithe stone," Rudder said, leaning back and raising his arms, relaxing with his hands pillowing his crown. The cuffs of his threadbare smock fell below his wrists revealing deep painful looking shackle imprints. Winter's eyes fell to Rudder's feet where there resided a matching set of marks on his ankles above the Church issued prisoner slippers.

Winter knew that it was pointless to ask about the specifics of his words, and opted to continue the tour without another non-sequitur. "Laives need their mothers just as much as we do," she affirmed, inclusively gesturing with her finger. "Especially ones that have..." Winter blinked. "Wait, did you say 'lithe stone'?" she asked before she could stop herself. *Here we go.*

Unexpectedly, Rudder simply nodded and kicked his feet in solitary amusement.

There had been a royal knight, Sir Rebekah, known as "the Lithe Stone." She had been killed or left for dead at Knotwithstadt, and now Winter began to sift through the verbal rubble that poured out in fragments before her. Rolling the dice, she pressed further, this time with specifics. "How many laives did you see last night?" she probed, hoping for some helpful mention of the missing orphan.

"Just the two stabby ears were all I did see, but that was not the only stabberings that were stabbed," Rudder answered, likely alluding to the murdered guards. He continued, "Shriveled and added to the cauldron, no one saw but me, and of course," he paused, skirling a finger toward the ceiling, "Him," he concluded with calm reverence.

"Of course, the Creator sees all," Winter acknowledged, impatiently tapping her foot.

"The creator of angry looks and unfettered anguish...during the night times," Rudder amended, forking a hand through his beard.

"The Creator saw me swipe the bread, but he didn't see me steal the baker's daughter!" the prisoner down the row interjected cheerily.

Winter shook her head, jotting a mental note and tucking it away, she would need to investigate that claim later. "I'll get to you some other day, rest assured!" she shouted to the prisoner.

Expecting a swift reply, Winter hesitated for a few breaths before she heard the prisoner answer quietly; "You know where I'll be."

Rolling her eyes, she returned her focus to the denizen of the cell in front of her. To her dismay, the pallet was bereft of its sitter. Raising the torch to illuminate the darker places, she investigated as best she could from where she was standing. He was not along the back of the wall or shivering in a corner, and as she continued to search, suddenly a remarkably white toothy grin enveloped the entire torchlight. Others would have jumped back a pace or two, but Winter did not give any ground.

"Hold the girl away from the wraith's gaze. It will feed upon your despair," Rudder advised darkly. Though his posture was menacing, the words were issued with an unexpected measure of kind assurance.

"I will be sure to do that," Winter replied. *I think I have gone as far as I can with this one,* she thought underneath the unwavering gaze of the feeble man before her. "Thank you very much for all your help, Rudder," the soon-to-be sheriff said, nodding warmly.

Before she turned away, Rudder raised a hand like a schoolboy and stood on his tiptoes, shaking eagerly to be called on. His face was fixed in a pained grimace, and he nodded as one struggling under a heavy burden.

Winter relented before departing, "Yes?" she prompted, inclining the torch. "The lad in the front row with the creepy smile and soiled trousers has a question."

"Have you ever been pretty?"

~ 3 ~

REMEMBRANCE

She could not fall asleep in this weird room inside this weird inn with all those loud and weird people downstairs carrying on like idiots. She had not gotten a decent night's rest since she had laid her head down on the cozy bed built by her father in the home of her mother's ancestors. The home deep within the forest of Knotwithstadt, well before the evil people showed up with swords and arrows, the home where she lived with her mother and father and brother. Thoughts of the home she had been forcefully taken from when everyone she knew and loved had been slaughtered before her, swirled ceaselessly in her mind, jumping from tragic end to tragic end. Closing her eyes did not help, nor did tossing and turning stir up any pleasant visions. There simply was no cure for what plagued her mind every night when the lights dimmed and cruel voices rose.

She wondered if it was bad that her most recent happy memory was when the werewolf in armour burst out from the night air and tore that mean guard into pieces. He rescued her from the misery that was the orphanage, the place where the children would gather around a patch of moonlight and take turns wishing on it, believing it was an angel.

As she reached for sleep, she tried once more to call forth happier memories. One time her older brother, Gaius, found a simple grass snake under a flowerpot. Believing it would terrify her, he concealed it behind his back before swiftly tossing it into her lap. To his severe disappointment, the slender reptilian did not garner the response he had wanted. Well, not immediately. When she picked it up at the base of its tail, the little creature unexpectedly regurgitated a worm that it had eaten earlier. Up until that point, she had simply regarded the snake with curiosity, but once that gelatinous mess gurgled out onto her knee, she screamed and scrabbled to get it off. Gaius' laughter could be heard clear through the trees, but it was not louder than her own screams, which reached their mother's ears first. Her brother received the fitting punishment one is due when one terrifies a mother's precious only daughter. Especially when the mother is Sir Rebekah of Camelot, recently retired from the killing fields.

The laif girl smiled as she pulled the pilled worn out blanket up to her chin. The werewolf, the knight who saved her, had brought her to this inn for a meal and safe haven. *Sir Percival?* She thought that was what the lady guard had called him before the conversation that had ended with her death. The werewolf could speak, but when he transformed back into a man he did not speak very much. In the darkness the girl had believed it was blood that soaked the man's features, but when the lamp-posts illuminated them, she discovered that she had been mistaken.

Those were tears streaming from his eyes, the laif girl realized, though he did not seem sad at all. Not in the least. The only time she saw his features soften had been for a split second, after he asked the mean guard why the Church was interested in this particular laif child.

The woman guard had carelessly replied, "This little runt claims to be the daughter of Rebekah the Lithe Stone," and the laif girl could not decide which was scarier: the expression on the knight's human face in that moment or his werewolf face. Needless to say, things got all shrieky right after the knight received that response. Why the guard's words had angered the knight so much, she could not say. She was just grateful to be away from anyone belonging to the Church.

Even though he was a beast and very terrifying, the laif girl was not afraid of him, not for one second. After he slew the guards, he took her hand and said the only words he had offered since they met.

"I knew your mother. You are safe with me."

She simply knew he was not lying. After that, he led her to this inn with the bright lights and the laughter. After a tasty meal of peppered grouse and sweet peas, the knight had pulled the inn master aside and exchanged a few calm words out of earshot. The inn master's wife, Aida, was a jolly woman with freckles that completely covered her face and any other patch of uncovered flesh. The laif girl began to wonder what the woman would look like if she were bald. She giggled under the covers and her nose was greeted by a startling prickly shock when she rolled over.

Aida was the one who led her up to this single bedroom, apologizing profusely, confessing that their inn did not entertain children often. The laif girl was not sure what the woman was so sorry about. Compared to the conditions of the orphanage, this room was practically a royal suite. She would not be kept up by the shuddering sobs of other children or the slapping of loose shutters or the squeaks and scratches of rodents in the walls and ceiling. This room was dry instead of damp and dreary. And the windows were secure and she felt safe. A feeling she had taken for granted, up until this point.

The tighter she squeezed her eyes closed, the more elusive sleep became. She could not force it, but she was going to try her hardest.

The laughter bubbling through the floorboards was not helping.

She tossed and turned. *What could possibly be so funny?!*

SHE FELT LIKE SHE HAD ONLY BEEN SLEEPING for five seconds when the door hastily swung open. Holding completely still, she cracked an eye open, the sight of a floating lantern causing her to sit up and take full notice. The knight, Sir Percival, appeared as grim as usual, but he looked hassled and rushed.

"We must be off!" he whispered harshly, extending a hand.

Without hesitating, she reached out, and he completed the extension, gripping her forearm and hoisting her to her feet. Percival quickly searched for her clothing, turning his head to and fro. The laif girl was wearing only a simple shift that Aida provided, which would not do in the cold conditions outside.

His eyes settled on her clothes for a moment, neatly folded atop a wobbly dresser that looked liable to topple should a stiff breeze come its way, and he pulled the girl close with one arm then snatched the bundle up. After thrusting her clothes into her chest, he placed a boot to the center of the window and forced it open with a kick. Chilled air swirled in, blowing the girl's hair over her face, and when the knight perched atop the sill, she was unable to see how far down the street was. As she tried in vain to move the clingy hair aside, a chorus of angry voices streamed through the door. The girl felt the knight rotate his hips to look back, then suddenly she was weightless. Percival uttered a deep grunt when his feet struck the earth. He had managed to stick the landing without stumbling, and he set off running into the night.

From far above and behind, she could hear the angry voices at the window shouting at him. Their voices thundered down, promising horrible fates, but he did not pay them any heed.

When the knight was satisfied with their distance, he ducked into an alley, setting the girl down. This alley appeared much like the one they had first met in, but this one smelled much worse. The girl understood without prodding that when he turned his back and folded his arms, she should put her warm clothing on. It was far too cold to be traipsing about in only a thin veil of fabric. She gently tugged his cloak when she was ready, afraid that if she pulled too hard the worn-out mantle would tear apart.

Percival turned toward the girl, kneeling down so he was eye to eye with her.

"No harm will befall you," he promised. The arrangement of scars under his eyes shifted slightly when his mouth moved. "But we must not tarry."

With that, he opened his arms and she entered his embrace. They set off once again, renewing the pace, but this time she was much less chilly. Their course now took them away from the lantern lit streets, opting for shadowed paths and crooked lanes, far from prying eyes.

She was just one orphan with the Church searching for her, so she couldn't even imagine who might be pursuing this knight. A knight like Sir Percival, one capable of murder without obvious reasons, must have surely gotten more than one group of enemies. After living in the city for less than a month, she could already sense a great deal of unrest, and sometimes, unhappy people do not make life easy for others wanting a gentle life. The jostling bounces of Percival's stride were harsh reminders that her gentle life was long gone and far away.

The sight of several men holding cudgels congregating around a well-lit fountain caused the knight to veer sharply from their trail. A deep growl rose from under his chest armour as he navigated the path, clearly agitated by the obstruction. Their new route led them over a stone bridge. When they were halfway across, the knight vaulted the rail, leaping over the edge into the streambed. The little girl clenched her teeth, preparing herself for an icy splash that never came. To her relief, the stream had completely dried up, and in a flash they were hidden under the bridge, hunkering down like a pair of trolls.

Sir Percival hastily lunged out to wipe away the deep impressions of their footprints in the snow. He returned with a swift motion, picking the girl up and heaving her onto a beam connected to the haunch of the bridge. The beam was a decent enough seat, but very cold. As the knight passed under her dangling feet, he whispered, "Stay out of sight. I will return." Dutifully, the laif pulled her legs up and sat cross-legged, burying her hands into the crook of her knees for warmth.

After what felt like an hour, though was likely only ten minutes, her protector returned. He tossed aside a long pine branch before reaching up to return the laif to the frozen soil. An excellent branch for covering one's tracks, no doubt.

The knight settled against the wall of the bridge as far from sight as possible, and the laif wriggled close, re-wrapping her scarf tighter around her face. Once he shrouded her with his mantle, the piercing wind ceased and the girl felt that she was huddled up inside a warm tent. She murmured a few words of thanks, which the knight did not hear, and drowsily prayed that the innkeeper's wife was safe. Within moments she was asleep, dreaming of roaring hearths.

* * *

WINTER PLUCKED AWAY AT HER HARP deep into the night, lost in thought, before being interrupted by a triplet of knocks resounding against her door. It was well known within the royal guard that when one heard the sound of the harp playing from the Lord Commander's solar, it was best to continue walking, and whatever you aimed to report had better be of the gravest import.

Winter clicked her finger picks together in irritation and loudly sighed.

"Enter," she said, her voice reverberating across the expansive room.

The heavy studded door tentatively cracked open and a young woman poked her head through the opening.

"My deepest apologies, Lord Commander— "

Winter cut her off. "Did you not hear the tonal harmonies of my harp through the door?" She stood and marched forward, her eyes narrowed at the intruder. "I believed the door to be dense, but who would have known that a member of my own company would have a head that could rival it!"

"Well," the woman began, stepping through the threshold and closing the door, pressing her back against it to seal it shut. "This member of your company may just be sick, all the way to the heavens, of her Lord Commander finger blasting her precious harp long into the wee hours of the morning, and scowling like a gargoyle, ignoring her charges!" She folded her arms and cocked her head at Winter, awaiting the response.

"Clarial! You dirty harlot!"

Neither woman could maintain the charade for long. They surged toward one another and met in a backslapping embrace. Winter was a head taller than the other woman, who was still resplendent in her uniform and smelled faintly of the stables.

"When did you get back?" Winter asked, taking a step back to admire the other woman with both hands on her shoulders. "I didn't think I would see you—"

"Until after you took the post as sheriff?" interjected Clarial, walking to an empty chair before the hearth. She doubled over and shrugged her riding mantle off, setting it on the back of the chair. Swiping loose hair from her face and straightening the hem of her tunic with a tug,

Clarial took a few steps toward the fire, rubbing her hands and extending them toward the blaze. "I wanted to make it back in time for your ceremony, but it appears that I may have misjudged the timing by a couple months."

"Six more weeks," Winter replied, setting a kettle on the iron stove. "Tea?" she offered, raising an eyebrow at the woman thawing by the hearth, who nodded in response.

"Do you have anything to add to it?" Clarial asked brightly, turning to face her old friend.

"Naturally," Winter placed her finger picks on a counter as she swept by, and reached into a nearby cupboard, sifting through an amalgam of spices. She was elbow deep before she concluded her search and withdrew, clasping a glass bottle of amber liquor. The contents sloshed around as she tucked it under her arm, bringing it to the hearth.

Clarial received the bottle and examined it, rotating it in her hands. "Without label or indication of proof," she pronounced, smiling devilishly. "Just the way I like it!"

The Lord Commander laughed as she walked back toward the kitchen.

"I believe I picked that up on the way back from my last trip out to the western fringes," mused Winter, settling onto her knees to rummage through the cupboard once again. Gadgets and utensils spilled out, clattering all over the hardwood as she clumsily reached inside.

"When was that?" Clarial asked, taking a seat. Shivering without warning, she eagerly edged closer to the fire.

Winter stood and fixed a calculating gaze upon the measuring cup that she had finally uncovered. "Three years?" she guessed distractedly. "Do you want to just eyeball the whiskey in the tea?"

"Of course! Who measures liquor?" Clarial crowed. She cast a disapproving look at her friend. "And try five years ago. It's been half a decade since you darkened the killing fields to see your old girl."

Retrieving the implements that had fallen from the cupboard, Winter laughed loudly and threw the items back into the cupboard before hastily closing the flimsy door. A resounding thud issued from inside as the contents settled, no doubt ready to pounce once she decided to open the pantry again.

"Five years?!" Winter scoffed, clinking a pair of teacups onto the counter. "Father Time waits for no one, does he?"

"Especially for us mortals," Clarial added, taking a swig of the liquor directly from the bottle.

"Whoa, whoa, when did you open that?"

Clarial wiped her pained grin with the back of her wrist, then spoke, ardently fighting back a fit of coughs. "That's some serious—" she coughed and pounded her chest. "Wow, that's some serious piss water you have here, Winny! Mighty fine stuff." She pitched the cork into the flames and pointed the neck of the bottle at her friend who accepted the challenge.

Snatching the offered bottle and placing her lips to the opening, Winter upended it with pageant flourish. Nearly choking, she brought it back down and recoiled as if she'd been stabbed in the belly.

After taking a few moments to gather herself, she cleared her throat and spoke, "That'll straighten a winding road!" Taking another swig with a look of utter revulsion, she passed the bottle back. "It gets better," she coughed encouragingly.

Clarial swirled the bottle and peered at the fire through the roiling contents. "The world seems much less sharp when looking at it this way," the bright-eyed guard said. "It feels strange to be here right now, you know? My hackles have been raised for so long while out on those ramparts, it's funny to feel at ease. To feel real cold again, to feel a proper break from all *that.*"

Before Winter could speak, Clarial anticipated what she would say next and beat her to it. "I know, I know. I signed up for the post. You don't have to remind me," Clarial continued half-heartedly, running a finger along the rim of the bottle.

Winter closed her mouth and decided not to add anything, instead choosing to settle into the chair opposite her friend.

"I probably shouldn't get too comfortable. The tea will be ready any moment," said Winter at length with eyebrows raised, expectantly poised for the teakettle's shrill whistle. A pregnant pause passed between them.

"It seems as though you're losing your—" A high-pitched shriek interrupted Clarial's intended insult.

"Ha!" Winter stood with a derisive laugh and made for the stove to silence the kettle.

"Forever the tactician," Clarial teased. "So where are we with a replacement once you leave all this?" she asked, gesturing to the room with a wide sweep of her hand.

"It's not up to me. I can only extend a letter of recommendation."

"And greasing palms is well below you, I am sure."

Winter pinched both cups at their rim and carried them over, the steam irritatingly moistening her palms. "You know me well enough," she admitted as she placed the tea on the solid chest between them. "Kay has the ultimate say in that business, and he has made inquiries, but I haven't indicated anyone in particular."

Clarial picked up her cup, singeing her fingers in the process, and waved her fingers through the air. "Damn! That's hot!" she cursed.

"Aye," Winter agreed, drawing her cup close and blowing the steam from it, unfazed by the heat. "Take a few sips before adding the piss water, I may have overfilled them," she added.

Clarial nodded, a devious smile blooming. "Do you think William Markman will be your replacement? Kay always oddly favored that git. Is he still lurking around?"

Winter nearly choked. "What do you think? That worthless pile is still employed, though the tasks I give him are well below menial."

"Are his underlings still used as scapegoats when he fails?"

Winter bobbed her head in agreement. "William believes himself quite clever."

"That prat is so incompetent."

"Yet somehow, Kay promotes him every season, despite my misgivings."

Clarial stood and arched her back, stretching with a yawning groan. "You should just reassign him out west to the front. He would eventually find the wrong end of an archenlaives' barbed arrow." Hesitantly, she grabbed her cup and continued, "but I'm sure you've already attempted that?" she questioned, bringing the cup to her lips with her eyebrows raised playfully.

"Attempted which one?" Winter inquired malevolently.

"Ah ha!" Clarial wagged a finger at her friend. "Well, let's just hope that he remains far below the station of Lord Commander. Remember that one knock-around lad, what was his name? He was cute with the scraggly hair...come on, you remember." She snapped her fingers, attempting to extract the memory.

"Anson," Winter offered.

"Yes! Anson!" Clarial pursed her lips. "And William, like the proper cheap fool he is, had advised that dreamy boy to reuse the tap screws instead of scrounging for fresh ones when he hung that heavy banner framed with battleaxes."

"I forgot all about that," Winter replied, rubbing her eyes at the recollection.

"Remember Fran and Mildred? How they jumped when the banner came crashing down? It almost obliterated Beaumains and his escort!" Clarial said laughingly.

"That poor knight was fresh from battle too," recalled Winter, with much less amusement than her friend. Beaumains had reached for his sword at his empty hip, and the look of pure panic on his face when he realized that he was unarmed for the festivities was not something to rejoice at.

"Of course, in proper coward fashion, William immediately pointed the finger at our handsome little angel." Clarial gazed into the flames. "Whatever happened to young Anson?"

"After that, he was sent to the scullery and I lost track of him."

"Probably eventually joined the red knights," Clarial calmly speculated, turning back to Winter. "If he managed to escape your keen eyes..."

"I should certainly hope not," Winter scolded, generously spilling liquor into her cup. "He's probably maintaining some high lord's stables down in the south, no doubt flanked by a plethora of offspring whelped by some pretty little farmer's daughter."

Clarial's eyes widened. "Well," she whispered, "I will unpack that later."

"What's that?" Winter asked.

"Nothing, nothing." The younger woman waved a hand dismissively. "So when I knocked earlier, I could hear you plucking away at your harp. What sort of mystery would cause you to ponder so late into the..." she trailed off, raising an eyebrow at the window, "...morning?"

Winter did not need to look outside for confirmation. Days and nights melded into one as far as she was concerned. Now that she had relinquished her daily duties, divvying them among the other commanders, she had abandoned her regular circadian rhythm. Instead, she chose to sleep when sleep chose her.

"Guards have been getting brutally murdered recently. A string of them, and they appear to be connected," Winter disclosed, taking a sip of the bitter tea and liquor concoction and wincing.

"Oh my! What are the names of those killed?"

"You wouldn't know them," Winter answered, pulling her legs up and tucking them against the arm of the chair. "They're all Church guards."

Clarial simply nodded in response, gulping another unpleasant tasting mouthful from her cup.

Winter continued, "I tried to speak with an eyewitness this afternoon. *Tried* being the operative word. The poor old sod seemed a witless wreck."

"Well, observing trauma can do that..."

Winter shook her head. "I don't think it was the trauma that rattled that wretch's noodle. Damage like that goes deep."

"You would know," Clarial stated, instantly wanting to take back her words as they left her mouth.

Winter did not seem bothered and went on, "There were brief moments of clarity among his nonsense and I keyed in on a few phrases that seemed important. I was ruminating on them right before your interruption," she remarked thoughtfully.

"Feel free to pitch a few at me like old times," Clarial urged, taking her seat. "But why do you care about this? The Church usually handles their own investigations."

"I'm bored."

"Ah, well. Still, let's hear some of this nonsense."

"He mentioned all sorts of things, trees and sailing, gorgons and crabs. But when he mentioned a gentleman and a werewolf, his demeanor shifted." Winter paused. "Noticeably," she emphasized. Setting her chin onto her knees, she stared into the hearth while her intertwined fingers drummed rhythmically against one another.

"A werewolf?" Clarial asked.

Winter rocked her chin back and forth in assent.

"Word trickled down from the killing fields," Clarial began, "now this is just rumor, but we heard that the king released his hound on the capital."

Winter's feet hit the floor, and she abruptly sat up, spilling her tea. "When?!" she demanded.

Clarial sucked air between her teeth. "Maybe a month?" she guessed, squinting at her own estimation.

"Sir Percival is here? In the city? And no one thought it necessary to notify the Lord Commander?!"

~ 4 ~

OLD FRIENDS, OLD SCARS

Sir Breunor's "cottage," was their destination, laying somewhere on the fringes of Fenrirfang forest. The pair traveled northeast on a stolen horse after exiting the northern gates of Camelot moments before morning's first light.

"Monsters are restless this time of the season," the gateman cautioned Sir Percival as they trotted past. The girl went completely unnoticed, enshrouded under the knight's cloak. "Food's getting mighty scarce out there with this endless cold snap, so I'd advise giving the forest a wide berth," the man added, expecting a response, but received none.

Percival and the laif child abandoned the main highway for the snowy meadows covered with a film of sharp ice that crunched with every step. Soon after, a thin, intermittent blood trail began to accent their tracks. Upon the realization that it came from their mount's pasterns, Percival alighted to the ground and began to mend the wounds with strips of pre-torn cloth that had been conveniently stowed inside a satchel secured to the saddle. The horse's owner was apparently very good at prepping for a trek, and the laif believed that Percival had selected this particular horse for a reason. When the knight had procured the mount outside the tavern, he had carefully weighed each tethered horse before selecting this mare.

As Percival tended to their horse, the girl noticed movement along the tree line, and had to blink several times to be sure that she was not imagining things. There was a variety of monsters staring longingly in their direction, some even up in the boughs of the trees. She could not identify all of them, but the ones standing upright with wagging tongues were most definitely faewolves. For reasons she could not understand, the predators were not killing each other. They just stood there ignoring one another, acting as though their faces were pressed to an invisible pane of glass, not daring to step out of the forest. One emaciated beast abruptly began to leap about excitedly; its loose fur flopping over a protruding rib cage and shriveled stomach. The sudden spurt of passion was swiftly subdued by a solid backhand to its snout from an elder of its kind.

"Percival," the girl whispered, raising a finger to the host. The knight had been returning the remaining strips of cloth into the saddlebag and gave the child a questioning glance before turning around. He regarded the scene with as much panic as he would a field of lilies and butterflies.

Hefting himself back into the saddle, the knight settled into place and spoke over the top of the girl's head. "Do not concern yourself with them," he said, urging the horse forward with a click of his teeth. "They know better."

The girl was unsure what that meant, but she swore she saw the monsters flinch when he spoke.

News of folk getting snatched along the outskirts of Fenrirfang by hosts of ogrekind, marauding goblins, or really any makeup of monster was commonplace year-round. Her mother had shared many stories of the horrors that existed in the forests of their people. The monsters she had described held many attributes, but restraint was definitely not one of them. Raising an eyebrow, her gaze unwavering from the tree line, the girl thought about asking more questions when she locked eyes with something that appeared to be a laif child. It was hunched and starving, wearing tattered garments that caught on the brambles as it followed their course through the meadow. The laif *thing* stuck out to her as an oddity from the rest of the horde. Now she had a new question to ask and did not know which was more pertinent.

Her head bounced against the knight's chest armour when the horse's hoof slipped on a discontinuity in the soil below the snow. "Percival?" she began, leaning forward and craning her head to look up at him.

His eyes darted down to meet hers. "That's a hob," he replied, answering her unspoken question.

How did he know? She scrunched her face in a puzzled look that garnered the first smile she had seen from the knight. "What's a hob?" she asked.

"Not entirely sure," Percival replied, squinting at the brightening horizon. "Your kind uses them to guard a few of the wards in the forest. And they spend most of their time underground."

The girl looked expectantly at the knight, waiting for him to continue. After a few moments of silence she realized that was all that he was going to offer, and she reluctantly turned her head forward once again.

"That one looks sick," she remarked, rocking with the horse's gait. "I'll keep my eyes on him." Though she could not see him, she felt the knight nod in response.

Earlier that morning, Percival had woken her, and the knight had asked her where she wanted to go. Until that point, she had been completely content to tag along, not believing she held the privilege of any choice. As long as the knight took her far from the Church and its wretched orphanages, she would be just fine. But when she had closed her eyes, contemplating her response, her mother's face flashed in her mind for just a moment, and she felt a brief sense of peace. "Home," had been her answer. "I want to go home," and the knight had gravely nodded his agreement.

As they continued on their course, larger flakes of snow began to fall and cling to her eyebrows. The hungry monsters were growing harder to discern, but a few flickers of movement in the high branches confirmed that their movements were still being mirrored, at least from the beasts who were scrambling in the treetops, avoiding the ground altogether. She had lost sight of the creepy hob, which was not comforting to say the least, but she couldn't say that she would miss the sight of that shambling mess.

Tugging her scarf below her mouth, the laif began to ask the knight how he could possibly see through the blinding snow, but instead offered a yelp when a tinge of brown and black pervaded the white swirling canvas.

She felt Percival's head turn, and the snow seemed to hang in the air, suspended before an updraft that never inhaled. Before she could even inch forward in the saddle, the knight was on the snowy meadow. She could not determine if it was the wind howling past her ears that had made the scraping noise, but the knight now held his longsword pointed at the earth as he walked forward into the blizzard. The tip almost kissed the icy sheen on the layers of snow, just barely maintaining a fractional distance. Soon all she could see clearly was the knight's footprints. The rest was a blur. The interloping creature was not moving fast at all on its two legs, and its gait appeared almost humanlike, though quite desperate from what she could tell.

A sudden gust of wind opened a window of clarity, and she watched the knight cross his blade over his left shoulder as the assailant drew near.

It was not a faewolf that approached him, nor was it the hob.

This was something else. Her hand involuntarily covered her mouth as she watched the pitiable scene unfold.

With a feint to the right, or perhaps a stumble, the creature sunk a step into the snow, buckling its kneecap. Percival somehow anticipated the next movement and when the pathetic beast weakly stumbled forward, the knight sliced clean through its clavicle in a diagonal arc. After a moment to allow life to drain from the foe, Percival wrenched his blade upward, lifting the creature off the ground like a lifeless puppet, attempting to free the entangled weapon from the creature's spine. Her last clear view was the knight planting his thumb and middle finger into the creature's eye sockets and dragging it by the head toward the tree line, a portal of swirling snow closing behind him.

Anticipating her question upon his return, Percival said, "That was a ghast." Settling into the saddle behind her, he spoke again. "And I don't know their origins, but I do know that they can be killed with steel."

"It didn't seem too ferocious," the laif shouted into the blowing snow. The horse was moving once again, but at a quicker trot.

"Winter is unpleasant." Percival's voice pierced the wind. "That one just wanted an end."

IF NOT FOR THE PLUMES OF SMOKE BILLOWING from the pile of snow on the outskirts of the forest, the laif would not have known that someone could possibly live here. Pillowy layers of snow sloughed from the door when it was finally heaved open. Sir Percival was the most ferocious looking man she had ever seen, but the man who answered the knock was definitely a runner up.

Sir Breunor appeared to live a lifestyle where sleep was entirely optional, but hygiene was paramount. His clothing was neat and tidy, and his beard was expertly cropped, the moustache hairs barely dangling below his upper lip. In contrast, his face looked extremely tired. The girl could not think of a better description of the man. *Tired*. Deep purple pockets surrounded his eyes, almost as if he had been in a brawl, yet she could tell he had not been scuffling with anything tangible.

When Breunor's gaze fell upon Percival, his countenance registered gladness, and he hastily ushered the travelers in, furtively glancing east and west before easing the door closed. The inside of the hovel was pristine and hardly looked lived in. The north wall, which skirted the hem of forest, had a simple sleeping cot that did not look like it had seen use. There was no bend or bow to it and the blankets were so tightly pinched they looked painted on. There was a rocking chair before the blazing hearth with a covered pot dangling above the flames. Aside from the rocking chair, the cot, and an empty table, the home had no other form of furniture.

For being so empty, this place is very warm. The girl thought whatever the lonely knight was cooking smelled amazing. The pot began to bubble, and she watched broth peek up and escape, spilling down the side and hissing onto the cinders below.

"Dinner should be ready very soon," Breunor said as he rushed to the fire. He lifted the lid, allowing an abundance of steam to escape, causing the bubbly contents to gently recede.

Dinner? The girl gave Percival a puzzled look, and the knight offered the slightest shake of his head, silently advising her not to ask. As Breunor stirred the pot, more aromas reached the laif, and she realized that although it smelled of supper, it would be a most welcome breakfast.

"It has been ages, old friend," Breunor proclaimed, still stirring. "What brings you here?" The knight raised a speculative eyebrow.

Percival took hold of the rocking chair and slid it over to the laif, gesturing for her to take a seat. "This girl's request," he replied.

"A child's request would so easily draw Sir Percival from the King's side? This should be good!" Breunor slapped his thighs and stood, folding his arms while awaiting a response.

"The child is not what took me from Arthur," Percival explained, removing his sword and scabbard and placing them onto the table. "I have matters to attend to in the city, but she takes precedence. The King would understand."

Breunor crossed the room and spoke as he passed them. "I am intrigued," he said, reaching into a cupboard to withdraw three wooden bowls. "Please go on."

"She is Rebekah's daughter."

This news sent a ripple through Breunor. "Ah," he sighed. His eyes darted to the girl, and she returned his look. The girl knew her mother had been very strong, but noticed that anytime her name was mentioned, there was always a visible reaction.

After an extended spell of silence, Sir Breunor scratched his jaw and finally spoke. "You aim to bury her bones?"

Percival tilted his head and curled his lip in silent agreement.

"It will not be an easy task," Breunor warned, shaking his head. "There are seven wards between here and Knotwithstadt. How do you plan on getting past them?"

The fire began to hiss as the soup bubbled over once again. Hopping over to the fire, the laif uncovered the pot and began stirring before Breunor had a chance to move. He thanked her before turning his attention back to Percival. In response to his question, Percival simply inclined his head toward the laif, raising both eyebrows.

"She's not..." Breunor began, trailing off before lowering his voice to a whisper. "She's a half laif, Percival. I do not think her blood will be accepted by the warding magics."

"How do you know?"

"How do I know what?" Breunor paced toward the fire, lifted the pot, and brought it over to the table. Glancing apprehensively at the laif behind him, he continued, "How do I know she's a half laif? Or how do I know that her blood will not be sufficient?"

Making her way to the table, the girl recognized the look on Percival's face as one she had seen often in the past. Many people were taken aback when they found out that her father was human.

"Both," Percival replied, accepting a bowl filled with soup in one hand while using the other to drag the rocking chair over to the table for the girl.

"Well, let's see." Breunor lowered a friendly gaze at the girl. "Was your father a human?"

"Yes," the girl replied, stirring her spoon in the thick broth, not bothering to look up.

"And did your mother ever teach you about the wards in the forests that keep humans from trespassing over your sacred grounds?"

Her mouth was full, so she politely nodded her response.

"What did she tell you?"

Placing the spoon aside, the girl wiped her hands on her mantle before answering the tired knight. "Not very much. It was one of those things she said she would teach me about when I got older."

"So you don't know how to bypass the ones leading to your home, I take it?" Breunor directed the question at the girl, but stared pointedly at Percival.

She shook her head, blowing steam from the surface of the soup while wrapping her hands around the warm bowl. She recalled the morning that Gaius had been shown the ward closest to the village. When he got back that evening dried tears had stained his cheeks, and he skulked to his room without uttering a word. Her mother had gently restrained her father from going to him. The next morning, she had asked her brother what happened, and in response he opened his palm to show a deep wound. The sides were already crusted brown where healing had begun overnight. That was all that he offered in explanation and he would not speak of what he had seen. She even asked him about it again weeks later, but he flat out refused to tell her anything. She would have asked yet another time, but shortly thereafter her brother had died on his knees before the blade of a Holy Knight.

"I think the soup is cool enough." Breunor's voice broke her from her reverie. "It's not a bad batch."

Her eyes blinked successively, returning her to the present. She ignored her spoon and instead tilted the soup directly into her mouth. After lowering the bowl an inch, she said, "It is. Thank you very much," then resumed slurping.

The girl wasn't sure why they had come here, especially as Percival did not seem to be the kind of man to make social calls. This Sir Breunor must have something important to offer. While she had narrowed down the possibilities, she hadn't figured out Sir Breunor's role. She decided they had certainly not come for horses, as they had released their own mount before approaching the cottage. She had offered a few silent prayers for the stolen mare's safety ever since, earnestly hoping she would make it home without getting eaten by that wall of monsters.

Though the soup was indeed very good, she knew that they were not here for the food. And he seemed to have only one bed, so they must not be here for quaint lodging. Looking around the space for clues, she noticed an arrangement of curved reeds hanging on the wall next to a collection of blades in varying lengths, widths, and shapes. Some had multiple blades protruding at hooked angles from their hafts and several resembled crude tridents. Breunor's ornate armour was resting on a t-shaped stand, propped up and oiled, and ready for use. Several of the helms decorating one shelf had a strange circular hole crafted into the faceplate where a knight's mouth would be.

I wonder if he has trouble breathing? The laif wondered, giving the knight another appraising look. He didn't seem unhealthy or weak...*just weary.*

Breunor reiterated his question to the other knight. "So how will you manage to get past the wards?"

"If she cannot dispel them with her blood, then we will press through regardless."

My blood? The girl listened more closely at that.

"We?" The pronoun choice was not lost on Breunor. "*We* will press through?"

Percival nodded. "You are coming with us."

"First of all," Breunor started, placing his bowl on the table and walking toward his wall of blades with his hands clasped behind his back. "Wards are far more than goblins with tiny blades and arrows. You can't just walk through them. This doesn't bear reminding, Percival. You know this."

"How do you get through them?" inquired Percival. "You can't possibly hire a ranger each and every time you go hunting for your prey."

Breunor laughed dryly and rolled his head against his shoulder, the ensuing pop reverberating against the wall, but when he turned toward them his eyes were narrowed into slits. "I have my ways. Sometimes I procure a vial of laif blood and cross my fingers. And I run like hell if it doesn't work. And *that* is a very rare occasion." He pointed at the laif. "She appears to be what? Ten? Eleven? Can she even wield a blade or a bow?"

"She has no need."

"You should be seeking a ranger's aid, not mine."

"That will not happen."

Breunor shook his fist and cursed loudly. "Forgive me for that," he said to the girl. Returning to the table, he centered his attention on the werewolf. "Alright! I'll help you," he sighed. "You know I can't just let you do this alone, you prick." Breunor chewed his lip thoughtfully. "First thing tomorrow morning before first light, we must head to the city for some important commodities."

"Breunor," Percival began, "it is morning."

The lone knight cocked his head like a confused hound. "Well then, we shall head out whenever the next morning comes around."

TALONS OF DESPAIR

The little girl pulled the covers up to her neck, and rolled over to watch the knights discussing her fate in hushed tones. Both men were standing, likely because Breunor lacked chairs, and the last sight she caught before rolling back over to face the wall had been Percival standing with his arms crossed while Breunor leaned on the table. After that, she knew that she was dreaming, but it all felt so real.

Off in the distance, a lantern was glowing, and she could hear a hum that swelled louder and louder as it moved closer and closer. An unseen hand gripped the lantern's handle as it swung like a pendulum, casting a whisper's strength of light against the darkness. The hallway between the girl and the lantern holder was framed by encroaching tree branches, giving her the sense that she was outside, though last she knew she was inside a knight's snow covered hut. The possible duality of locations only bothered her for a moment. The feeling of relief was fleeting when she opened her eyes to find that she was still on the cot indoors, however everything appeared to be coated with a hazy film. Rubbing her eyes with her thumbs did no good and blinking offered no relief.

She swung her legs to the floor and got up from the bed, compelled by an overwhelming urge to go outside and meet the lanternman. Under the greasy transparency clinging to everything, she could not see Percival or Breunor and thought that they must be outside waiting for her.

The hum continued to grow beyond the wall behind her as she approached the front door and sat down to pull Percival's boots onto her feet. The notion that the knight might be outside barefoot in the wintery conditions did not faze her in the least.

He's a werewolf, after all, she reconciled. Murky sludge ran upward along the baseboards bordering the threshold, and the door was not open...in fact, it was not there at all. With no door, the cold breezes should be blustering in, setting everything into disorder, yet that was not happening. The room was still a smudgy mess everywhere she looked, but it was not drafty. *It's a peaceful calm,* the girl thought as she sat back and clicked the toes of the ill-fitting boots together.

After passing through the doorway, she found that the world outside no longer held the smudges that the inside did, and it was crystal clear like normal. The winter moon hanging above caused the freshly fallen snow to glisten in contrast to the white blanket underneath, creating a welcoming pattern along the path to the lantern. *The lantern...*

Several things happened at once. The moon died, the path became a whirling tunnel, and the earth beneath her feet surged her toward the glowing light that had been invading her dream. She was standing still, yet she somehow was moving into the tunnel. The breezes whipped her hair around, tussling it over her face in an uncontrolled mess. When she looked back, the hut was still right behind her, but when she looked ahead, she was advancing. She wanted to sink to her knees and cling to the ground, but the ground itself was betraying her. Her body went rigid, and when she tried to open her mouth to shout, it felt like her lips had been sewn shut. With her arms locked at her sides and knees tightly buckled, she could only turn her head to steel herself from the radiance that seemed to pull her closer.

The hut had a front door again. And it was closed.

When she turned forward, the lantern was right before her eyes, and the once welcome light was now infused with terror. Tendrils of sickly mist escaped the pores all over the vein-covered carapace, eerily framing the throbbing bulb within.

Somehow the laif found her feet and ran from the path, albeit much clumsier than usual, as she was wearing boots that were a dozen sizes too big. Breunor's home was almost within reach, and if not for the root that snagged her left foot she would have made it. Like a clod, she fell to her knees in the slick snow. She tried to brace herself with her palms, but ended up slipping and sprawling out onto her stomach, coming to a sliding halt just below the roofline of the hut. She scrabbled to her feet but an invisible force suddenly clung to her shoulder and spun her around to face the light. The hum renewed its tone and she could feel her face soften, as if she were falling back to sleep. The lantern was not so scary anymore.

The humming ceased abruptly. She could feel her mouth hanging open, and after every labored blink of her eyes the light gradually suffused her head, tickling her scalp as it passed along its course. Voices began to utter phrases just beyond her comprehension. At first, there was only one, but then it was joined by another, then another, until it sounded like a hall at full capacity. The little girl began to feel like she was eavesdropping...Mother had told her it was rude to eavesdrop on adult conversation.

Mother...is that Mother's voice?

It sounded like they were speaking about the laif girl, narrating everything around her, but she was powerless to do anything about it.

"When her eyes finally close, we will be able to move," said one voice. The light's glimmer increased with each consonant. "Just sleep, little one. Your mother is waiting for you just beyond the veil. Just close your eyes..."

Her eyelids felt like millstones were strapped to them and her eyelids began to droop. Right before she submitted to the voices' wishes, a hideous skeletal face crested the top of the lantern. She thought maybe she had screamed, but she was not sure. Nevertheless, she could no longer resist, and as soon as she closed her eyes, her body felt like a melting candle. The warm liquid light that had encased her head suddenly became wickedly frigid, biting into her scalp like a host of pincher ants.

The skeleton appeared before her, hovering in the dark clouds, its jaw unhinged like a serpent preparing to swallow its prey. Her feet were frozen in place, and the same unseen force began to beckon her forward into the gaping maw with its putrid tongue grazing over a lipless mouth. She tried resisting, but found that any semblance of free will had been completely sapped from her. *Wake up! Wake up!* She silently screamed at herself, trying to convince her body to come back under her control.

Then Sir Percival was there. The werewolf.

At once, the loose wobbling jaw began to tremble uncontrollably before screeching and launching into flight. The ground rushed to meet the laif and she was suddenly on her hands and knees. Percival managed to deeply gouge the wraith with a wild swipe before the evil creature retreated. It stared at the werewolf with arms outstretched like a great bat, holding its fleshy coat taut as it retreated, and the lantern, which was not a lantern, but a disgusting tentacle-like extension of its body, dragged a snowy trail behind. Violently darting up into the air, the wraith sucked the lantern back into itself with an offensive slurp, then succinctly closed the flesh around it. After releasing another ear-piercing scream, the wraith spun in midair and flung itself away as though being tugged by an invisible thread. A few more shrieks were heard far away, sending shivers down the girl's spine, but Percival seemed unconcerned.

"What...what?" The laif struggled to form a coherent thought.

She looked up at the werewolf to find him appraising her with an examining gaze before scooping her up in his arms. Curling her toes in the large boots failed to hold them in place on her feet, and they plunked into the snowbank as the knight carried her back into the warm refuge. Over Percival's shoulder, the laif watched Sir Breunor appear from the darkness and pause over the fallen footwear.

"Fucking chilly wizards," he said, crudely identifying the monster, and cursing at the sky as another far away scream wafted over the quiet night air.

After stooping down to retrieve the boots, Breunor slowly rose to a stand. His eyes traced a gradual upward path to his roof, and the knight squinted and smiled gravely. He dropped the boots and placed a hand to his sword pommel, locking eyes with something over her head.

***

WINTER HAD SPENT THE BETTER PART of the morning feeling like she was spinning her wheels in the mud. Her connections within the Church had been very little help. Each of them told her the same thing: all hands were currently invested in the search for the orphaned daughter of the Lithe Stone, and none had heard of Sir Percival's arrival from the west, which would apparently be very near the bottom on their list of priorities. She inquired further about the orphan and was directed toward the barracks where she would find the patrolmen that had successfully tracked her to an inn the night before. Without wasting any more of the day, Winter made the trip to the barracks to see what sort of interesting yarn these guards would spin.

The dining hall where the members of the patrol were seated smelled of oil and sweat, even though they were dining with full plates of food before them. All the other tables were vacant, leaving Winter to pass through the hall to the center of the room without needing to offer any apologies or explain her presence. Her boots sunk into the thick carpet bisecting the tables, and she nearly bounced the remainder of her trek to the patrolmen.

All five were decked out in the livery of the Church, their long hoods pulled back and their leather gauntlets out on the table. Winter stared at their liripipes dangling only a foot from the carpet as she approached, avoiding their gazes until one of them spoke first. In the past she had found it helpful to wait for the other party to speak first in situations like this.

The conversation across the hall had clammed up as soon as Winter's boot first scuffed the hardwood under the archway. She felt them openly staring right at the onset, and as her scarred face was well known throughout the kingdom, she was certain that they were fully aware of who she was. After all, she would essentially be filling the role of their Lord Commander soon enough.

Winter stood at the head of the table and surveyed the crew, and one of the patrol looked at her reverently and flinched, moving to stand, but Winter motioned for her to stay seated.

"Are we supposed to salute you or something?" asked a pinch-faced patrolman, flicking a bone onto her plate.

Keeping her shoulders square, Winter turned her head to face the woman. "No," she said. "Not yet."

"What can we do for you?" another member of the patrol asked as she sat up and tucked her leg beneath her. She was clearly not as interested in confrontation as her comrade.

"She's probably here to bug us about that little orphan runt," pinch face sneered, sitting back with arms crossed. "You can go ask one of the majors, our story hasn't changed. We just want to eat our meal then hit the racks before another double shift tonight."

The arch in Winter's eyebrow held the menace of a cornered wolf. "There are details that I wish to hear directly from you."

Pinch face moved her mouth to respond, but another spoke up. "No offense or anything, but why do you care about this?" the woman asked meekly, twisting her scarf between her fingers. "I mean, this doesn't really concern the crown, does it?"

Winter strolled behind pinch face and rested her hands on the back of the chair. "I'm bored," she replied.

A few issued laughs at the response, one woman cackled like an overgrown imp.

"Look around you," pinch face snapped, sweeping her hand to the room. "Everyone else is out scouring the city. If you're so bored, why don't you just shuffle out of here and join them?"

Winter lowered her head down so she was an uncomfortably close distance from pinch face's ear. "What is your name?" she asked quietly while sweeping her gaze to the other participants at the table, a smirk on her lips.

"C-C-Carly," the woman responded, clearly rattled by Winter's intimate proximity.

"Well, Kuh Kuh Carly, that is a piece of my ultimate goal," Winter jeered, shooting back to an upright stance. "You see, this brief intermission from your meal is only a small stepping stone on my ascension to discovery. There is a puzzle rattling around in my head that I am trying to solve without the use of my fingers. And a big piece is missing, but it's staring me right in the face and right now I only need confirmation." She began to pace briskly around the table like a school marm at lecture. "And that is where you five lovely ladies come into play," the Lord Commander finished, cocking her head and awaiting a response.

"I don't—" Carly tried to speak but was interrupted almost immediately.

"Someone else!" Winter declared. She wiggled a finger as if testing the wind, then swiftly pointed it at the cackling woman. "You! Cackles!" she said with puckered lips.

"Me?"

Winter gave a single nod.

"Well," Cackles began, her eyes shifting uncomfortably back and forth at her companions. "We were following up on some curious information we got from an urchin on Millwright Avenue, said that he saw—"

Winter cut her off. "What was curious about it?"

"He said that he saw a tawdry looking knight walking hand-in-hand with a little girl. And the pair went into a tavern together."

"What's so strange about that?"

"The little girl was a laif."

"Ah," Winter scratched under her chin. "Continue."

"So we sprinted for the tavern—"

"Did you tip the urchin?"

A ripple of incredulity passed around the table.

"No," Cackles shook her head with a furrowed brow. "Why would we..." she trailed off as she noticed the scowl on Winter's face.

Oh Creator, so many changes will need to be made. Winter thought behind a silent glare.

"We sprinted to the tavern, *after kindly thanking the urchin,*" the woman continued, nodding emphatically at her fellow patrolmen, clearly jesting about thanking the urchin. "Once we got inside the place, we were immediately greeted by the over-friendly innkeeper and his wife. They strangely blocked our view of the main room by standing on tiptoes as we tried to look around. It was really annoying, but we saw through their dumb game immediately and forced our way past them to follow a blur of motion that had shot to the staircase as soon as we entered."

"This isn't our first joust," added Carly.

"Remember that one time we pursued that puppet-master," another woman piped in. "He was all slippery when we—"

"That sounds neat," Winter craned her neck at the woman, bringing her up short. "It sounds like a delightful tale, no doubt, and I would love to hear about greasy puppets some other day, but please can we stick to the current task?"

As the color drained from the cheerful woman's face, Cackles tapped the base of her fork against the table and continued.

"We weren't wrong," she said and the others grunted assent. "When we got to the room, the crazy bloke had the girl wrapped into his cloak and he plunged out the window, shattering glass everywhere."

"Remarkable." Winter was not excited. "Did you get a good look at the gentleman before he took that plunge?"

Cackles sucked air between her teeth, "Yeah, about that. This bloke was, well, he was not—"

"We would have chased him," another mentioned.

"I would *not* have chased that," another dissented.

"But," Cackles tugged her earlobe. "He was—"

"The scariest person I ever laid eyes on," Carly finished the statement and the others nodded in agreement. "He didn't quite look...*human*."

"We shouted insults from the window," the woman next to Carly offered, looking expectantly at Winter for approval.

"I'm sure that gave the scary man pause," Winter scoffed, but she was secretly excited. The puzzle was falling into place almost too easily.

That solves that. Sir Percival must be the one killing off the Holy men. Winter nodded to herself while the patrol began talking about the various threats they had hurled at the man's back as he escaped down the lane. *But why? Why is he on a murder spree...and why does he have this little girl...*

"'Crotch Goblin' was a good one," said Carly, admiring Cackle's wit.

"No, it's not," Winter disagreed, shaking her head. "Can you describe the man's attire?"

"Tattered."

"Savage."

"Unkempt, but somewhat handsome," said Cackles. "I don't know...in a rugged sort of way."

"Yes," Carly agreed, leaning forward. "He had the bearing of a powerful knight, but his armour and cloak seemed to be the sort you would find on the ground after a battle." Her face scrunched up tighter than Winter believed possible while pondering the memory. "And I caught a whiff of wet dog after he fell."

The other women nodded their heads with wistful looks on their faces, as if they all had experienced the same thing but were afraid to admit it.

If Winter held any doubts that this man was indeed Sir Percival, their description dispelled all uncertainty. Especially the last detail offered by the girl next to Carly.

"And that is all you saw last night?" Winter clarified.

"Of the girl and the man, yes," replied Carly while the others concurred with nods.

Alright." Winter pulled a chair back and sat with her elbows propped on the tabletop. "Let's hear about that puppet guy."

~ 6 ~

DISPELLING SHADOWS

"Get the girl inside!" Breunor urged fervently, his eyes fixed on something on the snow covered shingles. Percival assented and retreated into the doorway, the girl in tow. The girl thought she heard Breunor say something else but couldn't make it out. Percival had set her down near the hearth and told her to stay inside, but she could not remember whether she had nodded or not. The world had not quite ceased its upheaval, and it was strange hearing Percival's human voice come out of a werewolf, especially when the words were not at all threatening or scary.

The fire in the hearth was much more subdued than it had been the night before, so she inched closer to reach the stronger waves of heat. She could hear more voices coming from outside, but they did not sound strained or worried. Thankfully Percival had left the door open when he went back outside, and once she could feel her fingers again, she began to slowly stray closer to the center of the room to get a better view of the outside.

The laif could not see Percival from the doorway, but she could make out Breunor. From what she could tell, he had not moved at all. The boots that had fallen from her small feet were still directly in front of him, half buried in the snow. His pose, however, seemed more relaxed than before, his hand simply resting on his sword's pommel, still sheathed.

The voice coming from the rooftop resembled a proper laif. It reminded her of the wealthy laives that sometimes swaggered through her village during the midsummer months. They wore pretty clothes and spoke passionately while keeping their noses raised into the air.

Mother did not care for them much, but she did tolerate them. The girl could recall a terse conversation her mother had had once with one fancy looking laif; the laif was all decked out in greens and gold with a face painted up to match her nails.

"That's all well and good," Breunor shouted to the rooftop, glancing to his right. "But can we continue this conversation inside? My neck is growing stiff." The knight raised one hand to rub the back of his neck.

A response came from above. "That sounds acceptable."

As the creature leapt from the rooftop onto the snowy earth and came to a full stand, the meager light escaping the lodge accented thousands of glittery scales that dazzled the girl's eyes.

Sir Breunor tilted his head back to meet the creature's gaze. "Follow me," he said, then bent down to retrieve Percival's boots before making for his cabin. Sir Percival's entry behind the magnificent shiny knight with the massive wings went completely unnoticed by the girl. Her breath was trapped in her lungs and she gaped like a fool until Percival noticed her expression, then she straightened up as best she could.

Is he an angel? Trying not to stare, she peeked at the new knight's armour. It sparkled like a diamond and seemed to glide seamlessly over his body with every movement.

With his helm tucked in the crook of his arm, the winged knight surveyed the room with eyes that resembled a feline, the pupils vertical, widening and waning along their journey over the interior of Breunor's home. A scarf obscured the lower half of his face, and it shifted as he spoke. "Are you attempting a feeble re-creation of the round table here?" he asked, his eyebrows flitting upward at the end of his question.

"I don't…" Breunor trailed off shaking his head and looking to Percival, who had transformed back into his human form.

"Chairs," the shiny knight clarified. "Do you not possess proper furnishings?"

"Ah." Breunor turned his head and looked at his guest from the corner of his eyes. "I don't spend much time here, so it seems an unnecessary expense."

"How exceedingly practical," intoned the knight as he placed his helm on the tabletop and rested both armoured hands atop its dome.

The girl was captivated by the sparkly stranger and stared as if he were a statue come to life. She squinted her eyes and tried to imagine the face underneath the scarf. *I'll bet he looks like a kitty under there,* she speculated, not paying an ounce of attention to the conversation at hand.

"I believe Percival missed the first part of our conversation, Relic," Breunor said to the winged knight, brushing snow from his shoulder with a marked look of disgust. "Start from the beginning, then we can go from there."

"Sir Percival, eh?" Relic gave the knight an appraising glance then continued, "very well," he raised his chin and unfurled his left wing before quickly tucking it back into place. "I have been tracking that, what did you call it? A *Chilly Wizard?*" The girl imagined a sneer underneath the scarf when he turned to Breunor for confirmation. "I've been tracking it for a month or so, which in my opinion is far too long for a gargoyle to be away from his post, but orders are orders."

Gargoyle?! The laif cocked her head to the side in wonder.

Relic haughtily admired his claws as he spoke. "The *abowraith* was spotted shortly after the children from Knotwithstadt arrived as newly minted orphans. If this abowraith is the only repercussion the Church sustains, then I would consider the organization to be abundantly lucky."

"What is an abowraith?" queried the girl, tentatively approaching the gargoyle.

"Oh," Relic leaned away as if she were rotting flesh come to life. "It speaks," he drawled, extending the gap between them with a step around the table. "For those of us not well-versed on the dealings of abowraiths," he said, speaking to the knights, suspending attention from the laif. "The hideous creature that you clumsily dispelled would be an abowraith. It seems that they are conjured from the mass slaughter of innocents, as these ghastly apparitions do not appear from the ashes of a battle-field...well, unless the battle spills into a peaceful village..."

"And for some reason, they are more often seen during the winter months," Breunor added. "I'm not sure how much research has been done on them, but that seems to be the pattern. A village gets razed, then the next winter the nearby forests must be avoided until summer reclaims the land."

Relic gave Breunor a stern nod. "True, all true. And the wraiths invade the mind of their prey. Often they have a particular target in mind, but other times, it is seemingly at random. Once they successfully plant themselves deep in the host's head, that poor sod's mind becomes a veritable playground for whatever evil the wraith intends."

"Is it truly evil though, in the end?" asked Breunor, clenching his teeth in speculation.

"The wraith uses the host as a spirit of vengeance." Relic's cat eyes narrowed into slits. "But when free will is disposed of, I consider that act completely and utterly evil. I'm sure our good Sir Percival would agree with that?"

With an almost imperceptible nod, the knight inclined his head in agreement. The gargoyle continued, tugging at his laif-like ears. "It appears that the wraith has found its target." He released a heavy sigh as he looked at the girl. "Would I be drastically overreaching by asking whether *this creature* is either of your progeny?"

The girl felt a heated flash of indignation at being addressed as "this creature" but decided to keep her mouth shut.

"No, she is not," replied Breunor. "She was displaced when her village came to ruin."

"There must be more to this." Relic flicked his eyes in the girl's direction.

"Sir Rebekah was her mother," Breunor acknowledged.

"Ah, I see." The gargoyle's words were not tinged with disdain but spoken more gently this time. "And what, may I ask, brings her to this humble dwelling?"

Breunor looked toward Percival before responding. "Not really a what," he said, "More of a who."

"I am sure it is a tale that is as riveting as it is convoluted," Relic sounded bored. "But now I believe we are at an impasse."

"How so?" Breunor asked.

"You see, she has been marked by my quarry which makes her invaluable to me."

Breunor shifted his weight, resting a fist on the table. "You mean to use her as bait, don't you?" The knight peered at the gargoyle as if seeing him for the first time.

"More or less."

If Relic heard the low rumble emanating from under Percival's chest armour, then he was very good at acting bold. "Fear not," pronounced the gargoyle, raising a glittery palm at the knights and waving it as if casting a spell. "I do not aim to spirit her away from you as she was spirited from her home. No, that is not my intention in the least." The girl could hear that Percival's growling was not abated by this statement and continued to quietly thrum like a distant storm.

Relic muttered distractedly about wishing for a decent chair, then fixed his gaze on Percival. "Look, if you aid me in purging this forest of that wraith, which I might add, will continue to hunt her until the day she dies, then I will offer up my services for whatever your ends are. It does not require accelerated mathematics to understand why one would beseech Sir Breunor if one is planning an excursion to Knotwithstadt."

Stillness passed among them and the crackling from the hearth was the only sound pervading the room.

Relic's eyes bounced between Breunor and Percival, "Alright," he broke the silence. "I do not know if this requires—"

"When will the wraith return?" Breunor interrupted.

"Uh..." Relic was taken aback.

The knight continued to press. "How soon can we expect another attack?" he demanded.

"I don't know!" The gargoyle cleared his throat. "This is my first abowraith! Could be a few nights, could be a few weeks," he paused, thrusting a finger toward the door in emphasis. "And it could be right outside the door right now listening intently to our conversation!"

The laif did not like that implication and instinctively stepped closer to Percival.

"You're scaring her," Breunor warned.

"She should be scared," Relic said sharply. He abruptly turned toward the girl with what may have been a smile. "What did you see, little one? Not many escape a trap like that without sustaining some sort of mind scratch."

The girl bravely replied without hesitation, "Lights, mists..." She wrung her hands in the remembering. "I heard many voices, but I thought it was all a dream until Percival arrived."

"None of it was a dream," Relic stated. "Were any of the voices familiar?"

The laif nodded her head, but stayed silent for fear of crying in front of the knights.

"Did the wraith manage to touch your skin at all?"

She shook her head and the gargoyle exhaled in relief. "Now that I have found her...this actual physical link to the wraith, finding and gutting it will be much easier. Don't you see? Before I was blindly tossing darts into the ether, flying about the winter skies without any sort of reference point. This girl, this daughter of Knotwithstadt, is our best chance at ridding the forest of this curse."

"The curse that only seeks to kill the ones responsible for those innocent souls murdered at Knotwithstadt?" Breunor did not sound convinced. "I'm reluctant to stand in the way for this particular occasion."

Relic's fist shook in frustration. "That's not how it works!" he insisted. "If it were that simple, we would simply harness these demons right where they spawn!"

"Maybe you should," suggested Breunor.

"Gah!" Relic looked about ready to burst from his scales. "The host is obliterated! Changed! The host never survives! Never!"

"Oh."

"Very well," Percival finally spoke.

"No threats? No terms?" questioned Relic, sounding perplexed.

Breunor turned to Percival, which the gargoyle perceived as a slight. "Remember, we must make for the city soon. I have business to attend before we head north."

"Wait," Relic interjected. "That's it? I am joining you then? It is settled?"

Both knights turned their heads and appraised the gargoyle. Breunor scratched at his beard. "How difficult do you believe it will be to find a babysitter at this hour, Percival?" he asked with a sly grin.

The gargoyle's shoulders slumped in defeat and a wide smile broke across the werewolf's face.

* * *

"I DON'T KNOW WHAT TO TELL YOU," SAID SIR KAY for the fifth or sixth time, standing partially naked behind his dressing barrier.

Winter had interrupted him as he debated on which leggings to pair with an orange tunic that he was not entirely sure he would wear anyway. She was pacing around the room in a semicircle, allowing the dressing barrier to fulfill its duty. Throughout the entire discussion, which Kay might debate was more of an interrogation, she had not been able to make eye contact with the knight, making it difficult to read if he was lying or not. The whole business felt like a farce. She simply could not believe that Arthur had not sent word back to the capital about dismissing Sir Percival from the front.

"Doesn't your brother send dispatches?" Winter wanted to scream, but she somehow managed to dial it back.

"Half brother," Kay corrected. "Are you sure the aqua leggings with the ebony lacings would go well with the citrus top?"

Winter scraped her face with the palms of her hands. "Yes," she practically barked. "The black stitches will make the tunic appear much less radiant. You've been doing Arthur's kingly duties while he's been away, why don't you have a steward or something to help you pick out your socks and sandals?"

"I knighted my most recent squire last spring, and I have been much too busy to bring in another." Kay struggled with his reply as he wriggled the leggings up to his trunk. "And I have no interest in having a servant follow me around. Arthur managed without even a squire!"

*Well, Arthur is Arthur...*Winter wisely kept those thoughts to herself. Sir Kay did the best he could with the best intentions in mind. She held no ill will toward the laif at all, and she honestly respected him a great deal. Some of the decisions he had been forced to make over the centuries while his *half* brother has been far away, waist deep in the killing fields, would make most men abandon the post for the pub and never return from the bottom of the bottle.

"I don't believe you," Winter said to the barrier.

"That's fine," replied Kay, stepping out. "How does this look?" The laif twirled with his hands raised in surrender.

"You look gorgeous, my liege," answered Winter, a corner of her lip curled into a smile.

"You wish you were this beautiful," Kay joked, lightly patting her scar with his palm as he passed. "Now, I have nothing more to offer you in regards to this Percival business. If I knew anything, I would tell you." The knight ran his fingertips over the surface of his desk as he took a seat behind it. "I will make a few inquiries, see if any rumors tumble loose after I shake some boughs. How does that sound?" he asked, steepling his fingers under his chin.

"Why are you not more concerned by this?" Winter strode toward the desk with her fists clenched. "The King unleashed his hound on the city. This is earth shattering!" she exclaimed, no longer able to hide her frustration.

"I am concerned. Greatly, in fact." Kay's voice was quiet and calm as he placed one hand to his chest like a pledge. "The implications are not lost on me, Lord Commander. I do not like to be kept in the dark, but Arthur does the things he does and I am left to shout my protests at the wind. If the hound is loose, as you say, then I can only hope that it is for the good of the kingdom. There is nothing else I can do."

Winter wrinkled her nose, greatly dissatisfied, but was persuaded that Kay did not know more than he was letting on.

Kay's eyes swept over a particular sheet of vellum and he raised it to his eyes, scanning the words. "I don't have any answers for you," he murmured, lowering the page below his nose to meet Winter's gaze. "I don't know what to tell you."

"THAT WAS WHAT?" MUTTERED WINTER TO HERSELF as she stormed through the stone corridor, headed for her chambers. "Seven, eight times he said 'I don't know what to tell you?'"

"Afternoon, Lord Commander," a guard said to the breeze that Winter created as she swept past.

Shoving the door with her hand and accompanying it with a swift kick, the old door swung open with a bang that startled Clarial, who was sitting with her feet propped up on Winter's work bureau.

"No luck, I take it?" Clarial asked, restacking the papers she had sent fluttering.

"No!" Winter barked, stalking to the hearth and flinging a log onto the radiant ash. "Well, yes! But no!" She pinched the bridge of her nose in exasperation and turned to her friend. "Yes! It's all very interesting. Almost too interesting! Gah!" With that, she flung herself down onto her chair.

"Want some bread?" Clarial offered. Without waiting for an answer, she placed the half loaf on Winter's lap before sitting down across from her.

Winter peered down at the food, then stretched her neck back, staring at the ceiling while her hair dangled. "Thank you, Clare."

"Don't mention it," said Clarial with a crunchy mouthful, crumbs descending onto her lap.

Winter pantomimed placing items on shelves as she spoke, "First we have the cold blooded murders. Which are a puzzle unto themselves. Then we have the Church, which one would think would be concerned with the murders, demonstrably so, but it is actually diverting resources to apprehend some orphan girl that may or may not be running loose with a werewolf..."

"What's so important about this little girl?"

Winter frantically shoved herself upright. "There's so many layers!" Her bread tumbled from her lap and Clarial shot to the floor, snatching the bread before it struck the carpet. "Thank you," Winter said as she accepted the bread for the second time. She took a great bite and spoke through the soft goodness, "I'm just going to say forget it and find that werewolf," she grumbled, threateningly shaking the loaf at Clarial as if it had a lethal edge. "I wager that will get me to the bottom of this."

"Are you really this bored?"

Winter hungrily nodded, taking another bite.

"And what are you going to do when you find him?"

Feverishly, Winter's eyes panned right and left. She had not contemplated the repercussions of actually meeting Sir Percival in the flesh, only tracking him down.

"Good question."

7

PINK ON THE INSIDE

The highwaymen were circling the knights like an ill-advised cyclone. Breunor had suggested that he and Percival should leave their arms and weapons behind before trudging off for the city. And now they appeared to these fools as simple commoners with no allegiances, nor horses for that matter. It was strange though, why would anyone look to steal from folk with very little means? The knights' plan was to blend in once they entered the capital and avoid all attention, but they had failed before they even reached the highway.

Percival wore a mantle accidentally left behind by one of Breunor's female friends, and it was what apparently drew the highwaymen's attention. Before leaving, Relic had slyly commented on how well the pastels complemented Percival's eyes, which was received with a glance that merely hinted at the volumes of ire deep within the knight.

"That's no woman!" one highwayman sneered, turning his head to his companions, revealing a tattoo that resembled a blessed mark. "It's a felluh! And an ugly one at that!" The knights stood within sight of the city gates, but too far for shouts to be heard.

These brigands are apparently experienced in their craft, Breunor speculated as they stood in the epicenter of the horsemen's ring. The clouded breaths emanating from the horses as they huffed and protested was barely visible in the afternoon light. Days like these always appeared warm and inviting from inside, but the betrayal was immediate once the repellent sting of a frigid breeze slapped one full in the face as soon as one stepped outside.

Breunor quickly noticed that each of the men had marks on their necks in the precise location blessed marks could be found at birth. Some appeared legitimate, matching the warrior's symbol that both he and Percival bore, but others looked fake and conjured.

"Is that a seahorse?" Breunor asked, pointing at one of the riders, breaking the silence before any demands were made.

The man immediately thrust a finger to the side of his neck, clearly offended by the question. "No!" he spat, poking his finger on the mark. "It's a stickle-spined drake!"

"Ah, my apologies," Breunor laughed, bowing his head in mock sincerity.

The men were struggling to maintain control over their mounts. Each time one drew near, the horse would shy away and refuse to approach, no matter how much they spurred the poor animal's haunches. This made it difficult to appear formidable, and none of the men wanted to lose the advantage by dismounting, though they clearly outnumbered the perceived gentlemen. Frustrations were mounting and the scene began to grow awkward, made more so when one man began to bounce in the saddle like an angry infant bereft of its favorite toy.

"Close the circle boys!" shouted the bouncing man. He had a thick beard and was a head taller than the others, so Breunor pegged him as the leader. He also sported a legitimate looking warrior's mark on his barrel of a neck, leading Breunor to believe that he was the real deal.

The vultures circling above must have had a good chuckle when all at once the rogues spurred their mounts, but the horses were instantly repelled by the instinctual aura of terror the men were much too stupid to understand. The horses tore away from the knights at the center of the circle, screeching and bucking and tearing earthy clumps from under the snow, tainting the pure white landscape with chunky speckles of brown.

"Form up!" the leader managed to scream while he held onto his pommel with both hands, desperately trying not to further embarrass himself by taking a tumble. The horses reluctantly obeyed their riders and they slowly formed a single line between the knights and the city.

"Can we just?" Breunor asked, thumbing toward the city. "Can we be on our way?"

The situation had played out like bad theatre from the onset, and the knights were more than happy to forget that it had happened. No harm, no foul, they would continue their trek unimpeded. "We won't tell anyone..." Breunor promised.

"Quiet!" the leader shouted, something he was actually quite good at. "Dismount!"

"At least the men take orders well," Breunor murmured to Percival.

"What's that?!" The leader was shouting again.

Breunor rolled his eyes impatiently. "I was speaking to my friend here," he said, gesturing to Percival, who had thus far remained entirely placid throughout the ordeal.

"More like *wife!*" one of the quick-witted gents spouted as he led the left flank. The highwaymen began to form a proper circle with their various pointy weapons drawn. They came to a halt, their ring finally complete, and the leader broke from the ranks and began to casually speak as if they were sharing a meal.

"This does not have to be painful, but I want you both to know that you will not be surviving this," he said calmly to Breunor as he strolled past the knights, his broad shoulders nearly brushing their faces. "This has been a hard winter for us starving artists, and when we saw the fancy design on your friend's cloak, we just had to see what manner of beauty would sport such fineries in these harsh climes."

Twisting his mouth, Breunor bit back the warnings that were bubbling up inside his head. He had not yet bothered to count the fools, but he had also not wagered that Percival would allow them to get this close. *Perhaps he's getting soft?* he thought, looking around, taking a head count.

"It's true, we all shared the same disappointment," said the leader, who then eyed the scrawny panting man and amended his statement. "Well, not *all* of us, but the majority of us were disappointed when we discovered that you both are, well...men." The horses still formed an obedient wall, their tails swishing as nonchalantly as ever, their memories exceedingly short.

"After all," said the bearded brigand, towering over the knights. "We're all pink on the inside." This created a wave of exhilarated laughter that visibly startled Breunor. The knight blinked in disgust, and simply waited.

The leader licked the craters over his chapped lips. "On your knees. Now. I will not repeat myself," he growled, flicking the point of his sword toward the ground.

C'mon Percy...any time now...

When he finally spoke, Percival's voice was the sweetest sound in Breunor's ears. "Understand this," he began, and the leader looked impatiently toward the knight. A few of his men balked in their stances. Percival continued, "If you make one more movement..." he paused.

The old boy hasn't changed...

"That slightly hints of menace toward my companion," the knight wearing florals paused once more before concluding, "I will leave your bodies for the carrion birds. There will be no burial for your bones."

The highwaymen peered at one another in disbelief, their heads turning right and left. "The coward is crying!" one man shouted, thrusting a mocking finger in Percival's direction.

"Oh, shit." Breunor cursed, just before the horses screeched and scattered.

The turning heads locked forward, and instantly pure panic undulated like spreading venom, permeating the circle with terror.

Breunor immediately dropped to the ground and covered his head. That was when the snarling and tearing and ripping and pleading and screaming began. Something wet and sticky that felt like a dismembered elbow or perhaps a kneecap struck the back of Breunor's hands and he tucked his chin even further into the snow.

"But you said! You said!" pleaded one man, the next phrase coming out a trembling garbled mess, and it was not difficult for Breunor to imagine what prevented the man from normal articulation. *That's a claw in the lung.* Then a puckering sound right before a strangled gasp, *and that's the lung now apart from its body. Who's inside who now?* Breunor thought, smiling grimly. A few shouts from beyond the circle were silenced as a few tried to escape, and the only voice remaining was that of the leader. Well, not actually his voice...more like pained groans and whimpers, but Breunor did not need to lift his head to know exactly to whom they belonged.

"I have gold," promised the leader, though death tremors were slowly overtaking him. "Please, you don't have to—"

Breunor got to his feet and brushed the snow from the front of his garments. The dying man was sitting up with a chasm opened in his gut. Blood spurted out rhythmically, though weakly, from under the innards poking out. A faint mist swirled from the entrails exposed to the cold, as if they were breathing their last as well. He had no chance, yet he spoke as if he would be able walk away from this if only Percival were to leave him alone. Perhaps the man believed that a lampyr would be able to heal him, but Breunor did not need to look around to know that was not a possibility. Besides, a lampyr's healing magics were useless against wounds sustained from a werewolf.

The werewolf, soaked in the gore of the slain, plodded toward the leader. The pastels on the mantle were now caked in blood and mud and it created an oddly sinister appearance. *It really does compliment his eyes*, Breunor thought, admiring his old friend stalking toward the wounded prey.

"This doesn't—" began the leader, shaking uncontrollably. He made the mistake so often made by those before him; he tried to reason with a werewolf. Percival leaned down and buried his claws in the man's chest, snapping bone, then heaved him up onto his feet. Though Percival was a head shorter, he lifted the man so his feet dangled inches from the ice crusted snow. The man scrabbled at his own stomach, trying to tuck the dangling intestines back in, but air was escaping his lungs at a much faster rate, preventing him from staying alive much longer. Expiring within seconds, the man ceased all movement and dangled limp on the end of Percival's arm.

"You're growing soft," noted Breunor, approaching Percival who was wiping his claws on his tunic after unceremoniously discarding the corpse of the leader onto the frozen ground. "You gave them a chance."

"They were dead as soon as their boots struck the earth."

"If you say so," Breunor was not convinced. "Ten years ago you would have swept them up as soon as they first began circling us. You'd have eaten their horses right out from under them."

Percival was a man once more and was picking through the visceral debris all around them.

Fifteen! Breunor thought. *There were fifteen of the fools.* Had he not counted beforehand, the number would now be impossible to determine in all the carnage surrounding him. He watched Percival examining the dead and wondered what he was after.

"Did you lose a claw in one of them?"

The knight shook his head, "No." His eyes suddenly flickered with mild amusement when he spotted the object of his search. One particular corpse had a stump where his head should be, and Percival wrestled free the mantle that the dead man was still sporting. With measured grace, he rose and shook the debris from the article like one would snap a wet towel, flinging crystallized snow into the air. Twisting his neck and pulling with his other hand, he removed the pastel mantle and flung it aside with more vigor than he had shown to the leader of the dead idiots.

"IF I AM COMPLETELY HONEST," Breunor said after they had passed through the initial guard post at the entrance of the city. "I think I preferred you in that floral mantle."

"Heh," Percival grunted.

"But those boots are quite becoming!" commented Breunor, looking down to admire Percival's new proffered footwear. He had ripped the prior pair into strips when he transformed, which was a common hazard for his kind. "Is that the reason why you let them draw so close? So you could select your next wardrobe?"

The questions did not warrant a response, instead Percival moved the conversation to the task at hand. "Where are we going?" he asked, side stepping a pair of hunters with a deer carcass dangling from a pole they hefted from shoulder to shoulder.

"I have a couple places in mind, actually," Breunor said much more cheerfully than normal. "Try smiling at the people, Percival, just blend in." The knight advised through an overly toothy grin, nodding at a fruit vendor and his sour-looking wife. "Cast a few rays of sunshine for once in your life." Breunor's unnatural smile only deepened the recesses of the wife's frown.

"Is this better?" asked Percival, smiling widely at his companion.

"Oh my!" Breunor gaped at Percival's expression. "A smile resonates from the mouth, not the eyebrows," Breunor explained, shaking his head. "And keep your lips closed when you smile. You'll frighten the children."

Percival shrugged and stared at a passing woman with his eyebrows arched like a villain. "Where are we headed first?" he asked.

Breunor looked over his shoulder to see the woman glancing furtively at Percival before finally releasing the protective hold she had on her basket. "There's an architect I know who makes these wonderful contraptions that have proven exceedingly useful over the years," disclosed Breunor, a spring in his step, saluting a Church guard by bouncing a finger to his eyebrow.

"Sounds expensive."

"Oh, I managed to procure a decent amount of coin from your day's first slaughter before those hideous buzzards descended. It's so comforting to know that those great bald juncos still follow you around."

Percival blinked. "You mentioned a couple places?" he prompted, simultaneously shaking a fist at an infant in his mother's arms, the gesture reciprocated with matching ardor. The mother did not take any notice as she stooped over a vendor's booth brimming with gleaming baubles and necklaces.

"Yes, I did," answered Breunor, swirling a finger in the brisk air. "No big deal or anything, but to reach the second vendor we will need to visit a rather unseemly district of the capital." The sneer he received from Percival seemed to drop the temperature a few degrees. "Not to worry, though! I will only be in and out." As he spoke, he instantly regretted his choice of words.

"What exactly do you intend?" Percival growled, somehow continuing to maintain his less than stellar "gleeful" façade. "I will not be outside waiting while you express your carnal activities in some den of iniquity."

"Oh, you don't have to wait outside, you're more than welcome to join us!" Breunor quipped, knowing full well he was traversing into dangerous territory. Before Percival could react to the comment, his companion slapped him on the back and laughed heartily. "I jest, I jest!" he chuckled. "There's a laif harlot that I can sometimes procure some blood from. Depends on her mood and all that though. Lass leads a tough life."

"The contraptions are for?"

"The wards."

"Then what is the blood for?"

"The wards."

Percival looked as if he were chewing on his tongue, utterly perplexed.

Smiling politely at another Church guard, Breunor met the woman's eyes for a split second before darting forward. "If we manage to obtain a few vials, the blood should work just fine," he said, looking up at the midday shadows cast by the eaves on the stonework buildings.

"Why don't we start there then? Makes no sense to spend coin on devices that we may not require."

"Whoa!" Breunor scoffed, placing a hand to his heart as if deeply offended. "You have no idea what you are saying. We are getting explosives, no matter what," he shook his head vigorously. "I am not leaving this city without them."

"STARK MALICE?" THE SCORN WAS EVIDENT in Percival's voice as they began to ascend a second flight of creaky stairs. "That was the name given to him at birth?"

"I don't know," Breunor shrugged, taking a careful step over a particularly rotted stair. "I have never asked him about such matters. Our relationship is strictly business. I bring coin. He gives me explosions."

Breunor heard a pained groan in response and he could not tell whether it was Percival or one of the decaying planks that had issued the noise. He had been coming to this architect for just shy of a decade, watching the building slowly grow further into disrepair with each passing season. For someone gifted as a designer and builder, Stark did not pay much attention to the integrity of the structure he lived in. Breunor knew the client list was rather short, but Stark charged a hefty bit of gold for his wares. Never once had a product failed, and on multiple occasions the spectacular display over-exceeded all expectations. The man was a true artist in every sense.

The first time the knight had employed one of Stark's devices, he had purchased only a single caltrop for experimental purposes. The artist had strongly encouraged him to buy at least four for the maximum effect, but the hefty price tag dissuaded the knight from spending any more on something he was not certain would work. *But, oh my, did it work!*

He had nestled the caltrop into the side of a riverbank worn nearly flat by the large amount of kapreta traffic that passed through. That was all he had to do. Set it and forget it. As he watched from an overhead branch, far enough to avoid any possible debris (at least he thought it was far enough), the first monster slogging from the water managed to avoid triggering the mechanism, but the second one...*Oh my!* The liquid shockwave that peppered his face nearly tore him from his perch. It was one of the most glorious spectacles he had ever witnessed. A tear began to form under his eyelid at the mere memory.

"Breunor?" inquired Percival, a look of disdain painting his face.

Quickly blinking and swiping at his face, Breunor sniffed. "It's so musty in here, isn't it?" Managing to compose himself, he saw they had arrived at Stark's unremarkable shop door.

Three taps on the door elicited a response from the inside.

"Who is it?" the voice sounded distracted, but not irritated.

"Breunor."

There was a sound of sprockets and gears getting disconnected just beyond the hinges. "Alright, come in. It's unlocked."

The room was pleasantly bright, the windows nearly overtaking the west wall from floor to ceiling. The sun poured onto the shiny fragments of wire and various metals used as casings for the deadly toys arranged in a simple fruit vendor's booth. The rest of the room was a crafter's paradise, covered with all manner of tools, and precision calipers, squares, and measuring devices arranged meticulously on work benches specifically built for each type of explosive. One had a ventilation port like a chimney that reached the ceiling and vented out into the clear blue atmosphere above. Unlike the rest of the dilapidated building, this room looked like it could survive even the strongest of gale force winds.

"This isn't your first visit, so just go ahead and pick whatever you want from the shelves there," Stark said as he walked back to a central station covered in trinkets with a strapless purse at the center. "I don't think I have concocted anything new since you were last here." He sat down, lowering a magnifier from the selection adorning his head like a crown and fixed his attention on the purse. His tongue flicked out as he concentrated on his work.

"I hope you are faring well over these cold months." Breunor remarked, regarding an orb shaped device with a white fuse protruding from its top. The shape of the explosive fit very nicely in his hands.

"Yes, yes, very well," Stark stated absently. He looked up with a start, suddenly noticing that Breunor had brought company. His left eye, which was greatly magnified, blinked in rapid succession before he snapped the lens up. "I see you have ignored one of my rules," he fumed, standing up, his normally steady hands quivering. The artist fixed an angry look on Breunor. "But that's okay," he continued, "If he starts any funny business, I have back up." With that, Stark abruptly raised his hand and snapped dramatically.

The unarmed knights quickly looked around the space, expecting an explosion or a cavalcade of muscled guardians to appear, but there was nothing except rough silence settling over the room.

"Ha!" Stark roared, reaching under his jacket to produce a flask from his breast pocket. With a wink, the artist threw his head back and took a swig. "Focuses my mind!" he insisted. Even though the tension in the room had been deflated, the knights still waited for something lethal to happen. Seeing the paired look of concern on their faces, Stark spoke again, taking his seat.

"I'm only playing with you," he chuckled reassuringly. "You may bring as many people as you wish, as long as your coin remains good."

8

NO WEAPONS, NO EXCEPTIONS

B reunor was not the least bit surprised when Percival opted to remain outside while he ran the last of the morning's errands. The werewolf had not been convinced that it was a simple procurement of blood, believing that there would be *other* fluids involved. It was probably a smart decision on his part, in the end.

After all, Breunor ruminated as he walked into the only halfway decent looking building on the block. *I did say that it was up to her mood at the time...*

As very few still living creatures had ever cast eyes upon Percival, most having only heard tales and scatter-brained reports, Breunor was unconcerned that the were-wolf-knight would be recognized as he stood waiting in this shady, grimy district of less than desirables. Camelot was a bold and booming region, despite its ruler leaving the throne bereft. Beneath its majesty teemed an under-world of crooked schemers and lazy drifters, which was to be expected any place where mortals made up the main populace.

Breunor approached the pulpit situated a few steps into the lobby, much like a hostess station at a fine restaurant, where a woman leaned heavily on its surface, somehow remaining on her feet. Breunor was unsure whether this brothel hostess was still among the living, and as he raised a tentative hand to her unmoving shoulder, the woman suddenly shot up with a loud snort.

"Geeze!" yelped Breunor, faltering a pace backward.

The woman sloppily ran a wrist across her nose, heedless of her present state and drawled, "Can I interest you in upgrading from the 'Single Slam' to a 'Daemonic Triple' for a mere sod's pittance of fifty gold?" She made a feeble attempt at batting her eyelashes seductively. "It's our 'Blow Life into Winter' special."

Breunor's mind whirled at the offer, but he knew that he did not have the time for that type of fun today. He smoothed the corner of his moustache and turned his head, looking at the woman sideways. "I'm afraid I must decline," he said, conveying disappointment at refusing the woman's enticing offer. "Is the minimum still an hour's time..." he paused, squinting at the woman's nametag. "Chelsea?"

The hostess looked puzzled for an instant, then glanced down and looked back up with a confident expression. "Yep, Chelsea, that's me..." Her voice trailed off as she stared at something in the distance.

Breunor followed her fixed eyes over his shoulder. "So, uh, is it still an hour minimum?" He swiveled his head to the other corners of the empty room, feeling less than assured by her demeanor. "I don't need much time, honestly."

Chelsea appraised him from head to toe. "Ah, I see...yes, it's still an hour minimum. Payment up front," she said with a yawn. "Most of the girls and boys are still cleaning up after the lunch rush, so if you have a particular partner in mind, please ask and I can check their availability."

Check their availability? Breunor blinked. *That's new.*

He cleared his throat, "Is—"

She cut him off, "Ah, I see you'll need someone sturdy," she remarked, tapping her own neck, indicating Breunor's warrior's mark. Scaling the paper on the dais with her spindly finger, her lips moved silently through the list of names.

"I'm actually looking for Silvien?" Breunor stated, the phrase rising in pitch at the end making it sound like a question.

The hostess' finger stopped its incremental descent. "She's a two-hour minimum."

Already rummaging through his purse, Breunor began to work over the coins inside to produce twice the amount he had anticipated. "Fine, fine," he muttered, clinking gold onto the wood.

The woman inclined her head toward a set of benches along the wall. "If you'll just take a seat, she won't keep you hanging for long," she promised, sliding the coins toward herself with a hungry smile.

These are also new, thought Breunor with a sigh, trudging for the newly crafted benches lining the wall like a lowered tavern bar. His mind wandered back to Percival, who was holding the bags of explosives outside. *Maybe I went a little crazy with the fuseless snaps, but you can't go wrong with them, really...well, as long as Percival doesn't shake them too hard.*

Chelsea had returned to her unnatural pose, sleeping upright with her upper body pressed onto the dais, arms flung out so her fingertips dangled. The building was quiet, not a squeak of a mattress nor the moan of a client could be heard through the floors and thin walls.

A few years ago, Silvien had let the knight in on the secret. "Trinkets imbued with silencing magic," she had told him, indicating with her eyes a sapphire chain and locket dangling from a nail several feet above the headboard. He remembered slapping a palm to his forehead, feigning that he "should have thought of that," but really the idea of magic rarely crossed his mind. At the time he had been consumed, and actually still was consumed with his goal. His goal, which did not require the use of spells or incantations. This jaunt to Knotwithstadt would be the first break in many years, and honestly the village was on his to-do list anyhow. No harm in bumping its priority up a few notches.

From the corner of his eye, Chelsea suddenly sprang to an alert pose, looking a bit like a puppet whose strings are jerked all at once. Her arms fell limply to her sides, which complemented the illusion quite nicely. Light from the open door flooded the dais.

"We've been expecting you," she said with an unnatural lurch forward, as if her feet were nailed to the floor. The sound of several pairs of boots thudded through the entryway.

I thought I beat the lunch rush? Breunor was puzzled. He slowly pressed his back to the wall in a vain attempt to remain hidden from the army of newcomers. Several blazing sconces flickered around him, abundantly illuminating the space. His eyes darted to the torches, wishing he could extinguish them, though he knew the odds that he would be recognized were slim. He had not attended a tourney or gala in many seasons, and he believed that his reputation had dwindled to rumor once he had made the decision to abandon the Round Table for a life of violent purpose and solitude.

Five Church guards stood before the hostess, swords sheathed in their scabbards. The helmetless leader stood on tiptoes to press her gauntleted hands on the dais and scanned Chelsea's face. "Where?" the guard inquired with a sneer.

"Over there," Chelsea pointed at Breunor and all five heads swung toward him at the same time.

Pointing at his own chest and looking around in confused disbelief, Breunor rose to his feet. At that moment, another group of five azure guards emerged from the curtained room beyond the lobby, effectively blocking all means of escape. He noticed each guard was heavily armed.

"Hey, they aren't obeying the rules!" he complained, pointing an accusatory finger at the approaching guards.

"We've made an exception," Chelsea said coldly, her eyes flickering to the sign over her shoulder, which read **NO WEAPONS, NO EXCEPTIONS**. As a further insult, she flipped the wooden rectangle over revealing a crudely drawn phallus with a hand protruding from the shaft offering a thumbs down.

"Oh, come on," Breunor whined as he was led away.

PERCIVAL SAW THE GUARD DETAIL enter the establishment, and chose to follow the second set that traversed the alley leading to the rear of the building. After a few moments spent lingering in the fenced backyard, surrounded by refuse and acrid odors activated by the sunlight pouring atop the mess, the sounds of rattling armour and stern protests splintered the air from the front of the building.

"Things are never simple," he angrily lamented to a goblin standing on a ledge overlooking the heaps of trash. The creature peered down at the knight for a moment and gave a single nod of agreement before returning to his task. He performed a flawless swan dive into the pile, leaving the entry point relatively undisturbed.

***

DIDN'T THINK I'D BE ON THESE STAIRS again so soon, thought Winter, carefully placing her feet one after the other on the stone staircase. She had been engrossed in a spirited debate with a table of perspective deputies when word reached them that a patrol had picked up Sir Breunor. The Church had been pursuing the knight for at least half a decade regarding some suspicious activity he was reported to have been embroiled in. Winter had raised an eyebrow at the report, wondering aloud why the Church still cared after all these years.

The only explanation from the stocky middle-aged guard with a thick moustache and equally thick eyebrows was some nonsense about the census.

"Why do all roads seem to lead to the orphanages?" Winter had huffed as she rose to her feet, a little unsteady after consuming five and half pints of some bitter brew. She had theatrically swallowed the remainder of her current pint in one go, announcing, "Never leave a man behind!" and had followed with, "Where are they holding this knight...Sir...Sir...what was his name? Sir...Sir..." She snapped her fingers less than an inch from the stocky guard's nose.

"Breunor," he finished, leaning far from her intruding finger snaps. "I imagine they'll be keeping him in the holding cells under the old barracks. That's where we routinely keep—"

"Thank you!" Winter spun on her heel. "That name sounds so familiar," she remarked, placing her fingers to her chin in contemplation as she made for the door. Walking through the city streets deep in thought, she still could not recall why that name was so familiar.

She was just a hair more sober by the time she reached the bottom of the mossy staircase leading to the holding cells.

"Where's Kirk?" she asked, staring at the gaoler on the landing.

"What the—" the startled man tried to respond but was cut off when she placed her forefinger on his lips.

"Shhh, it's alright," she slurred, removing her finger and wiping it on the gaoler's tunic. "Which cell is Sir Bray-oh-nee-nor in?" Her lips felt like they were working overtime attempting to correctly form the knight's name.

The gaoler's confusion only increased. "Who?"

His eyes shot up to the stairs behind her and he instantly straightened. "Sir Breunor!" the gaoler whispered, hearing the rattling of armour coming from the downward stony grade. The man in question was having a bit of difficulty on the slippery stones with his hands bound behind him. And he was apparently notorious enough for the gaoler to know him based on sight. The pairing sets of guards to his front and back were of no help concerning support and the knight slipped more than once on the gradient leading into the prison.

Perhaps destroying those stairs and replacing them with a slide would prove safer, considered Winter as she pressed herself against the wall, allowing the prisoner and his retinue to crack the ancient door open and enter the cells. When the last of the guard disappeared into the dank dungeon, Winter followed behind. She paused to glance back at the gaoler, but he simply smiled and waved as she crossed the threshold.

The group stopped midway and unlocked cell eleven. The shortest of the guard gave the knight an overeager shove of encouragement to enter, which unfortunately did not have the disheartening effect she intended. The knight simply shrugged the force away, redirecting the guard's weight. She tripped on her own feet causing her to be the first to arrive in the cell while he remained standing outside, completely unfazed by the aggressive push.

Winter could not contain her amusement and snickered through her covered mouth. At once five heads spun toward the noise, previously unaware that there was someone behind them. Before they could respond, she assumed the air of Lord Commander and spoke, "Alright, patrol." She pushed her way through the group and clamped a hand on Breunor's bicep. "I can take the prisoner from here. Good work. All of you. You should be proud." The statements fell way more formal than she intended, so she grinned and added, "First round at the Stableyard is on me!" This proclamation was met with broad smiles, and one patrolman even clapped a few times before slowly petering off when he realized he was alone in his fervor.

"Who are you?" the short guard demanded. She was not smiling from where she stood in the cell.

The guard who was inclined to clap spoke up, "She's the Lord Commander of the royal guard and she'll soon be *our* Lord Commander," he paused, beseeching Winter for an answer. "In what? Five or six weeks, something like that?"

"Yeah," Winter said with a shameless hiccup. "Something like that."

"I can't even pretend to care anymore," the short guard responded wearily and made her exit from the cage. She continued walking to the main door, leaving the others behind. The three remaining guards watched their comrade's departure and stood awkwardly for a few seconds as Winter stood rigidly clutching Breunor's arm.

"Are we?" one guard began.

Winter waved a hand. "Dismissed." She watched the blue cloaks depart, the last heaving the door closed behind him, which significantly dimmed the atmosphere. "Ooh, setting the mood..." Winter giggled under her breath as she urged Breunor into the cell.

"What was that?" the well-groomed knight asked with an arched brow.

"Nothing for you to worry your pretty face about," Winter said, pulling the cell gate closed with more momentum than was necessary. The resounding clash rattled the bars all along the jail, humming vibrations throughout the basement.

"Hey! I'm trying to sleep!" a familiar voice shouted from two cells to Winter's right.

*The baker's daughter's kidnapper...*Eyes bulging, Winter shouted, "You pipe down, sir! I'm still coming for you one of these days!" she warned.

Silence hung for a moment while the bars of cell eleven gradually diminished their rattles, then the voice softly replied, "I'll be here."

Breunor raised his shackled wrists. "I would shake your hand," he said with a smirk. "Which is something that you may find much different after you serve your term in public office."

"Yeah, yeah," Winter waved the air as if a host of gnats swirled at her face. "I get it, yeah, and before you ask, I will be having my left hand removed, so shaking hands won't be any different than how it is now."

"I had no idea anyone was stepping up as sheriff," admitted Breunor, crossing his arms with a shrug. "I'm a little out of touch with politics."

"And I don't really know who you are," said Winter, leaning against the closed cell door. "If you can't tell, I'm nursing a bit of a buzz right now."

"You don't say."

Winter wrinkled her nose. "Don't judge me, you're the last one between us who can judge anything right now."

Breunor's eyes traced the bars from floor to ceiling as he took a few meandering steps around his new accommodations. "If you say so."

"Look, I'm going to level with you here," Winter began, picking at a flake of rust on the door lock. "I don't do well with 'down time', and if I'm idle for too long I begin to lose my mind. I'm here for a pleasant conversation, no interrogations. I just want to know why they dragged you down here is all."

"I have no idea."

"You're a knight, right?" Winter rolled her wrist as she began the list. "Are you...royal, holy, errant..." she scowled, "are there any other kinds? I'm drawing a blank here."

Breunor raised his palms and shrugged, offering no help.

"Well, which are you?"

"A little of column A and column C, I suppose."

"So you're a royal knight who no longer serves the Crown, but serves himself instead, eh?" She nodded her head as if she had received an affirmative response and continued, "And somewhere along the way you offended the Church and made them sad."

Squinting in recollection, the prisoner searched his memory but came up empty.

Winter noticed the knight was deep in thought and decided to continue, hoping that a few more specific details might jog his memory. "A weird little blond birdie told me that you dropped trow and peed in a member of the census office's oatmeal cakes a few years ago."

"You're a weird bird," murmured Breunor as he moved to flop onto the provided cot, but thought better of it when he noticed the trail of mold beginning on a slit in the mattress and running upward along the wall, disappearing in some damp crevice out of sight. He imagined with horror the vast swath of spores that would have issued from the depths of that worn out cushion if he had partaken in its intended use. "Not today!" he whispered to the cot.

"Come on! Tell me what you did to make them bring you in for questioning!" Winter could feel sobriety creeping up and wished for another drink. "What did you do?" she pressed again.

"I don't remember peeing on anyone, and I don't remember committing any untoward act in the census office," admitted Breunor, returning to the front of the cell to face her. "After I left the Crown I have been keeping to myself. I live on the outskirts of Fenrirfang and hunt. That's all, really. They probably nabbed the wrong guy."

"Another case of mistaken identity, huh?"

Breunor nodded.

"Why did you leave the Crown and why do you live by yourself?"

"Those are two questions that actually share a single answer, but I'm not in the mood to give a history lesson right now."

"Awww," Winter rolled her eyes, then rolled them further as the atmosphere brightened. Light seeped into the massive room as the door opened across the expanse, the loud creaking out of sync with the movement.

A man in the basic azure mantle of the Church guard approached them, the hood drawn up and shadows obscuring his face. He had a powerful bearing that unsettled Winter. It made her feel oddly outranked for the first time since becoming Lord Commander. The man abruptly stopped several paces from Breunor's cell, but Winter still could not make out his face, only a stubbled chin below a tight-set mouth.

"Perc—!" exclaimed Breunor, stopping himself short. "My purse!" He attempted to correct the slip and decided to ramble as a cover. "Those hoodlums took my purse when they arrested me! I have some important personal items in it and I would greatly appreciate it being returned to me. Is that why you are here, Sir?" He pointed an accusatory finger at the newly arrived Church official. "Are you here to return my purse?!"

The man ignored Breunor's demands. "Ma'am," he said politely, striding directly in front of Winter to stand before the gate. She shuffled a pace backward, granting him access. A sudden primal instinct surged in her veins, repressing any urges to question this particular man.

The guard spoke with his back to her. "I was sent to release the prisoner."

"Don't you need keys?" she queried, hesitancy lilting her voice.

With two hands positioned above the lock, the man straightened his back and bent at the knees as if preparing to heave a blacksmith's anvil.

"Keys work better..." Winter quietly advised, trailing off.

The man lowered his head and when his chin settled, he violently jerked the gate forward, causing it to rattle in protest. He arched back with tremendous force and snapped the hinges free. Metal dust and shavings cascaded to the floor, their soft tinkling the only sound filling the silence.

Winter stood in shock, locked in place, staring as the man's arms began to diminish in size and the clawed hands that had deftly set the door aside returned to a less hairy, human form.

~ 9 ~

SWORDS ARE BORING

"Well, that was easy," stated Breunor as he stepped into the daylight.

Winter followed behind the pair, pausing to nudge the prostrate form of the gaoler tucked inside the dungeon's entryway. *Still alive...glad it wasn't my sweet Kirk on duty today.* She thoughtfully glanced to the heavens in gratitude for the indulgence.

The gaoler's cloak had been stripped and his keys were still strung to his hip. His sword remained sheathed as well. *Caught by surprise.* Winter lifted her eyes to the back of the imposter as he led the still shackled Breunor up the slick stairs. The man was no doubt Sir Percival in the flesh...*or fur?* She shook her head and opened her mouth to protest, or offer advice, or simply ask that they allow her to tag along in whatever outlandish nonsense they were embroiled in. Before she could speak, another voice entered the space. The voice came from merely a handful of paces ahead of the knights at the top of the landing. She could not make out who was speaking, but she immediately recognized their affiliation.

"Who authorized this prisoner's release?" The husky female voice carried quite a way and no doubt drew attention from all passersby. Winter could sense the collective of heads turning and feet stopping to check the scene.

Percival looked at Breunor, and Breunor looked back at Percival and shrugged.

"I...I was told to release the prisoner," Percival stammered, clearly out of his depth when it came to deception.

"By whom?"

"By...by..." Percival turned to Breunor, who only offered another shrug. "By Antonio," the knight finished, hoping this would satiate her curiosity.

Winter watched the guard's face crinkle like a crumpled parchment, "Antonio...who the bloody—" she said, confused and angered by the feeble attempt at trickery.

"Come now, guard man," Winter interjected, stepping between the knights. She gave Percival a patronizing pat on the shoulder as she passed, navigating the stairs. Her eyes scanned the retinue of Church guards, finally falling on the angry guard whose countenance did not brighten at Winter's arrival. "I gave them clearance. We are moving the prisoner to dryer accommodations. The damp environment is giving him a fever, you know."

The guard wiped the corners of her mouth in exasperation, and paused to let the information settle, trying to decide which question to ask first. "And *who* are you?" she snapped, folding her arms and awaiting another clever response. Before Winter could respond, another guard leaned close and whispered in the angry guard's ear. A flash of recognition passed over her face, but her features did not soften. "So you're to be our new commander? Why are you getting involved before your tenure begins?"

Though still in an alcoholic haze, Winter bristled at the inquisition. She magnificently maneuvered the stairs without sliding an inch and stormed toward the guard, bringing her face level with the woman. "The real question is who the hekk are *you?*" Each word was dripping with indignation. *If you can't give a proper response, then take offense and shame the other person into submission.* Before the guard could reply, Winter spoke again. "If any of *my* court guards spoke to me with half the amount of disdain in their voice, I would reach into their anus and pull their tongue back out through the cork hole."

The guard's veneer began to crack and she faltered. "My... my deepest apologies...It's just that this situation is a bit—" she stammered.

Winter drove a forearm into her chest, effectively silencing the guard. "I don't answer to you," Winter spat, forcing the guard aside. The blue cloaks parted, and she turned and gestured for the knights to follow.

"Thank you for your service," Breunor jeered as he passed. "Really first class. Top rate." His wink was interrupted by a tug from Percival.

Percival approached Winter, pulling Breunor along behind. The recently released knight was blowing kisses at his captors and stumbled to keep up.

"Thank you for that," Percival said, walking next to Winter. "But we must part ways."

Winter gave a nod and peered into the crowds ahead as if they were shrouded in darkness. "Where is the orphan girl?" she asked, not mincing words.

This snapped Breunor's focus onto the conversation. "Wait. How do you—?"

Percival's cowl was drawn, but Breunor wagered that the werewolf's ears were beginning to grow pointy under the fabric.

"I know a great many things," Winter said with a toothy smile. "One of those being that you are going to need me in order to get out of the capital."

"I highly doubt that," scoffed Breunor as they approached the busy street laden with foot traffic. The alleyway they traversed offered a limited view of the market, the brick on both sides smeared with crusted ice and snow. "We'll be parting ways like my friend told you."

They were about three steps from entering the fray when, right on cue, a young guard took notice of them and stepped into the alley.

"Hey!" he said, holding a hand up, signaling stop. With his other hand he gestured to his companions down the lane. "We just arrested this fellow. I don't recall hearing word of a transfer." The guard locked eyes with Percival and began to nervously twirl the wispy beard hairs springing from under his chin. "And I don't recognize—" he began.

"The prisoner is under my care now..." Winter trailed off, hoping the guard would offer his name.

"Hamitch," the neck beard replied. Recognizing Winter as soon as she spoke, he continued, "My apologies, Lord Commander. I saw him and I just..."

"It's perfectly alright. You were just doing your job, Hammock," Winter said. She glanced at Percival and tilted her head in a silent 'I told you so.'

The neck beard guard's smile faltered. "It's Hamitch, sir," he quietly corrected, stepping aside with a signal for his fellow guards to go back to whatever it was they were doing. The guards watched Breunor pass by, and one raised a finger in protest, but neck beard waved and shouted, "They are cleared!"

"Alright!" Breunor had to shout to be heard over the myriad of noises around them. Vendors shouting their wares, customers rigorously haggling prices, children screeching and running between legs, and livestock mewling and braying in their respective tongues. "What's your game?" the shackled knight demanded.

"No games," replied Winter, placing a careful hand atop a scurrying child who was chasing another. "Well, kind of..."

Breunor tripped on the flagstone and growled a curse. "Speak plain, Commander!" he shouted. "We aren't blessed with unending time!"

"I know who you both are, and to be quite frank, I want to come along."

Percival and Breunor swiveled their heads at one another.

Winter sensed their disapproval and continued, "I can be of great help. I have a lot of resources at my disposal."

"That's precisely why we must part ways," Percival began to walk faster, dragging Breunor for a few steps before he increased his pace.

Winter jogged forward and placed a hand on Percival's shoulder. "If you are skeptical of my motives, then ask yourself this: why would I be helping you to leave the city?"

"That is yet to be seen," Percival replied.

"What?!" Winter squawked. "I could have easily summoned guards to plunk this knight back in his cell. The Lord Commander of Arthur's court holds quite a bit of sway in these parts, my friend. I am a valuable ally."

"Then why come with us? Would that not place you in some sort of political peril?" asked Breunor, not buying into her logic.

"Oh, most definitely." Winter's face took on a savage look that caused Breunor to pause. It seemed that the ale was finally leaving her system. "But you see, my reasons are my own!" she roared, turning a few heads in their direction; quite a feat as the general din surrounding them was just a few knocks shy of a battle roar.

"For all that is holy!" yelled Breunor, his eyes scanning the crowd for Church livery. "Just get us to the north gate and then we will talk further!"

Suppertime smells began to pervade the street, rich broths simmering and warm breads baking as households began to wind down before twilight. Men and women were returning from their labors, children wandering back from lessons, all playing their daily part. Each famished and ready for a hot meal and smiling faces sharing tales from the day's toil. Complaints of lazy workmates and triumphs over difficulties, the conversations varying but all welcome once one crossed under the threshold leading inside *home*. Comforts that Percival and Breunor, nor Winter, for that matter, had felt in a long time.

Winter's stomach began to growl, and she noticed with great relief that the gates were just short of thirty paces away. The temperature had dropped at least ten degrees during their walk and heavy flakes of snow began tumbling down.

When they passed the last stall, Percival turned to Winter without breaking stride. "What can you do for us?" the knight asked, surprising both people flanking him.

"What do you need?" Winter said, distractedly brushing a massive snowflake from her eyebrow.

At that moment, a cluster of a sheep entered the gate, much later in the day than the herder would have preferred. When the forefront of the fluffy creatures spotted Percival, they began to bleat and break. Bounding in all directions, it was every sheep for herself, their eyes as wide as dinner plates. The herdsmen struggled to bring the small flock under control. Their dogs, however, seemed to be in their glory, nipping and urging the animals back into order.

"First of all," Breunor began, his eyes bouncing between the pair of guard towers looming ahead. "We need discretion. And second," he paused, sidestepping a shepherd dog on its course to reclaim one of its lost charges. Straightening his collar, he continued, "We need a jug of laif blood."

***

CLARIAL, UNLIKE WINTER, enjoyed having nothing to do. After years of service on the front lines without a holiday, patrolling makeshift ramparts and sleeping in shifts, she was more than ready for a spell of relaxation. This was her first paid leave, and she had most definitely earned it.

Winter had been gracious enough to allow her unconditional reign of her solar, and she was taking full advantage of the comforts that accompanied sharing a space with the Lord Commander of Camelot's palace guard. Fresh game was readily available, all she had to do was beseech a passing servant or page and the hot meal would arrive piping hot within an hour's time...sometimes less.

And the best part, she was not compelled to share with anyone, the food was all hers.

As she was settling down by the hearth, looking forward to a quiet evening accompanied by a warm blanket and a savory meat pie filled with grouse and potatoes, Winter whirled into the room spouting questions about laif blood and vials. Sir Percival's name was mentioned several times amidst the other nonsense. Clarial could not decipher what her friend was going on about.

"Go slower," she implored, leaning forward to place her pie on a short table before the hearth. "Wait, have you been drinking?"

"What?" Winter tried to blink the room back into focus. "Yeah, so what? I stopped at a pub for a quick pint on the way back, but that's not important at all right now."

Clarial rested her chin in her hands. "Start from the beginning and go slow," she said calmly, as if she were speaking to a child who had just seen a ghost. "I'm not going anywhere."

Taking a deep breath and when her shoulders settled, Winter noticed the pie. "Ooh, is there another pie?" she asked with hungry eyes. "Hold on, nevermind, I don't have time for food. Or do I?"

Clarial watched her friend pace, and after she passed for the sixth or seventh time, placed the pie in Winter's hands. "Thank you," Winter said without looking down. "Alright, so long story short," she paused to chew her first bite, "This is excellent! Is it squab?"

Nodding, Clarial decided that any clarification would only prove a distraction.

The Lord Commander continued, "I met Sir Percival." The words were near indistinguishable through the mouthful of food, but Clarial somehow managed to understand.

"You met Sir Percival?"

"Yes," Winter pointed her spoon at Clarial, sending several globs of gravy onto the carpet. "And he needs a vial of laif blood. Well, he actually requested a jug, but I believe he was being hyperbolic...now that I think about it, it actually wasn't Percival that made the request but his friend that he had just busted out of jail."

A loud aggravated sigh escaped from Clarial as she brought the blanket up over her head. "You're not making any sense!"

"Sorry, sorry!" Winter said, settling into the seat across from her shrouded friend. After gathering her thoughts for a few moments, she drew the day's events into clear descriptions and even managed to answer the barrage of questions Clarial threw at her.

"So you led them all the way to the gate and past the guard houses, and when you asked them for a map or directions to Breunor's cottage they told you that they would leave you *a trail of bread crumbs?*" Clarial asked, incredulous.

Winter had to pause for that one. "Metaphorically, of course," she replied with a measure of uncertainty. "They will probably leave some other sort of indicator."

Clarial spoke under her breath. "Let's hope so," she muttered. "I am curious, though. Where do you intend to procure a bucket of laif blood? That's not something you'll find at even the creepiest apothecary."

Winter shrugged and shoveled another bite into her mouth.

"I mean, you could just get some goat blood or something, right? Who cares? You'll be traveling with a werewolf and a master hunter," remarked Clarial, twirling a lock of her hair. "How many wards are there between here and Knotwithstadt?"

Placing her spoon into the bowl, Winter held both hands up to display the answer. She did not want to be rude and respond with a full mouth.

"Seven?" Clarial asked, sinking back into her chair. "I hope you'll make it back in time for your ceremony."

"You mean, you hope *we'll* make it back in time," Winter said.

"Why are you looking at me like that?"

"Oh, you know why."

"No way," Clarial stated and tossed the blanket aside as she stood.

Winter spoke through a full mouth. "Yes."

"I just got back from the West, Winter," Clarial argued, throwing another log into the hearth. "This is my holiday.

I don't want to do anything but eat, sleep, and eat. And maybe drink," she paused for a moment. "Nope, definitely drink. That is my aim until I am summoned to return."

"How long will that be?" Winter asked, watching the embers burst around the fresh log on the flames.

"None of your business," Clarial replied, wiping her hands on her leggings.

"Will it be after I am made sheriff?" Winter persisted. "Come on, give me a hint."

Folding her arms with a scowl, Clarial planted her feet and spoke to her friend. "As much fun as all this sounds," she sighed, exasperated. "Running around the forest, splashing laif blood everywhere, and traveling to a kapreta infested forest village with an orphan, a disgraced knight, and a werewolf..." Clarial trailed off.

"Wait!" she suddenly exclaimed. "That does sound like fun."

Winter clapped her hands and shouted in triumph.

"On one condition," Clarial said, pointing toward the armoury at the back of the solar. "You let me use the *Tide Shifter*."

"I was just about to offer her to you," Winter answered casually. "There's no way I would leave her behind."

"Excellent!" Clarial cheered. "Swords are boring."

THE PAIR SET OFF FROM WINTER'S CHAMBERS as soon as the sun crested the horizon. Spending the evening preparing for a quest had made sleeping difficult, and the morning had arrived much faster than they felt was fair. The snow had stopped falling overnight, making Winter optimistic that the trail left behind by the knights would still be visible.

"The butcher is this way," Clarial said, tugging the cuff of Winter's gambeson.

"Oh, right," replied Winter, still in a sleepy daze. She spun toward the direction Clarial pointed. It was too early for most vendors and shops, only the bakeries seemed to be awake and ready for the day. The scent of the fresh bread baking was nearly overwhelming to Winter. "Mind if we stop in for a breakfast loaf?" She slowed her pace, pausing to gaze longingly into the window.

"We have enough provisions," Clarial countered. "And we don't have time to wait in line for the day's first pumpernickel."

Bowing her head in agreement, Winter stepped quickly to keep up. "Mmmm, pumpernickel," she mumbled, "but you are correct, time is of the essence."

The butcher shop was located three doors from the bakery and Winter knew that it opened well before the crack of dawn. "The early-rising louts and mouth breathers desperately need their bacon," Winter had told her friend the night before. "So our tight timetable shouldn't be disturbed at all if we go in there before sunrise."

A pair of squat, balding middle-aged men pushed through the door into the street as Winter and Clarial approached the shop. One of the men had his face pressed inside a pouch and was loudly inhaling the contents inside. The other man held a look of desperate wonder as his greedy eyes locked onto the pouch in his friend's hands. With a healthy bang, the door swung shut the instant Winter reached the front stoop.

She shook her head and pushed the door open. "Mouth breathers!" she hissed.

The frail-looking skeleton of a man behind the counter offered them an exhausted smile. "Greetings, ladies," he said without an ounce of enthusiasm, wiping his hands on his bloodied apron. "That's a mean looking poleaxe you've got there..." he paused, eyeing the weapon. "So how many pounds would you like?"

"It's a halberd," stated Winter, unimpressed with the man's lack of weapon knowledge.

"Pounds of what?" Clarial interrupted, placing her hands on the counter and surveying the plethora of meats on display.

The butcher shrugged. "Bacon, of course," he twirled a finger at the pile of thick-cut slabs of raw marbled meat on a wooden platter.

"I imagine we'll need—" Clarial tried to place an order but was blocked by her companion.

"We are not here for bacon or sausage, or any other meat, for that matter," Winter said sharply, folding her arms.

The man's eyebrows shot up on his high forehead, causing the skin to wrinkle below his receding hairline. Meanwhile, a woman entered leading a little girl by the hand, causing the man's eyes to flash to the entry door.

"I will be with you in a moment, Mrs. Pendlebrick," the man called out. He leaned closer to Winter and closed one eye as if the gesture required a great deal of concentration. "What is it that you are looking for?"

Her wrist briefly caught on her scale maille as she reached into her mantle and produced a corked wine skin. "It's empty," she announced, placing it on the counter and slowly sliding it toward the butcher in fractional increments.

"Alright..." The man appeared uneasy by the creeping increments. "We don't sell wine here, miss."

The wine skin continued its crawling pace as she spoke. "I am not looking for wine, my good man."

"What is it that you are looking for?" he asked, his eyes apprehensively following the wine skin on its lethargic course toward the edge of the counter. Winter ignored the saltshaker toppled by her elbow, but it broke the butcher out of his reverie and the man jumped to catch it before it tumbled onto the floor.

"I need you," Winter said softly, removing her hands from the leather receptacle. "To fill this with blood, please."

The woman in line behind them released a startled gasp and quickly covered her daughter's ears. Winter's eyes rattled as they rolled. "Oh, come on, Mrs. Pendlebrick, it's only blood! It's not like I'm asking for anything remotely offensive...like the life essence of a virgin or something."

Mrs. Pendlebrick released another defiant gasp at that, and Clarial slapped the back of Winter's shoulder, urging her to leave the woman alone. "Winter..." she cautioned.

Winter relented and turned back to the butcher. "How much will this cost me?" she inquired, curling up one corner of her lip.

"I'll do it for free," he replied, giving Clarial an obvious wink. "As long as you buy two pounds of our fresh bacon." His hand swept over the pile of breakfast meat with the flourish of a drunken mummer.

Exhaling as if she had been punched in the gut, Winter replied with pained acquiescence. "Fine."

~ 10 ~

AS LAMBS

"I thought you said it would be a *metaphorical* trail of bread crumbs?" Clarial cried in disbelief.

Standing at the gate with her halberd planted in several inches of shifting snow, the wind billowing her mantle, Winter laughed, grinning at the sight greeting her on the snowy plain. Her eyes were filled with delight, gazing at the knuckle-sized chunks of bread peeking out from below the white drifts along a northeast trail of footprints. Just above the snow, thin wisps of icy powder played and twirled, threatening to cover the *crumbs*.

"Apparently not," Winter chuckled. "Now, what did that drover say about controlling the herd? Square my shoulders in the direction I intend, and the dog will do the rest?" she asked Clarial, looking down at the scruffy-looking mutt staring back at her.

"Yeah, something like that," Clarial replied. "Do you think that sheep like to eat bread?"

"Not sure, but that would be most fortuitous," stated Winter, giving the sack on her shoulder a reassuring tug.

"Let's hope that this works." With that, the Lord Commander squared her shoulders to the trail of *actual* breadcrumbs. Instantly the dog bounded to the flock's right flank and the reluctant livestock began to plod along, gingerly at first but soon assuming a trot.

The drover had been extremely reluctant to part with any of his herding dogs, even after Winter had foregone the urge to haggle and had settled on the initial price he promoted. When it started to look like the deal may not have been brokered, Clarial stepped in to tell the man that the herd was on a one-way trip, and they would try their best to return the dogs. The man began to ask questions that neither Clarial nor Winter were willing to answer, but he finally agreed to part with the cleverest of his herders as long as they put up thirteen gold as collateral.

"I want to get old Twiggy back in one piece," he had stated, giving the women a wary once over with his good eye (the other was foggily obscured with a milky sheen, which had been admittedly a bit off-putting). "If you don't, then I'm keeping the gold." He made a feeble attempt to wink with his milky eye, but the muscles around it only twitched and the eyelid did not close, so he just stared into the beyond. After an uncomfortable period of time had passed, Winter extended a hand and the deal was set.

The early morning's sunlight was blinding against the snow, and both travelers squinted as hard as they could against the nearly overwhelming brilliance. The trail the knights had left turned out to be easier to follow than expected, and on several occasions, Twiggy nipped a few sheep that had slowed to nibble on the more generous hunks of bread littering the ground. As they drew closer to Fenrirfang Forest and the wilds and evils that lay inside its near endless boundary, Clarial and Winter slowed their pace, affording more distance between themselves and the flock.

Once they passed the toppled battlements that riddled the meadow, snowy fields stretched before them like untouched vellum. Twiggy drifted inside the gap between the herd and the women, sometimes slowing just enough for Clarial to give him a quick scratch behind one of his pointy ears.

Suddenly, the dog bristled and snarled as the fur on his neck shot up into a ridge. With teeth bared, the dog lowered himself as if to pounce, staring with heated distaste at the forest. Clarial and Winter shared a look and without exchanging words came to a halt, watching the oblivious herd continue on.

The skinniest faewolves and goblins Winter had ever seen broke from the treeline first, followed by a handful of carrion-feeding monsters, mostly ghouls and wendigos, but other less-than-desirables were included in the mix. Winter and Clarial had no desire to stick around to observe the forthcoming slaughter, so they abandoned the flock just as quickly as they abandoned their path. Sprinting away, the women cut a safe arc around the small herd that was now breaking and running desperately in all directions.

The snow proved to be quite the inhibiting factor for Winter, but Clarial, who had been blessed at birth with the sign of a runner, slowed her pace to allow her friend to keep up. The women fixed their gazes on the horizon, trying not to look toward their squealing flock being picked off and torn asunder.

An excellent diversion, Winter thought as she sucked frigid air into her lungs. *But what a cripplingly sad sacrifice.* After reaching a safe distance, the women turned back to see that the dark forms had completely overtaken the white and were greedily feasting upon them. More and more starved monsters poured from the forest as if a signal arrow had burst in the sky. The chase had ended.

Winter could hear Twiggy desperately barking somewhere in the fray, but she could not see him. As they crested the plain out of sight, she offered a prayer to the Creator. *Make that loyal dog's end a swift one...*

THE BREADCRUMBS HAD CONTINUED TO BE PLACED, though the spacing was further apart along the knights' footprints. "How much bread did these men have on them?" Clarial asked incredulously, admiring a curved length of softened crust between her fingers. "We have been following the trail for what, three miles now?"

Winter ignored her and focused on the trees in the distance.

Clarial continued, "It's a wonder the crows didn't gobble up the trail."

"Sniff that crust," said Winter distractedly, still looking into the forest.

After bringing the morsel to her nose, Clarial flung it aside with disgust and bent down to wipe her fingers in the snow.

"If you ever wondered what werewolf piss smells like..." Winter said wryly, looking down at her friend.

"I almost ate a piece of that a few minutes ago!"

"I would have stopped you," Winter lied. "I think we're almost there."

Clarial was less than amused. "What makes you think that?" she asked, furtively bringing her fingertips to her nose.

Winter tilted the halberd toward a funneling mist that stained the clear blue atmosphere a distinct shade of gray. "That looks like chimney smoke to me."

***

THE ABRUPT KNOCK AT THE DOOR startled the laif girl into spilling her hot tea right onto Relic's lap. The knights collectively shouted in horror, expecting a display of agony from the gargoyle, but he did not react as one who just had their groin doused in boiling liquid. Without even a flinch of pain, the gargoyle simply gazed down at the stain seeping across his tunic.

"Is someone going to get that?" he queried as he watched the tea dribble onto the floor.

"I'll get a towel," offered Breunor, walking toward a rack of linens.

"No, not that," the gargoyle clarified, pointing at the door. Another set of knocks resounded, and the girl bounced up from her chair.

Relic stood and brushed at his wet tunic. "Alright, the babysitter will get it."

Before the girl could see who was at the door, she heard Percival mutter a string of curses under his breath. The door opened, revealing a pair of women in light armour carrying bundles of what the girl assumed were provisions for a journey. Their uncovered heads were tinged with flecks of snow, and their long hair was pulled back into matching knots. One of the women had a heavy scar on her face, and the girl recalled what her mother had taught her about commenting on a person's defects. *Only speak of it if they bring it up, and even then, it's best to say as little as possible.*

Despite her scar the woman appeared friendly, though at the moment she looked rather startled. Suddenly her friend tugged at her sleeve and exclaimed, "You didn't tell me that there would be gargoyles involved!"

Realization dawned on the scarred woman a bit more slowly than her friend, and she leaned around the gargoyle to shout at Breunor, "You didn't tell me that there would be gargoyles involved!"

"Well, just one, actually—" Relic stammered as the women shoved their way inside. The look of awe dissipated on the scarred woman's face considerably faster than her companion, who was gawking while shaking the gargoyle's hand. She muttered a few phrases that the little girl only caught fragments of, but it sounded like she had never been this close to a real live royal gargoyle before.

"Come on in, please," said Breunor, crossing the room to take the women's traveling sacks, making a valiant attempt to appear as the gracious host. "Feel free to warm yourselves by the fire in my..." his eyes darted around at the meager furnishings surrounding them. "Humble dwelling."

The scarred woman ignored the hearth and knelt down, looking the laif girl in the eyes and extending a hand. "My name is Winter, what's yours?" The firelight caused the scales on her armour to glimmer.

"Netty," the girl replied.

"That's such an interesting name," Winter commented, taking a seat on the floor and gazing around her while speaking to the girl. "I knew your mother before you were born. She was brave and strong and overflowing with kindness," she hesitated for moment. "For the people she loved and protected."

The girl scooted to the edge of her seat, her face aglow. "Can you tell me stories of her?" she asked. "Tell me stories of my mother?"

"Of course," Winter replied, tears welling in her eyes. "I will tell you as many as I can remember." She managed to choke the phrase out as Netty beamed at her, clearly delighted by the offer.

On the other side of the room, Breunor approached the woman warming herself by the fire.

"You must be Clarial?"

"I am," she replied, "and you must be Sir Breunor?"

He nodded.

"Do you have a cooking pan of some sort?"

He nodded again.

"Good, because I have some fresh bacon," she announced, indicating the pouch in her hand.

Winter was still seated on the floor playing a childish hand tickling game with the orphan and she looked up at Breunor on his way past. "Where do we go from here?" she asked as the little girl recoiled and giggled, waving a hand.

"We will get to all that shortly," said Breunor offhandedly, foraging for a clean pan. "I'm actually quite impressed that you made it here without a ranger."

"Oh, I have my ways, Sir Knight," Winter replied.

Relic snorted loudly and looked over at Percival who was also observing. If Winter had heard the sound of derision, she did not give the gargoyle any attention.

"If your *ways* include the use of that halberd over there," Breunor flicked his wrist at the weapon leaning against the wall. "Then I will be greatly interested in observing them." The knight rose and raised a pan in victory. "Found it," he said and moved toward the waiting Clarial.

"I am sorry to hear about your betrothed," said Breunor reverently, handing Clarial the pan. "I believe what happened at Knotwithstadt will have repercussions that the kingdom will be feeling for many years to come."

The girl saw Winter straighten up when Breunor mentioned her friend's paramour. Clarial's face held an uneasy look for a moment, which could be interpreted as sadness, but the girl sensed it for what it was; confusion. Whether Breunor picked up on it or not, she could not be certain.

"Oh, yes," Clarial scowled at Winter for an instant, then continued, facing Breunor. "We will definitely feel its effect for a long time." Clarial set the pan down and began to lay out the strips of bacon on its surface.

Unknown to Clarial, Winter had decided to take it upon herself to spin a tale or two in order to get the knights to let them join. One of those being that Clarial had a beau who had been slain at Knotwithstadt and she desired safe passage north to bury his bones.

Netty overheard Clarial's statement to Breunor and leaned close to Winter. "Like the abowraith," she whispered.

Winter cocked her head. "Wait, what?"

"The abowraith," repeated Relic.

Winter rotated her trunk to face the gargoyle standing over the table. "I heard what she said. Why is she talking about them?"

"Questions that begin with 'why' are usually the saddest and most difficult to maneuver," replied Relic cryptically, admiring his claws and flexing the hand as if he had been dueling for hours. "You understand what an abowraith represents. Now look at the young one before you and piece it together for yourself."

A shadow passed over Winter's visage. "You are being pursued?" she asked the girl.

Netty nodded but did not withdraw from their game, placing both palms down onto Winter's open hands. The Lord Commander looked up at the gargoyle who was scratching his chest, crinkling the royal emblem emblazoned in his tunic. He gave a tilted nod.

"That is why I am here," said Relic darkly. "It chases Netty, and I hunt it."

A silence fell in the shack, only the sound of crackling bacon filling the air. Relic began a quiet discussion with Percival out of earshot, a difficult task to manage considering the size of the room. Clarial turned to Breunor to discuss the western front and the pushes and drawbacks while Breunor listened in rapt attention.

"May I braid your hair?" Winter asked. Netty had seated herself on the woman's lap, and she vigorously nodded her head in agreement.

"Can you bundle it all back like yours and Clarial's?" she requested turning back to meet Winter's eyes.

"I was thinking that exact same thing," Winter replied, running her fingers through the girl's hair, brushing it as best she could. Miraculously there were not as many tangles as expected. "You have gorgeous hair, Netty."

"My father always liked to claim that's the gift his bloodline gave me."

Winter chuckled. "I think we know otherwise," she said. "Your mother was stunning."

Netty tucked her chin and winced as Winter worked out a knot in a bundle of strands. "You never saw my father," she spoke distantly with admiration.

"True," Winter agreed. "He must have been a looker to catch the Lithe Stone's eye."

Bringing the pan over, Breunor offered a few slabs of bacon to the Lord Commander and the orphan. The surface was still sizzling when Winter reached her fingers in and gingerly plucked a few strips, avoiding the bursting grease bubbles. Relic and Percival declined the offer, dismissively waving when the knight inclined the food in their direction.

"Suit yourselves," said Breunor to the creatures in the corner, popping a crisp corner of the pig meat into his mouth.

Winter had wrongly assumed that Netty would want some bacon, so when Breunor swung back around, she tossed the strips back into the traveling pan. "Heathens," the knight remarked under his breath. "That just means there's more for us," said Breunor to Clarial, extending the pan her way.

"Thank you, sir!" Clarial scooped up more of the offered food and began crunching away, chewing with a mouthful and leering at Winter.

Netty's shoulders trembled as she laughed. "I like your friend."

"Yeah," said Winter, pinching several strands of the girl's hair between her fingers and layering them one atop the other. "She's a delight."

After the entire two pounds of bacon was devoured by Breunor and Clarial, the knight rubbed his hands together and spoke to Winter, though the statement was meant for all. "I have something to show you, but its secret must remain within these walls." Striding to a floorboard, the man bent down and wrenched at it with his fingertips. He gained purchase after a few attempts, the grease from his late breakfast lingered on his hands, adding to his struggle.

"Here we go," he announced, producing a roll of vellum that was half as tall as the knight. A silvery cord was wrapped three times around the bundled sheet, and it slid off like silk when the knight removed it. Clearing a space on the table, he plunked it down and took a step back as it gradually unfolded itself. Invisible hands seemed to be parting the parchment, the separate rolls spreading in unison, revealing an immaculately clear map of Fenrirfang Forest. Even some of the surrounding areas, like the canton of Knotwithstadt, were included. The very top of the map was completely covered in blue and continued endlessly off the map. "Lake Humiel" was scrawled diagonal over the massive body of water.

Winter inhaled sharply. "Where did you get this?"

"Not important," Breunor brushed the question aside and continued, "as you can see, this map denotes the wards all throughout the forest with those hand scribbled symbols. Most were there when I obtained it, but I added a few myself. I tried to respect the artistic craftsmanship, while also making clear what sort of danger one can expect when crossing the various thresholds."

Clarial pointed at a crude depiction of a woman with absurdly frizzy hair. "This kind of seems out of place to me."

"As it should," Breunor clarified. "That's not a ward. That's an area occupied by gorgons."

"Ah," Clarial squinted at the drawing, "I see it now."

"Not all the marks and symbols are wards," Breunor explained, pointing at a winged creature with big fangs and a ring around it. "The wards are circled, anything else is just a hazard or some other noteworthy landmark."

Winter leveled a finger over the map and hesitated. "May I touch it?" she asked Breunor. The knight waved encouragingly in response, and Winter placed her finger on the parchment, tracing a path around the Crescent Marshes. "It's going to take forever to go around the marshlands here," she said, her finger tapping the map, "and that's not taking into account the seven wards between here and there. There are pine and leaf copses, bogs, canyons, gullies, swamps, and I imagine some highlands that we'll be crossing to get around it..." she trailed off, noticing Breunor's face resembled a schoolboy hiding a frog behind his back.

"Winter," he said cheerfully.

"What?" She shook her head, agitated by his demeanor.

"No," said Breunor, pointing to the door. "The season outside. It's *winter.*"

"So?"

"The marshes are frozen over."

Clarial leaned in and traipsed her fingers over the large green puddle, "We'll just walk across it," she said with admiration, patting Winter on the back.

EVEN THOUGH NETTY IS ONLY HALF LAIF, her laif side seems to prevail over her mortal one, Winter ruminated, rolling over and stretching her legs under the surprisingly cushiony blanket that the host-knight had provided. For instance, she does not require much rest. At least that is what she claims.

There were many open spaces available on the cabin floor for sleeping, and the particular one Winter had selected was the perfect distance from the hearth. Not too far so she would not catch a chill, and not too close, to avoid getting all sweaty and gross. All was quiet, save for the occasional scraping of Relic's taloned feet on the hardwood when he rose to stoke the fire.

As she began to feel her body drift away to the far away fuzzy dreamlands, a sudden sharp stab in her lower back startled her awake.

"Gah! Clarial!" Winter whispered, sitting up and craning her arm back to rub at the stinging spot. "Trim your toenails once in awhile!"

Clarial appeared offended by the remark. "I'm still wearing my boots," she muttered, crouching down to Winter's level.

Winter returned Clarial's defensive statement with a look of disgust, peering down at her friend's feet.

"Don't you try to shame me, you little liar," Clarial hissed, adjusting the blanket she had draped over shoulders as a cape. "Next time you tell a pair of knights that I am betrothed to a fictional dead man, at least grant me the courtesy of mentioning it beforehand."

Clarial jabbed a pointy forefinger right below Winter's sternum. "Ah!" Winter wheezed in shock.

"Got it?!" demanded Clarial, jabbing again, but Winter deflected this renewed attack with her forearm.

Raising her hands in surrender, Winter apologized, "Alright, alright, alright. I'm sorry about that!" She reclined back onto her elbows. "I should have keyed you in on that, but it slipped my mind, what with all the happenings...happening—"

Clarial interrupted. "Is there anything else I should be made aware of? What other lies did you concoct so they would let you tag along? Did you tell them that you can speak kapreta? Or that you're immune to basilisk venom?" She reached out and gripped the fabric around Winter's collar. "Did you tell them about my third nipple?"

The question took Winter by complete surprise. "You have a third..." She trailed off, scanning her friend's face and trying to discern if it was a jest or not.

"Winter," Clarial intoned humorlessly, tilting her head.

"That was it!" Winter settled back onto her pillow and gazed up at her friend. "I swear."

"Alright," said Clarial, turning to walk away.

"Clarial?"

"Yeah?" She stopped.

"Do you have a...a..." Winter giggled, pointing to her friend's bosom.

"Get some rest, you idiot."

~ 11 ~

THE FIRST WARD

A hazy film on the morning horizon reduced the amount of sunlight penetrating the trees, and the travelers were greeted with a healthy burst of snow as soon as they stepped out of Breunor's cottage. The wind rudely whipped the icy particles into their faces causing them to raise their scarves a bit higher.

Breunor lifted his chin to the sky. "Good morning, Fenrirfang!" he shouted, greeting the naked treetops as he led the party north into the forest.

They had spent the better part of the night pouring over the map and discussing the best course of action. Netty had fallen asleep well before anything was decided, nestled into Winter's shoulder and uninterested with the workings of the journey. All she was concerned with was the end point when she would be able to lay her family's bones to rest in proper laif fashion. The wards did not concern her. The faewolves, goblins, ghasts, and any other pest did not concern her. The abowraith sometimes seeped into her dreams, but even that did not really scare her...well, maybe just a little bit.

It was not the fact that grown adults surrounded her on all sides. It was not the weapons and armour that they wore that gave her the most comfort. Nor was it how kindly they treated her, making her feel wanted and important. No, none of these gave her more solace above the others. It was Sir Percival. Even though she knew nothing of his tales, his legendary deeds and the ones embellished by lesser men. She *knew*. She knew he would bring down an aelder dragon for her, climb up its armoured hide and rip its eyes from its sockets. He would raze a village of goblins with a single torch for her. And he would unearth the Questing Beast itself and reach into its maw and wrench all its fangs free if need be. He never said as much to her. But he did not need to.

She trudged beside him now, one hand in his and her other inside Winter's. They agreed that they would let her walk until she began to slow the group down. Winter promoted the idea, suggesting that the exertion would help the girl sleep at night. Every once in a while Percival and Winter would joyously pull her up simultaneously, bringing her completely off the ground and she would swing weightlessly, kicking her feet, slugging the snow from her boots. She imagined what the forest was like when it was in bloom and thought that walking through it while maintaining her direction would be nigh impossible.

The forest was very quiet. No rustling leaves could be heard, and there were very few birds even chirping. Only the staunchest of avians sat hunched on branches, and even those only silently watched the travelers pass beneath them.

Maybe they thought they were being sneaky, but the girl definitely noticed the flock of vultures following behind them right after setting out in the morning. The dark villains had speckled the snowy boughs of a skinny, tall solitary tree occupying the field almost out of eyeshot from Breunor's cottage. Every once in a while, she would look back and catch a glimpse of one alighting onto a branch far behind them. Always following behind them.

"How far until we reach the first ward?" Clarial asked, taking a sip from her flask and brushing the drops from her lips, lest they freeze.

Breunor continued walking, but turned his head to reply. "Not much further."

"I still think we should have brought that map with us," Clarial insisted, passing her flask to Winter. "That thing is handy."

"No," Breunor countered. "It's too valuable," he turned to face her, walking backwards. "Besides, it's all here." The knight tapped the side of his head with a grin and spun back around to continue leading.

"How many times have you made this trip again?" called Winter, returning the flask to her friend.

There was a pause for several moments, and right as Winter was about to repeat the question, the knight finally replied, "*This* trip? Never. I have always gone around the marshlands, but this is more of a straight line, so it should be much easier." The knight gave a shrug that rattled his armour, accenting just how quiet the landscape was.

Up ahead, a ribbon of snow cascaded to the ground. Tracing it upward, Netty spotted Relic seated on a huge branch. The gargoyle's feet dangled freely as if he were patiently waiting for a midsummer carriage ride. "The ward is two hundred or so paces ahead, Breunor," Relic shouted, lifting an invisible bottle to his covered mouth.

Netty was not the only one confused by the pantomime and she saw Clarial shoot Winter a puzzled glance.

"Hand me the blood wineskin," Breunor requested with a hand stretched toward Winter. The Lord Commander fumbled for a moment to withdraw the wineskin, the strap briefly catching on her left pauldron, but after a few shakes, she managed to release it.

From what Netty understood of wards, they were basically invisible lines all over the forest and crossing over one was like springing a trap. Sprinkling fresh laif blood on the line would satisfy whatever kind of horror guarded the wards, but as she was not a pure laif, her blood would not suffice, though pouring older blood from a wineskin seemed just as useless.

As she wondered about these things, she watched Breunor tilt his head back and wrap his lips around the mouth of the wineskin. To her shock, he took a heavy swig and brought the skin back down, gagging as he swiped at his beard.

"Oi!" he shouted, his eyes darting between the women, glaring daggers into them. "Who did you get this blood from?! It tastes like the bloke ate nothing but thistle and hayseed!"

"Well, I, uh, you see..." Clarial and Winter both stammered incoherently trying to produce a sufficient reply.

"It's delicious!" Breunor interrupted their stutters. "The usual swill I get tastes like soot."

Winter was the first to recover, "Oh, well where do you usually get your laif blood?" she asked with an air of certainty, as if she were well versed in the lore.

"A brothel," Percival replied for the knight.

Netty tugged on Percival's hand, drawing his attention downward. "What's a brothel?" she asked, her face scrunching in confusion.

"A den of iniquity," Percival replied without any hesitation.

The girl nodded her head, pretending to understand the explanation.

Winter and Clarial shared a look of admiration and relief. They had briefly tried to conceive a tame response that would not garner any further speculation from the girl, and Percival succeeded perfectly. A connection between the werewolf and the orphan had already been apparent, but the way he spoke to her only solidified it.

Breunor corked the wineskin and handed it back to Winter with a look of gratitude.

"I imagine you have done this before then?" Winter asked meekly, placing the strap over her head and tucking the pouch back into its place under her cloak.

"Hundreds of times."

"Has it worked everytime?"

"More often than not."

Clarial could sense the growing unease in Winter and spoke for her friend, "And what do you do when it doesn't work?"

"Fucking run," Breunor replied, "not much else to do when you're venturing alone and you spring an ancient laif curse from its slumber."

Netty did not like the sound of that and neither did Clarial and Winter. The laif looked up to Percival for comfort, hoping his demeanor was not one of despair. To her immense relief, the knight looked just as serious and angry as usual. The conversation did not appear to have impacted him in the least.

A soft thud from behind startled the girl, but she was pleasantly surprised to find Relic striding behind them. The gargoyle was grounded for the first time that day, having acted as their overhead scout. His breath escaped in a mist through his scarf as he gave her a reassuring nod, the bat-like wings on his back slowly retracting as he did so.

"Alright," Breunor stopped and turned to everyone behind him. "Wait here."

The knight strode forward, the only sound filling the harsh silence was his feet crunching in the fresh snow.

"Fingers crossed," whispered Winter to Clarial.

Clarial had leaned her halberd against her shoulder, and she raised both hands displaying that her fingers were indeed already crossed.

"What can we expect from this ward?" Winter asked the group. "You know, just in case this doesn't work."

"Hobs," Relic replied, as casually as if she had been inquiring about which ale was on tap that evening.

Clarial released the crossed fingers on her left hand and gripped the halberd. "Oh, that's all?" she asked, only the faintest hint of trepidation in her voice.

Percival bent down and scooped the girl up into his arms. She clung to his neck and he adjusted her position so that she resembled a satchel on his back.

A brief gap in the trees allowed the party clear sight of Breunor walking alone with a dagger in his hand. The knight slowed his steps while staring downward at the ground, both knees bent as if preparing for a great tremor. He clenched the blade in his fist and appeared to ruminate on the proper moment to make the cut. Behind the girl, Relic cleared his throat and only a moment lapsed before Breunor sliced downward causing blood to dribble out onto the pure white ground. When he tightened the muscles in his arm, squeezing his fist like a vise, a scarlet deluge issued forth to join the newly tainted snow.

After littering the ground with blood for a minute or so, Breunor shouted back to the group, "We're good!" He waved a cloth that he produced from his satchel, intending to wrap it around his fresh wound.

Winter and Clarial sighed in unison as they took their first steps, but their relief did not last. Thin muscular arms exploded from the earth. A sinister host of limbs gripped Breunor below his knees and used the knight's limbs as leverage to pull themselves up. All around, creatures pierced the snow's surface, their appearance equal parts daemon and child, eyes intent on murder. With pointy ears and pointy fangs, they were completely naked save for a loincloth wrapped around their waists, and the first clutch overtook Breunor within the span of a breath.

Percival instantly swung Netty to his chest and shouted for Relic. The gargoyle, already aloft, instantly darted to Percival. "Take the girl!" commanded Percival, heaving the child upward with his hands under her armpits. As soon as the fabric of Netty's mantle left his fingers, a host of hobs tackled him to the ground, snow bursting like dust upon impact.

Blinking her eyes against the cold wind, Netty watched Sir Percival go down and her heart sank as her body soared through the air. But when he rose, swirled in a snowy blood mist, he was no longer a man, but a wolf.

He was tearing the hobs that had assailed him into shreds and jamming their limbs down into their throats. One hob foolishly approached the werewolf from behind and was greeted by a fanged maw that completely overtook its head. With one snap, Percival rendered the hob headless. After a sickening crunch, the werewolf spat the remnants of the hob's head onto the snowy pitch and whirled around seeking his next victims.

Relic placed Netty on a branch safely above the chaos. "Stay put," he instructed.

"Do I have any other choice?" she asked, settling onto the bumpy surface.

The gargoyle glanced at her wryly as he hovered before her, and she imagined a smile spreading across his kitty mouth. He wheeled away and dove downward into the raging field below. A sickle-like claw adorned the tip of each gargoyle wing, and he used them with wicked precision, dropping dozens of unaware hobs in one pendulating swoop.

Clarial was carving a path with her halberd, piercing some with the spear point and flinging them aside, while others met their end with the blade of the axehead. Breunor, somehow among them, was screaming, "Run! The tide is endless! We must run!" He tugged at Winter's sleeve while she yanked her sword free from a hob's clavicle. The creature crumpled under their feet, and Winter almost stumbled over its dying form, but Breunor held her up.

"Run!" he screamed again.

"I heard you!" Winter yelled.

A hob abruptly struck the earth like a meteor, blasting debris up into the trees. Winter and Breunor looked up to see Relic spiking hobs from several hundred feet in the skies. He held one like a javelin and was aiming the throw far off into the distance. "Follow this one!" he shouted down to his companions in the fray. "He will lead you to safety!" he promised, launching the creature in an easterly direction.

Everyone other than Percival paused to follow the hob's arc across the sky, their heads rotating in unison. They pressed in the direction that Relic had indicated, Clarial leading with her halberd and Breunor close behind, Winter at his back. Detecting an opening in the horde, Clarial spun the halberd in a horizontal arc that left a dozen hobs bereft of their torsos, and sprinted for the gap.

Breunor deftly followed suit, running behind in her wake toward safety, but Winter was unaware of her companion's escape. An emerging arm gripped the Lord Commander's ankle and she lost her balance, falling and struggling to rise after smashing into the snow. Using her sword as leverage, she pulled herself up, but the daemon host had seen her collapse and swarmed toward her like frenzied ants. She could not locate Breunor or Clarial with the hobs all around, but when she looked to the sky, she saw Relic making for her. But the gargoyle came up short on his dive and hovered in the air, gazing down at her with sorrow in his eyes.

She clambered to her feet, shook the grasping hands from her legs, and began slashing at the hobs that closed the gap. There was no wall to back up to, nor was there a corner she could edge into for protection. On all sides a teeming mass of dark magic-infused hobs closed in, existing solely to kill any who dared traverse the forest without a laif willing to shed a blood sacrifice.

And then a force like nothing she had ever experienced hurtled into her, throttling her neck, snapping it back. Stars invaded her optics, her feet left the ground and she felt like the ornament on the prow of a ship, plowing a course through a sea of flesh and bone.

There were snarling hobs surrounding her, but in the span of one blink, they were gone and nothing but quiet forest surrounded her. The forward momentum slowed and she teetered on the edge of consciousness. The force of the saving blow had nearly knocked her out. As the blood began to rush back, she watched the tunnel close and slumped into the furry arms that held her.

WINTER WOKE TO A CRACKLING ORANGE FIRE shooting cinders into the starlit atmosphere. When she sat up and tried to turn her head, the base of her skull felt like it had painfully sewn to her spine. *So this is how one feels after being rescued by a werewolf.* Moving even a fraction proved utterly painful, so she returned to the reclined position she had found herself in.

"So what was in the wine skin?" asked Breunor pensively, taking a long pull from his pipe. The cherry burning inside the bowl carved a path of light to his solemn features.

Winter sat up and winced. "Uh, yeah," she began, massaging the back of her neck with one hand. "I am not entirely sure what's in there..." She looked around the fire and saw that everyone was glaring at her.

"But you know what is *not* in there," stated Breunor.

Clarial held a look of contempt that matched the others, and Winter felt utterly betrayed. *That hussy knows perfectly well that we scammed them with a butcher's cocktail!* She scrambled for an adequate explanation. "Well, you see, it was experimental—"

She was cut off when Percival abruptly rose from his seat on a felled log, growled something under his breath, and stalked off into the forest.

Breunor ignored the knight's abrupt departure, and leaned closer to the flames. "An experiment, you say?" his voice stayed flat and serious and sounded quite severe.

The logs shifted causing the moisture inside of them to be released, and the hiss of liquid escaping interrupted Winter's reply. She sat with her mouth open waiting for the sizzling to cease. Once she felt an appropriate amount of time had passed, she cautiously spoke. "I'm just...well, I'm just going to come clean." Straightening up, she cleared her throat, preparing herself for their response. *I hope they don't toss me back to the hobs.*

"I thought," she squeaked. Her mouth was dry and she could feel her face reddening. As Lord Commander, she was unaccustomed to being at the raw end of an interrogation.

Winter tried to lock eyes with Clarial. *Wait, why is that skinny twit giggling?* She scowled at her friend and continued, "I thought that it wouldn't matter. That perhaps the fact that we would be traveling with—"

"I can't do it anymore!" Clarial interrupted, tilting her head back and laughing into the night sky. "I already told them all about the pig blood!" Clarial confessed, wiping at the river of tears pouring down her face. A round of guffaws cascaded down from the trees, and Winter assumed that it was what a stupid gargoyle sounded like when he found something amusing.

Breunor gave an honest chuckle. "I didn't think it was *that* funny," he admitted, taking another draw of his pipe, "but that look on your face was pretty ridiculous."

THE TWINS

"What was your betrothed's name again?" Breunor asked Clarial, breaking the morning's gloomy silence.

They had risen and departed quickly, leaving the campfire still burning. Their supply had been hamstrung, losing well over half when the hobs had sprung the day before. The only remaining provisions were the ones that Relic had smartly stuffed high up in the bole of a tree before the bloodshed began. His portion was mainly bedding and soft goods, which proved most handy throughout the cold night, but did not fill anyone's belly.

"I don't recall you ever asking," replied Clarial harshly. She was torn between being grateful for having less of a burden to carry and being upset about the stabbing hunger pangs. "And his name was...Bernard," she lied, ignoring the cringing expression on Winter's face.

"I don't remember anyone named Bernard in my village," said Netty, glancing up at Winter who was holding her hand. Percival had set off earlier than everyone else, having held the last guard that night. He had awoken Breunor before daybreak and departed for parts unknown.

Relic had taken to flying further ahead of the group, as was his habit. Their ever-present reconnaissance.

"He was just passing through at the time of the attack," Clarial spat, not looking at the child. She was trying to sell the falsehood and the growing starvation spurred her frustration, making it easier to appear upset with the current topic.

Breunor pressed on, "What was his occupation?" He produced a flask and took a drink. "Was he an errant knight, or perhaps some other sort of sellsword?"

"Are you implying that he was on the Church side of the slaughter?" Clarial snarled, and Winter's eyes widened at the sudden burst of indignation.

"Well, I—" Breunor attempted to backpedal but was quickly cut off.

"How dare you!" Clarial hissed, tears began to form under her eyelids. Winter admired the performance, and pulled her scarf over her mouth, unable to control the smirk that was gradually morphing into a grin. "My Bernard was a journeyman blacksmith! Would never even hurt a wisp! He struggled with even shaking spiders out of his boots in the morning for fear of disturbing their slumber! He was a gentle sort! Didn't even want to turn out insignificant bugs!"

She's really going for it, Winter struggled to hold back her laughter. *Perhaps I should step in before...*

Breunor looked as if he'd just shattered a priceless antique. "I'm so sorry, Clarial, I meant no harm! Honestly!" The knight looked to Winter and Netty for assistance, but neither seemed ready to offer any help. "I was only asking if he were a man of arms because it seems to me that only a man of prowess would be able to court someone like you."

Nice save, Winter's grin softened.

"Someone like me?" Clarial sniffed and wiped her nose. Her anger seemed to be cooling.

"Yeah," Breunor paused a moment to collect his thoughts. After gaining traction on removing himself from the hole he dug himself into, he did not want to sink back down with another unintended insult. "Sharp and fast." The words were meant as a statement of fact, but he accidentally raised his voice at the end as if he were uncertain.

Winter winced and expected another fake tirade.

"Thank you," softly Clarial replied, wiping the last of her tears with her vambrace. Winter imagined that her friend did not have the energy to maintain such a performance for much longer and had accepted the apology so they could discuss something else for the time being.

The four trudged along in relative silence after that, the only conversation being their stomachs taking turns growling, offering steady reminders that they had skipped the previous night's dinner as well as this morning's breakfast. It was perhaps two hours or so until midday and the sun, just as the day before, was engulfed by a thick, murky haze.

"Winter..." Netty tugged on Winter's hand. "Have you noticed those big birds following us?" she asked, rotating her torso to indicate the treetops behind.

Winter shook her head and glanced at Breunor and Clarial. "What big birds?"

Breunor cleared his throat to respond, but Clarial was quicker.

"Carrion birds trail Percival," the woman explained.

Winter rolled her eyes. "Of course they do." Pausing to stare at the trees, she waited for a hint of black against the endless whiteness that littered the boughs. She did not need to wait long. Soon the flicker of a dark wing broke the horizon and an ensuing snowy crunch came from the tall branch under the movement. "Well, that is a comforting notion," Winter commented, giving Netty's hand a squeeze and walking once more.

They had two more wards to cross before they reached the Crescent Marshland and the terrain so far had been relatively flat, plain, and of course, filled with trees as far as the eye could fathom. When the snow retreated and the flora appeared, perhaps this patch of Fenrirfang would be more remarkable. But currently it all looked the same to Winter.

"Hey," Breunor said. "Just so everyone is aware, I had kapreta antidote in my satchel that got stripped by those hobs...so try not to get bitten."

Clarial coughed. "Good advice," she said. "It's not like Knotwithstadt has an infestation or anything."

"Luckily, I managed to keep hold of my explosives," Breunor continued brightly. "So there's that."

"See, it's not all dreary news," said Winter, looking at Netty and playfully swinging her arm. "If we get bitten, then Breunor can blow us up!"

Suddenly a sharp, smoky scent carried to them on the wind. Their mouths began to water and Clarial could not help but shout, "Someone is cooking up ahead!"

A surge of energy filled their famished limbs, and they hurried toward the smoky trail. A solitary figure stood near a fire in a small clearing. As they drew nearer, Winter noticed some sort of handcrafted contraption surrounding the fire. It appeared to be a frame constructed with sticks, and when she entered the clearing, she found that it was a cooking frame cobbled together with branches and skinny tree limbs.

Strips of meat lay on the top, dripping juices and receiving appetizing sear marks by the lapping flames. The carcass of a tremendous stag lay discarded on the outskirts of the ring, placed at the base of an ancient looking birch. Seeing the dead beast's antler, Winter stared in amazement. They were the biggest set she had ever seen and dwarfed all of the trophies she had viewed in any lord or duke's hall. It was an odd feeling that passed over her as she stared at the hollow colossus that was simply a harvest for Sir Percival, and nothing more.

So that was where he went off to before sunrise, thought Winter with gratitude. *Just another perk of traveling with a werewolf.*

"I have dibs on a back strap!" Winter announced, beaming at Netty who returned her expression with equal excitement.

"OH, WHOA," CLARIAL BREATHED, lifting the tender branches that acted as a canopy gently barring entry into a wintry spectacle. "Breunor, where are we?" The forest floor was no longer covered in snow, but instead light blue blades of grass sprouted, but Winter was wary to set foot on them. Breunor was the first to tread forward, then Clarial, and both had survived thus far.

The grassy carpet began at the roots of the trees hemming the trail and continued for further than Winter could see from where she hesitantly stood. Orchid-like flowers covered the trees in strands like wedding garland, their petals pale hues of blues, purples, and silvers. Birds matching the colors of the flowers chirped in the snowless boughs above, and an array of shiny insects hummed and weaved around the landscape, but ignored the travelers. The place appeared to be a sanctuary offering a reprieve from the harsh climate surrounding.

Breunor turned his head toward Clarial. "The plants and animals here are nourished by snow. In the other seasons, this place actually appears rather barren. Save for the trees, of course, but they do not flower like this the rest of the year."

"What do the trees look like without the pretty flowers?" Netty inquired.

"They look like trees," Breunor answered, appearing puzzled by the question. He tilted his head and scratched behind his ear in contemplation. "Just imagine them naked and that's what they look like."

Netty giggled at Breunor's words, and she looked up at Percival to share in the joke, though he was not at all amused with the other knight's statement. But when the little girl caught his eye, he smiled down at her as best he could. For a moment she removed her hand from Winter's and brought it over to squeeze Percival's hand. "Can I roll in the grass for a little bit?" she asked, her request imbued with so much hope that Percival could not refuse.

"Go for it," Percival conceded, letting go of her hands.

The little girl began to tumble and somersault around, plucking up grass in fistfuls. "The ground is so warm!" she exclaimed. "I hope this road leads all the way home!"

The travelers smiled at the girl's spirit, side-stepping her tumbling body when she almost bumped into them, though Winter's mind was hovering elsewhere. She squinted her eyes, blurring her vision just a bit as she tried to bring the image of the map to the forefront of her mind.

"Isn't there a laif village beyond the second ward?" Winter asked.

"There is," Breunor replied. "It's west of the line we are following, but it's a bit out of the way." He looked to Relic for confirmation.

"Perhaps we can restock some our lost provisions there?" suggested Winter.

The gargoyle shook his head, unsure. "If they welcome us," he said, shrugging and gesturing at Percival. "Netty will definitely be permitted, but I cannot speak for the rest of us with any certainty. No offense, Percival, but they may not let you in at all, and may even request that we chain you to a tree outside."

Netty appeared more offended than Percival but before she could object, Relic continued, "That, however, is not an immediate concern." He turned his shoulders, gesturing to the path ahead. "There's a pair of laives approaching, occupying the same trail we are following."

The others waited for more details, and after a long pause, Breunor spoke up. "And?" he queried impatiently, waving a hand and urging the gargoyle to continue.

"Oh." The gargoyle peered at them with his vertical pupils. "That's it...and they're dragging a bovine carcass behind them."

"How far are they from us?" Winter asked their scout, pausing when his last statement suddenly sunk in. "A bovine carcass?" she arched one eyebrow at Percival.

Relic rubbed his scarf shrouded chin. "They are probably more than an acre away," he speculated. "They are beyond this magical respite that we currently find ourselves in and trudging through snow." Flexing his wings, readying for a return to flight, he added, "I did not get too close, but the carcass appeared to be speaking." With that, the gargoyle shot into the air, returning to his duty.

"An undead ox?" Winter glanced at Clarial. "That sounds pretty...neat."

Clarial nodded, pursing her lips in concern.

"Come on, little one," said Percival, lowering a hand down to Netty. The child was fastidiously plucking petals from a daisy with her back against a tree. She placed the flower behind her pointy left ear and reached out to the knight who scooped her up easily, as if she weighed no more than a cloud. "I will be carrying you for now."

The warm, snowless path ended sooner than any of them wanted, and the party was greeted with an icy blast of wind as soon as they pushed the fragile branches aside.

"It was nice while it lasted," Clarial sighed, grabbing hold of her collar and shrugging her chest armour up. Netty shared the woman's disappointment, but did not say anything, instead burying her face in the crook of Percival's neck and curling the rest of her body tighter to him. She shivered for only a moment before the knight concealed her with his mantle.

From above, a creature cleared his throat, and Winter looked up to see Relic perched overhead with his feet dangling. He was chewing on a round piece of fruit, and he swiped the juices from his mouth and inclined the fruit toward the path ahead.

Before Winter returned her gaze forward, she heard Breunor solemnly speak. "Yep, we have company," he announced.

Without leaf or petal, the forest was easily transparent, and off in the distance two forms were indeed working their way toward them, each sharing a heavy burden. Their shoulders were encumbered with a rope attached to a great lump that carved a trench in the snow behind them as they pulled and tugged with each labored step. It appeared to be an uphill battle waged on a relatively flat terrain that had seemingly been going on for quite some time. Noticing the party approaching, the pair eased their ropes and straightened up.

"Hail!" A male voice came from one of the laives, and both raised their hands in greeting.

"Hail," replied Breunor, returning the salute with much less enthusiasm.

Standing across a gap, both parties stood and regarded the other from a safe distance. Winter felt uneasy with this new encounter, and she noticed that she was not alone in her feelings of trepidation; Breunor's hand had not left the pommel of his sword for even a heartbeat.

"We have been traveling toward the vultures!" a female voice proclaimed, and the laif slowly drew her scarf down revealing a thin face ringed with exhaustion. "Have you noticed them?" she asked, pointing over Clarial's head.

"We have," replied Breunor dryly.

"Allow us to introduce ourselves! My name is Melfina, and this is my brother Lamben," the laif announced, indicating the lad next to her. He lowered his scarf showing that his face matched his sister's perfectly. "Most folk just call me Mel and they call him Ben," she said.

Twins! Winter shook her head in disgust. *For crying out loud.*

Breunor decided to forego introductions and ask the question on the forefront of everyone's minds. "Why are you pulling that cow?"

Melfina twitched as if she were startled by the question. "Oh, that?" she thumbed behind her, and the shaking carcass mumbled something from beneath the stitches that held the beast together along its stomach.

"It's vulture feed," Lamben answered. "Don't mind that."

"Wait, what?" Clarial fixed the male laif with a puzzled look. "What's inside that dead husk?"

The twins shared a devious look and nodded in unison.

Twins! Winter squeezed her eyes tight.

It was at that moment that Netty peered from beneath Percival's cloak causing both laives to snap their attention to her immediately.

Melfina slowly tilted her head as she spoke. "You travel without guide but bring a child instead to help you pass our protected borders?" Her voice lilted dramatically as if reciting a sad piece of poetry. "Do they maim you, little one, and draw your blood for their own ends?"

Netty responded by burying her face into Percival's neck.

Their strange new acquaintances' eyes darted around seeking an answer.

"Her blood is no good for that," Breunor said at length. "She is only half laif."

Lamben's eyes had not left the little girl. "Her mother's side?" he queried, the question registering as more of a statement.

"Alright," Winter interjected, stepping forward and urging Clarial to join her. "It has been nice meeting you, Mel and Bean—"

"Ben."

"Whatever. Well, we have business to attend over yonder." Winter looked at the others for support, but to her dismay, they remained rooted in place. "So, yeah, we're going to just continue on our merry way, if you'll just..." she tipped her head, urging everyone to follow her lead.

Melfina regarded Winter with delight in her eyes. "And how do you plan on obfuscating the coming wards?" she cheerfully inquired. "They are quite formidable."

"We'll figure something out," Winter snapped, retreating toward her companions with a long backward step.

Breunor's hand finally left the pommel of his sword and he squinted at Lamben as an idea formed in his mind. "You owe us," the knight stated causing the laif's eyes to flit to him in curiosity. "We are providing vultures for whatever it is you are intending. No need to explain—" he said quickly, but was interrupted by Lamben.

"The human stowed inside the heifer is an outsider that we kindly welcomed into our village. His guide told us he was merely passing through and requested to stay with us until spring. We agreed to offer him aid in return for labor. For a while he proved a most valuable addition, tending our fires and dismantling the game brought down by our hunters. But two nights hence, he decided to enter our home and *kiss* my sister!" The laif curled his lip and glanced back at the carcass-filled death sentence. Melfina shifted uncomfortably and her brother continued, "But do not worry, we gave him a generous amount of wine, so he hardly knows what is about to happen to him."

From inside the carcass came a faint singsong voice, the words indistinguishable but happy sounding. As the laif had been reciting his tale, powdery snow began to sprinkle down around them as the host of carrion fowl gathered in the boughs above, smattering the treetops with their inky black frames. Lamben's eyes lifted to the hungry vultures and his mouth began to twitch maliciously. "You said that we owe you a favor?" he said, focused on Breunor. "Name it."

~ 13 ~

THE TOURNEY

"This village of yours?" Winter began, rushing to catch up with Lamben. The laif slowly turned his head to regard the woman. He was leading the group, walking astride Breunor as they made their way westward toward the twins' home. The laives had agreed to help the travelers through the second ward, and they readily assented to Breunor's request to lead the party to their village. Melfina had informed them that gaining entry would not be a problem as long as outsiders simply passed through and did not overstay their welcome.

The Lord Commander removed a dagger from her hip and held it to the laif. "Does it have a smithy?" she asked. Lamben's eyes scanned the blade and lingered on a heavy notch near the blade's pommel.

"Did you sustain that damage crossing over our first ward?" the laif inquired, pulling his mantle tight to his chest as a stiff breeze careened through the party, the locks of his hair softly battering his face. Winter nodded and tucked the blade out of sight. Lamben continued,

"Yes, we have three forges. One belongs to a farrier, and the other two deal with arms and armour...both of which should serve to be more than adequate for your purpose."

Winter thanked the laif and slowed her pace, not wishing to be at the vanguard in case the next ward went awry like the last. Following behind Breunor and Lamben were Clarial and Melfina, but their conversation did not interest her in the least. They were discussing the finer points of harvesting hartwood for armour. The idea that certain ancient woods could be harvested and turned into armour was utter foolishness to Winter, but there were craftsmen who claimed otherwise. Winter had actually brought up the concept to Clarial last week, hoping that her friend would join in the mockery, but she was gravely mistaken.

She's one of them, Winter thought as she side-eyed her friend, *a cork champion.*

"I don't know about that, but I heard if you manage to fell a hemlock just over five hundred years, it's equally as good as a larch just past its millennium," said Clarial rather pretentiously to Melfina. Winter quickly moved away, not interested in hearing more of the dull conversation, but did manage to hear the beginning of it.

"Oh, so you're in the coniferous camp, eh?" Melfina retorted. "Well, if that..." And that was all Winter could stomach. She drifted to the rearguard and found herself near Percival and Netty who were walking side by side. The girl was waving a heavy stick while receiving prompts from the knight regarding proper sword stances.

"Low guard now!" Percival coached with moderate intensity, and Netty responded properly, twisting the makeshift training blade to protect her legs.

"Well done," Winter exclaimed, applauding the display. "High thrust!"

Netty rebounded from the pose to a quick upward stab.

"You'll have a host of goblins fleeing from you in no time," Winter praised. "What will you name your blade when you receive it?"

Percival corrected her statement, "When you *earn* it."

Netty smiled and began stabbing invisible ghouls and ghasts and exclaimed amidst the flourish, "Malichar!"

The announcement stopped Winter in her tracks. Percival appeared unfazed by the declaration, showing no reaction, though it was possible he had already heard the intended title of the girl's future blade. Historically, *Malichar* was the name of the cursed blade that had been used to execute Yaval, the first Warrior, centuries ago. Such knowledge for one so young, was quite off-putting. She caught up with the pair and critically scanned the knight's face for any recognition, but found nothing. *Either he has the finest straight face I have ever seen or he is ignorant.*

"What a..." Winter began. "What a lovely moniker, little one."

"The big birds are back," reported Netty, changing the subject.

"As is their way," Percival stated plain.

The screaming from the man inside the carcass pie had ceased some time ago, either from sheer distance or expiration. More than likely from the latter. *And now the host hath returned,* Winter looked back, regarding the creatures, *appearing just as famished as always.*

"Does it bother you?" Winter asked Percival.

The knight looked at the woman, the scars on his face wrinkling when he smirked at the question. Winter continued, "The buzzards following you..." she clarified, pointing at the boughs behind. "It must get annoying."

"They don't bother me," he replied, shrugging.

"They know better," said Netty, twirling the stick like a baton and rolling her wrist in an imitation of those with greater experience.

Winter puckered her lips and nodded. "I see..."

LAMBEN AND BREUNOR THRUST THEIR FISTS into the air in the same moment, demanding a halt.

It appeared to Winter that the knight was the first to react by mere fractions, but she was probably biased. Everyone stopped, with the exception of Melfina, who continued striding forward to join her brother, clasping hands and continuing toward the invisible threshold.

Removing short blades from under their mantles, the twins intertwined their wrists like lovers sharing glasses of cherry cordial. Instead of taking a sip, they each placed the tip of their blades to the other's tongue and seductively dragged the tip over the spongy surface, drawing thin trickles of blood, reddening the pink flesh. Winter felt the urge to cover Netty's eyes, but when she turned, she saw that Percival had already taken the liberty. She caught the werewolf's eye and winked before returning her gaze to the skin-crawling performance before them. *Facking twins...*

Lamben and Melfina inclined their heads toward each other as if they were about to kiss, but to Winter's great relief, they simply pressed their foreheads together and squeezed their eyes shut. Rolling their necks and snapping their heads in opposite directions, the laives spat the blood out in a circular pattern, moving their bodies like cogs in a clock, before finally standing back-to-back with their arms laced at the elbows.

"Well, that's one way to do it," Breunor remarked quietly to Clarial.

The twins shared another awkward moment, coming together in an airtight embrace that lasted far longer than Winter felt was appropriate for blood siblings. As if noticing the party for the first time, Melfina finally lifted her head from her brother's shoulder and spoke. "The way is safe now," she announced, gradually removing herself from Lamben's embrace. "If we hurry, we will be in time for the opening tilt at our winter tourney!"

THE VILLAGE WAS MUCH LARGER than the map had indicated. Having spent much of her life in the capital, Winter had no idea what the size of a village would actually be. After walking inside the gates, she found it to be rather wonderful. She detected no guards when they first entered, and the homes were built into the trees atop the snowy carpet, the forest continuing completely undisturbed. Here and there, Winter saw a few shacks wedged into the boughs above their heads, but it seemed that the primary dwellings were on the ground.

"This is remarkable," Winter whispered in awe to Melfina.

Both laives turned to stare at her. "Specifically?" queried Lamben, replying for his sister and flicking a clump of snow off his cloak.

Winter surveyed the twins, looking back and forth between them. "The homes and forest co-exist completely naturally. Seamlessly, really. It's, well, it's remarkable."

"Is this your first time visiting a proper forest canton?" inquired Melfina, speaking with that irritating lilt that Winter felt was a bit too patronizing.

"It is," Winter replied.

It was apparently Lamben's turn to speak again. "Unlike you mortals, laives do not need to tear down in order to build up."

Winter felt a bit offended and also guilty all at the same time. "Also remarkable," she said.

The village was completely barren of life, the homes and shops had been abandoned, though fires could be seen still burning inside the few that they passed by. The silence was suddenly ruptured by a clashing of steel less than a league away.

"They have begun!" shouted Melfina with glee, squeezing her brother's hand and running toward the violent sounds, nearly jerking Lamben's shoulder free from its socket. "Everybody, come quickly!" She pivoted, backpedaling, and waved her hand, beckoning them to follow with haste.

As one, they trailed behind, realizing that they currently had no other choice. The troubles they could encounter if they were seen without the twins was something they all hoped to avoid completely.

And besides, Winter thought, watching the back of Melfina's mantle kiss at her heels as she rushed in front of the group, carving fresh tracks in the snow. *Who wouldn't want to watch an actual laif tournament?!*

A flat meadow rimmed with a rolling hill opened up before them, the midday sun pouring down onto the tourney ground. The crafted grandstands ornamenting both sides of the pitch were completely filled with cheering and laughing spectators. Banners waved from posts along the bleachers, and pennants languidly fell from atop lances held by squires, indicating which knight they served.

Watching this familiar feeling spectacle, Winter idly wondered which culture had started these traditions. It resembled every tournament she had ever witnessed, but somehow, it felt much more *normal* out here. The way the knights carried themselves with noble bearing and how the onlookers cupped their mouths to jeer at their knight's opposition was customary for the occasion, and yet, foreign. *Remarkable.* The word flashed again in Winter's mind, fast becoming a recurring theme since she crossed into the laif...*village?* The word seemed much too quaint to describe the place she found herself in. *City? Kingdom?* She shook her head. *I'll have to ask one of the creepy twins how they formally refer to this place.*

"There's a space over there!" Melfina pointed, brimming with joy at the sight of an unoccupied length of ground. The space was along the fence under a crimson banner emblazoned with a black rat holding curved blades in each hand underneath three circled stars. "Quick before someone takes it! There! Beneath Trobarkljova's colors!" The female twin broke her brother's grip and surged to save the spot.

"Ugh!" Lamben remarked, protesting. "Folk will think we are cheering for that delusional knight!"

The party passed the laif as he stood with folded arms in clear objection, but after a minute or so, he reluctantly joined the group after hearing Breunor remark on the incredible view.

"What's so bad about this rat banner, Ben?" Breunor asked as the laif sidled next him, clearing the snow atop the fence rail.

"It's an opossum," Lamben corrected glumly. "The Trobarkljovas believe they are immune to becoming *undead*."

"I'm not going to even pretend to understand what that means."

"I will speak candidly," Lamben promised, leaning closer to Breunor than the knight was comfortable with. "I am surprised that they would travel all this way to grace us with their presence. The fact that they have a knight in the lists is equally surprising. I wonder if they even have a proper squire to accompany this laif-ahorseback." Lamben gestured at the banner and spat. "Every single Trobarkljova sent to become a lampyr has perished at the fountain, which I believe the triple stars indicate. Honestly, I'm only slightly versed in the *lesser* laif sigils, so forgive me if I'm a tad inaccurate in my representations. But, anyhow, every laif sent..." Lamben paused, miming a knife slitting his own throat and following it with a gagging noise. "Died. Which should bring shame upon any household. But not the Trobarkljovas. No! They wear it on their sleeves as an honor, but it should bring them nothing but shame," he finished with disgust.

"So they defy the culture?" Breunor asked, keeping his eyes locked on the Trobarkljova knight directly on the other side of the barricade.

Lamben nodded gravely. "With every breath they breathe."

"Sounds like I found my knight!" Breunor laughed, shooting a friendly yet defiant look at Lamben, who was unprepared for such a statement. Initially, the laif returned the look with displeasure, but upon realizing that the knight was not being insolent, his face fractured into an evil grin, and he began to laugh from his nostrils. Breunor clapped Lamben's shoulder and the pair shared a brief moment of friendship, quickly interrupted by the next challengers colliding on the field.

Steel clanged and lances exploded into particles. The sound of the impact resonated into the crowds and beyond, registering high into the boughs of the surrounding forest.

Winter was absolutely thrilled. "Oh shit!" she shouted, the phrase bursting from her mouth unbidden.

Neither knight had been unhorsed, but both lances were shattered which should earn points, but Winter noticed that there were no flags to display the score for each side. "Hey Mel," Winter nudged the laif, breaking her from her seemingly mesmerized state. "How do you keep track of who is winning?" she asked, sweeping a hand over the field.

Melfina returned the question with a puzzled stare, her eyes darting between Winter's eyes and her scar. "This is not a tourney for mortals, Winter," the laif was speaking in *that tone* again, and if Winter had hackles, she would have a hekk of a time keeping them from rising. "The knights joust until one of them yields." Melfina noticed Winter's perplexed expression and continued, "Often knights will joust a single opponent for more than a day and a night without giving in. You must know that *we* do not require the rest that *you* do. A scoring system would bring nothing but dishonor."

There were some things that Winter took for granted, and when she ruled sleep out of the equation, variables arose from outside of her normal reasoning. "So how long does this tourney last?" she asked with awe.

Without sparing a glance for the woman, Melfina shrugged. "Until spring."

The laif probably thought she was being clever, but Winter saw the eye roll that succeeded her reply. Deciding to ignore the pretentious laif, Winter turned her attention back to the field where the knights were now preparing for the next tilt. Their laifhorses pawed at the earth, staining any snow that had not been trampled into oblivion, awaiting the signal to charge. Honestly, laifhorses had always creeped Winter out. They were a thinner horse, lither, and their eyes held sentience. In addition, their teeth weren't blocky and square like those their mortal counterparts sported, but appeared pointy and more canine-like. A shiver cascaded her body, not from the temperature, but from the laifhorse that she swore had just winked at her.

The squire standing next to the knight with the winky laifhorse deftly handed a fresh lance to his knight. A few brisk words were exchanged between the knight and squire, the laifhorse following the conversation with its eye darting between the pair and snorting a response as the knight slammed his visor down. Rhythmically bouncing the top rim of his shield against his faceplate, the knight waited for the horn to blow.

Winter visually swept the field and focused on the opposing knight. "Do you know who these knights are?" she asked Melfina without turning her head.

"The one before us in the black and gold armour is Sir Lhandon of the Gentle March. He hails from a small, but noble canton in the western region of Fenrirfang, south of Lake Humiel," she offered, admiration in her voice. Within a breath, however, her demeanor hardened as she regarded the knight at the far end of the barricade. "The other is Sir Lenebra. A lickspittle twit not fit for her spurs."

"Well..." Winter trailed off, unsure whether she should inquire further, but the decision was made for her when the horn bellowed its demand. The knights spurred their mounts and surged forward, leaning hard in the saddle, lances slowly descending as they drew near each other. The scarf wrapped around Sir Lhandon's helm gallantly billowed behind him as he charged. The previous encounter had created such an impressive spectacle, and

Winter wrapped her hands tight to the fence post bracing for their next concussive impact.

She was not disappointed.

A tremor of shock split the atmosphere when the knights met, the force rolling into the spectators, sweeping away any untamed locks of hair on uncovered heads. The sheer force of this blow seemed to be completely focused, absorbed, and transferred into Sir Lhandon's cantle. Brown liquid erupted from the knight like a muddy geyser, spewing out below his back plate and out onto his crupper.

"Yikes!" Winter yelped, covering her mouth. Sensing Clarial's shocked stare from her periphery, she turned to face her friend. As soon as they made eye contact, the two began roaring with laughter, Clarial dropping to a knee, using the fence as her only means to prevent a total collapse. It seemed, however, that Clarial and Winter were the only ones to find humor in this embarrassing display of weak bowel control. Melfina desperately tugged Clarial back up to her feet while swiveling her head all around, an uneasy expression etched on her haughty visage.

"You embarrass us!" she hissed, placing her spindly fingers behind Clarial's neck and squeezing. "There is no humor to be found when a knight releases." Freeing her taloned grip on Clarial's neck, the laif adjusted her brocade scarf and offered placating nods at the handful of onlookers.

To her delight, Winter noticed that there were gleeful looks in both Breunor and Percival's eyes, but the knights had had the wherewithal to discreetly pull their scarves over their mouths. Turning around and regarding the treetops, Winter found Relic. The gargoyle's shoulders were quaking, his laughter quivering the branch he was perched upon. She mouthed the phrase, "Did you see that?" at him. He nodded in reply, then doubled over in silent laughter, his locked claws all that prevented the creature from taking a tumble.

In stark contrast, the laives hardly reacted at all. Most acted as if someone had simply spilled a glass of milk or dropped a loaf of bread on the floor. A minor incident, and once cleanup was over and done with, it was back to business as usual.

Once Winter had gained a modicum of composure, she attempted to ask Melfina a question, but as soon as a few words spilled from her mouth, she was overcome with giggles. Each time Winter made an attempt and failed, the laif grew more and more displeased. Finally, with an exaggerated groan, she pulled away from Winter and stalked over to her brother to watch the rest of the tourney in peace.

Taking Melfina's place next to Winter, Clarial nudged her friend's shoulder. "What were you trying to say to her?" she asked.

"I was—" the scar faced woman interrupted herself with another fit of giggles. Fanning her face with one hand, Winter cleared her throat and tried as hard as she could to get the notion out into the air. "I was trying—" she dissolved into yet another bout of laughter.

"Out with it!" Clarial urged, shaking Winter's vambrace.

"Alright, alright," Winter sighed and swiped a loose lock of hair that was invading her eyebrow. "That, phew...that laif with the broom up her ass explained to me that they don't keep score in laif tourneys—"

"I know, I know," Clarial waved a hand, prodding for the punch line.

"Well, I was going to suggest that instead of determining the winner by whoever *yields* first that they should just..." Winter's eyes shimmered deviously as she looked over at Sir Lhandon's squire working away diligently with a bucket and sponge.

A sea of heads turned when the women lost all strength in their knees and collapsed into each other. A cackling issued from the boughs above them, and through tear-streamed eyes, Winter watched Relic in flight bobbing away, his wing control hindered with laughter.

* * *

THE UPROARIOUS LAUGHTER JOLTED THE SPECTATORS attention to a pair of buffoons near the fence, happily grappling with each other, more than likely fueled by a copious amount of ale or some other stronger spirit.

A bit premature, the elder laif looked to the heavens, regarding the sun in its midday climb. *That pair must have received hearty libations accompanying their late breakfast.* She shrugged and heaved a heavy sigh. *Mortals.* Settling back in her seat, swaddled in fur trimmed blankets, the laif wrapped her fingers around her goblet filled with spirits of her own and raised it to her lips.

Elgora, the elder's daughter, leaned in, nearly spilling the drink on her mother's lap, and spoke. "I wonder who invited them?" she asked, pointing a furry mitten in the direction of the Trobarkljovas' banner. Before the elder could respond, a hand clasped her shoulder, fingers biting uncomfortably, and a familiar male voice whispered in her ear.

"Mudarfael," the man murmured, addressing her by her title. "Do you sense what I sense in that recently arrived pack of mortals?"

The elder had not yet taken stock of the group, only noticing the cackling women and their guides, the Neprodjan twins. Nothing seemed amiss to her in that initial moment, but now as she passed her gaze over the others leaning against the fence, a tickle of fear latched onto her trachea.

"A kletfae!"

REQUIREMENT

"**W**ood is good for hafts, not for blades!" Winter argued, her eyelids drooping. The local ale was quite a bit stronger than what she was used to and was hitting her rather hard. Melfina and Clarial shook their heads in unison, both wearing matching looks of disapproval.

It had been several hours since the episode involving the shitting knight. The sun was still casting light, but slowly drawing closer and closer to the horizon. Winter felt that at a regular *mortal* tournament, this would be the time for the finalists to prepare for the final tilt. For a race like the laives, however, who slept at most twice a year, the festivities were just beginning.

Another pair of knights collided, shattering their lances into twigs and sending a shockwave through the crowd. Winter winced and shook her head, the novelty having worn off after an entire day of jousts. Bringing her cup to her mouth brought only disappointment as mere dregs flowed towards her expectant lips. *Another empty!* "Fack!" she cursed.

Unnoticed during the commotion, four laives in formal raiment had paired up and flanked the party and stood behind them waiting to be recognized. The laif nearest to Winter cleared his throat, and Winter distractedly turned and handed him her empty cup. "Bring another, if you please?" she requested, turning her attention back to the tiltyard.

The formal-looking laif peered into the cup and gazed back up at Winter with disgust on his face. He looked as if he would very much like to smash the back of Winter's head with it, but fortunately a much older laif appeared behind him and took the cup before any irreparable damage could be done.

"I think you have had enough, my dear," the matron drawled. She gently pressed the cup against Winter's shoulder, drawing her attention.

Winter did a double take. Only a moment ago there had been a regal laif with dreadlocks cascading past his scapulas, now there stood the oldest laif she had ever seen. *She must be beyond ancient! I've never seen a laif appear older than thirty-five, and this broad looks like she held the Creator's hand while he formed the mountains.*

"Perhaps you are right," agreed Winter, sighing loudly.

"I most certainly am," the old laif agreed. "We would like to hold audience with your protector," she stated, inclining her head toward the rest of the party.

"You'll need to be more specific," Winter slurred.

"You *know* of whom I speak."

"No, I really do not."

"The beast of a man."

"Well, that narrows it down to two suspects..."

"The..." the Mudarfael's jaw tightened. "The *werewolf*," she hissed impatiently.

"Alright, alright!" Winter wiped away the spittle mist that had struck below her left eye. "I'll get him for you," she turned her back to the laif and waved her arms wildly. "Percival! Hey! Percival!"

The knight snapped his focus from the pitch to the woman making a fool of herself for the hundredth time that day. As soon as his eyes fixed on her, Winter spun back to the Mudarfael. "You have his attention," she said, turning back to the tourney.

The matron had not finished with the group and pressed closer. "I think it would be best if you all came with us," she announced loudly, sweeping one hand behind her to indicate a second clutch of armed laives approaching, all bearing serious countenances along with rather sharp looking swords.

Breunor shared an uneasy look with Clarial and stepped forward to address the matron, but Winter, who was not their appointed or desired spokesman, was quicker. As the first words escaped her lips, the entire party loudly groaned. "Anything you need to talk with Percy about, you can do right here!" she proclaimed, emphatically pointing toward the snowy soil. "Right out in the open!"

As if on cue, the jousting knights met with a shuddering crash, interrupting the conversation. The Mudarfael blinked for several rounds with one finger raised to her lips in contemplation. The serious laives looked at one another apprehensively, and the one with dreadlocks glowered murderously at Winter, his hand resting on his blade.

"She does not speak for us," interjected Breunor, holding his palms out submissively toward the laives, "If you—"

"Very well." The Mudarfael cut the knight's speech short. Nodding at the most youthful of the serious laives, who immediately set off at a trot away from the field, she spoke again, "We will await Alistair's return."

"I assume that was Alistair—oof!" Winter managed to get in a few words before receiving a startling jab to her ribs delivered by Clarial's elbow.

The Mudarfael ignored the question and turned her attention toward Lamben and Melfina. "Where are these travelers lodging this night?" she inquired.

Melfina shrugged. "Once the sconces were lit against the darkness, I was going to beseech you or one of the other elders to see if shelter could be provided for them."

"Sounds agreeable," the Mudarfael nodded in satisfaction and raised one wrinkly eyebrow. "And I see that you have successfully removed the interloper from our lands."

The twins gravely nodded in unison, and Winter curled her lip in revulsion. *So creepy all the time!*

"Excellent. We do not need that sort of ilk traipsing about."

A small sneeze brought the Mudarfael's attention toward the feet of Sir Percival where Netty was wiping her nose on the cuff of her mantle. Noticing the focus of the woman's attention, Percival placed a gauntleted hand to the little laif's shoulder, drawing her closer to him.

"And who might you be?" the Mudarfael asked, her voice rising an octave or two as she bent down to Netty's level. "Of all the folk within this canton that you could fear, I'm the very last name on that list."

Netty squinted at the old matron, holding her gaze for several seconds before pulling tighter to the hem of Percival's tunic. The steel of his greaves was chilly, but she preferred their icy familiarity to these strangers surrounding them.

"We are looking to resupply what we lost on our journey," said Breunor, attempting to draw the focus away from Netty. "Perhaps there are some shops you could recommend that we could peruse in the morning? After that, we will be on our way."

"Are you traveling north?"

"Aye," Breunor replied, "also, if there is a ranger we could commission for the next ward before we reach the Crescent Marshes..." he trailed off as he noticed the matron was no longer listening.

The Mudarfael was smiling affectionately at Netty and responded dismissively to the knight, "I am sure we can accommodate whatever you seek." Leaning closer to Netty, the woman spoke again, "What is your name, pretty one?"

Winter was not the only one growing uncomfortable with the matron's fresh obsession with Netty. A few of her guards shared confusing sideways glances with one another.

"Her name is her own," Percival answered tersely.

"No need to be standoffish." The Mudarfael stood upright and quickly backed up a pace, finally noticing the sprouting fangs in the mouth of the knight. "My name is Ringuil," she announced, placing a hand to her breast. "This girl and I share a few things in common. You see, my father was human and my mother is a laif, just like yours." The laif paused. "You and I will age the same. Very, very slowly compared with humans, but much faster than our full laif families, who do not show signs of age at all. Can you guess how old I am, little one?"

Netty shook her head, retreating further into the folds of Percival's cloak.

"Seven hundred and twenty-three," the matron proudly stated, the skin around her eyes crinkling as she gazed into the beyond. "The scholars believe I have another three hundred years or so, as long as I continue to avoid dire confrontation." Her eyes flicked to the werewolf for a moment before resting on Netty again, "You see, we are not immortal like our mothers, but we do enjoy a very long life."

"My mother *was* immortal," intoned Netty, staring at the dirt encrusted snow on the ground at her feet.

Ringuil was momentarily taken aback by the implication, believing that the girl's mother must surely be alive, and opened her mouth to respond but was interrupted by both Alistair's return and yet another shockwave from the pitch. Winter's eyes followed the young laif as he led a foreboding laifhorse toward them, the sight of it sending chills up her spine. Strapped to its saddle was an expertly crafted suit of gleaming armour and set atop the armour, like a king's crown, sat a glorious tourney helm. Alistair handed the reins to Ringuil, who gave the laifhorse a scratch under its chin and mumbled something in the beast's ear.

Standing before Percival, Alistair spoke solemnly and carefully sounding like he had received strict tutelage beforehand. "It has been requested by those greater than us that you accept this gift," stated the laif, extending a hand toward the laifhorse resplendent with exemplary arms.

Percival appeared beleaguered by the offer, his eyes resting on the laif who had been speaking, waiting for further explanation.

"For what and why?" Breunor demanded.

"Why?" Alistair looked at the knights as if he had been flicked across the tip of his nose. "Why, to join the tourney, of course."

"Out of the question," Breunor protested with cold certainty. "This must be a jest," he said.

"This is no joke," Alistair assured them, his hands reverently clasped below his belt. "And it is not a *request* as you seem to understand the term."

Lowering her chin and staring deep into Breunor's eyes, Ringuil clarified Alistair's statement. "It is a demand."

PERCIVAL HAD REFUSED THE PROVIDED ARMOUR, claiming that accepting foreign armour was akin to accepting a drink poured in secret. He did, however, relent to wearing the helm, having no desire to lose an eye. The offered helm had a fixed face and a single slit for the eyes that rested just below the curvature of the visor. The idea was to allow the knight clear vision as he leaned forward in the saddle charging his opponent, but before any lances broke, the knight could tilt his head back to protect his eyes from any harmful debris. It was a great and simple invention, but it had little use outside of the tourney grounds.

The rest of the party was led toward the central grandstand that overlooked the tournament, positioned equidistant from both starting points.

"What is this village called?" Clarial asked Breunor as they moved onto the first set of steps.

"I don't know," admitted the knight, shaking his head.

"How do you not know? Surely you have been here before?"

"I tend to avoid civilization."

"Don't you have the map memorized?"

"On the map it's called 'Laif Dwelling' or 'Laif Village', or something along those lines."

"*Or something along those lines?* It's *that* nondescript?"

The knight offered a solitary nod.

Winter, walking behind the pair, overheard the debate, and took it upon herself to alleviate the query. "Hey Mel," she said, turning to the female half of the twins. "What exactly is the name of your village?"

"This dwelling is known as Malupraevo, it is where we call home."

I'm fully aware that you live here, you twit. Winter responded with a thin smile, trying to exude admiration, but felt it likely came across as a grimace.

The laif continued unabated, her eyes skimming over Winter's scar. "It is one of three villages that lay nestled inside the canton of Centarpaetfen. Ringuil is the matriarch of Malupraevo, and soon you will meet the other leaders and elders of the canton."

Sounds neat. "Thank you so much for clearing that up, Mel." *You smarmy donkey.*

The looks they received from the sea of laives seated on the bleachers were mixed to say the least. Ringuil was leading them single file at a pace that Winter wished could be a bit faster than a wounded snail slogging through a trail of salt. One little girl tugged at her mantle and said, "You're pretty," but when Winter turned her scarred face to thank the little girl, the little girl's expression of horror seemed an instant retraction. *Making friends everywhere you go.*

"By the time we get to the box, Percival's joust will be a distant memory, and spring will be upon us in full bloom," Winter mocked, an aside meant for Clarial, who was marching in front of her. If Clarial heard the jape, she made no response that Winter could perceive. Deciding not to repeat herself, Winter felt a bit deflated, and chose to remain silent until their eventual arrival to their destination.

A musky, though not entirely unpleasant aroma greeted them as they entered the central grandstand. *Smells of moss and bracken locked in a trunk,* Winter mused.

Winter wanted to locate the mayor, duke, viscount, or whatever the title was for those in charge of the entire canton, but this proved impossible by sight alone. As was the culture among ruling laives, power was usually shared and there were not any specific chairs denoting chief prominence.

Five seats had been left open for the new guests in a regal compartment typically set aside for the laives of station within Centarpaetfen. A few heads turned with smiles and nods, and swept back to whatever it was they were occupied with before the brief interruption.

Five chairs? Winter looked about in confusion, pointing one finger to her chest before pointing at the others, making an obvious tally. "There are only four of us," she stated. Melfina and Lamben had not been extended a formal invitation and were no longer with them. Ringuil slowly took her seat and patted the cushion next to her in an inviting manner, locking eyes with Netty and smiling.

"Ah, yes," Ringuil commented, her eyes twinkling as Netty climbed up onto the chair. "I asked to have a seat set aside for your friend *above.*" The matron gestured with a gnarled digit toward the skies.

"I think he would much prefer the view he is currently enjoying," Winter offered a tight smile as she took her seat next to Netty. *No way I'm going to let this old bag alone with her.* "But I am sure he will appreciate the gesture when we tell him."

Ringuil returned a similar tight-lipped smile and gestured to her left at a striking female laif with hard angled features. *That's a jaw that could take a punch,* Winter wagered to herself.

"This is my daughter, Elgora."

"Greetings," said Elgora dryly, sweeping a haughty look of appraisal over the party.

"I'm Winter," the woman began introductions, pointing a finger to her chin, then pointing to the others in turn. "And this is Clarial and Sir Breunor of..." she snapped her fingers, hoping the knight would conclude her statement with some impressive title.

"Of the Cold Hearth," he lied feebly, the phrase executed with as much fervor as one prodding a skeleton to life with a sapling. Clarial covered her mouth with her fingertips, her shoulders shuddering with laughter.

Winter silently mouthed "Cold Hearth?" at the knight with a look of pained despair. "You're killing me!" she mouthed.

"And this is Netty!" Ringuil announced to Elgora as she unfurled her fur blankets, extending them across the little girl so the pair could share warmth. Winter bristled, skimming a fingertip across her scar.

A trumpet blasted just below them, vibrating the planks under the soles of their boots. The unexpected interruption snapped everyone's attention back to the field, and a hush fell over the grounds for the first time that day. A herald in glittery coats marched onto the field, his cape mere inches from slapping the muddied snow that caked the ground. The laif seemed to be concentrating on something on the turf, but suddenly his whole body went rigid and he spread his arms as wide as possible as he began his announcement. "MY DEAR LAIVES OF MALUPRAEVO," he paused to allow for an eruption of cheers, "MY PROUD LAIVES OF NEVOLAESPEN." There was another pause to allow for raucous applause. Then, as if the tips of his fingers were being tugged by invisible strings, he swept his arms up in a tremulous gesture to everyone. "AND, OF COURSE, THE RULERS AND THE EXQUISITE LAIVES WITHIN CENTARPAETFEN!" he finished, his pronouncement sending the entire population into a frenzy of cheers, shouts, and inarticulate screams.

The occupants of the grandstand merely clapped politely, but the surrounding atmosphere was deafening. Netty covered her ears and nestled closer to Winter, who extended a sheltering arm over the little girl.

Once a semblance of quiet prevailed, the herald continued, "We have a unique, dare I say, *enigmatic* challenger on our illustrious field this day! Not for centuries have we allowed a mortal to pick up lance and tilt in our games! But this day we have lifted the veil for this man! This knight! This champion of the Table Round!"

The reaction was still quite exuberant indeed, but more tempered than before as some of the laives exhibited perplexed expressions in lieu of shouts.

"May I introduce to you, here for the first time at Centarpaetfen's annual winter tourney," the herald paused, hunching over with his hands on his knees to catch his breath for a few moments before arching back violently and screaming, "SIR PERCIVAL!" The invisible strings were cut and the laif's arms fell to his sides as an icy silence sliced through his melodramatic proclamation. Not one laif stirred and the hands that had been speculatively rubbing chins or fussing with curly locks were abruptly stilled.

A vicious snort from the far side of the field absorbed Winter's attention, where, mounted atop that skeleton of a laifhorse, was Sir Percival in his armour. The knight steered his borrowed steed toward the gate, and leading the laifhorse was Alistair, acting as squire. Clenched under the crook of Alistair's arm was that exemplary helm and in the other hand was clutched a lance without a pennant.

He looks completely pissed, Winter thought. Observing Percival's overall bearing, she could tell that this was clearly not his first tournament.

Turning her attention back to the group, she caught the tail end of something Breunor was explaining to Clarial, "...and that's why the court won't allow him to joust anymore—" he said, right before the crowd erupted in exhilaration. Percival's opponent had finally emerged from his tent.

"THIS KNIGHT DOES NOT SEEM TO REQUIRE INTRODUCTION, BUT I WILL ANNOUNCE HIS NAME REGARDLESS!" It was nothing short of miraculous that the herald could somehow manage to be heard above the violent din surrounding him. "SIR GUUUUUUUUUUUULARION!" he shouted, holding the "guuuuuu" much longer than Winter felt appropriate, but the spectators ate it up like a prime meat stew.

Elgora leaned over her mother to speak to Winter. "Sir Gularion has yet to be bested on the field," she boasted, "he has never even fallen from his saddle."

"We usually save him for the final joust," added Ringuil, "but we made an exception for today."

Something about the way the matron exhaled the word *today,* caused a wave of unease to wash over Winter.

"This is not a good idea..." Breunor murmured to Clarial, and Winter overheard, though was unsure of what exactly the knight was remarking about. She leaned over the empty seat between her and Clarial, trying to catch the rest of what he was saying. The timbre of his voice exuded an air of grave apprehension, and Winter suspected it was well-placed fear for his friend in the saddle.

"Not good at all," he reiterated.

The flags dropped and the knights spurred their mounts forward.

~ 15 ~

THE ORACLE

There had been no earth rending crash, no shuddering shiver rolling over the crowd, no great clamor as the knights collided.

IT HAD ALL HAPPENED SO FAST. Too fast for Winter to immediately gain full comprehension. The gravity of the dreadful scene only began to settle into her consciousness as an armed contingent of guards rushed the party out of the grandstand and into a cathedral sized building directly behind the platform. The enraged crowd focused their ire upon the armoured guards, peppering them with stones and other implements. Gallantly shielding Winter and the others from the unjust onslaught raining down upon them, the guards ushered the group forward. Once safe inside the edifice, Winter made a terrible discovery. *Where's Netty?!*

"Where's Netty?!" she shouted.

* * *

AS SOON AS NETTY SAW WHAT SIR PERCIVAL DID, she noticed that a deafening silence dropped all through the village. It permeated every stand, every bench, and every concession. Laives occupying taprooms within shouting distance of the lists hushed their speech. Even the mice and rodents huddled in their harborages grew silent. Netty wasn't actually certain about that last detail, but she believed it was true.

The last she had seen before Ringuil threw the mountain of blankets over her had been a group of enraged laives rushing Percival, and Relic descending upon the laives. She heard Winter, Clarial, and Breunor being rushed past, hastily and firmly escorted by the guards stationed in the grandstand.

The villagers had almost immediately shifted from disbelief to aggression, and all their rage was focused on her friends.

"Who can even stand against such blind hatred?" Netty heard Ringuil comment to someone nearby, probably her daughter. The response was muffled, the speaker too far for Netty to clearly hear. Plus the heated demands for murder cancelled out quite a lot of conversation. As hard as she tried to focus on hearing what was happening with her knight out on the field, she was unable to hear anything of consequence. One particular female laif was screeching and weeping inconsolably directly behind her, and Netty privately wished, only for the briefest moment, that someone would just slap the woman across the face.

Several minutes passed and the panic surrounding Percival had quieted. Netty wished above all else that someone would take these mounds of blankets from her. When she had tried to rid herself from their oppressive nature, a firm hand had clamped down and a stranger's male voice intoned that it would be in her best interest to remain hidden for the time being.

Where is Percival?! And my other friends?! What has become of them? Panic, a most unwelcome feeling, began to rise inside her. She absolutely did not want to be left in this village. *What if they forget about me?* Steadying herself, she grew as still as possible. The girl pictured her muscles as a coiled spring, waiting for the perfect moment to tear the shrouds off in a decisive flourish.

"Meet me in the cathedral."

Netty recognized Ringuil's voice coming from several paces away, seemingly near the side exit.

Ringuil continued, her stern voice growing gradually dimmer, but Netty managed to catch the first part. "Bring the kletfae once you notice..."

Kletfae??

* * *

WINTER HAD BEEN SPINNING IN PLACE, shouting for Netty. The cathedral they had been ushered into for safety had a chilly draft permeating the large room. The vaulted ceiling above them was entirely covered in painted scenes, though well-worn and desperately in need of a few touch ups.

The banging on the massive arched door had not stopped for even a solitary moment since their arrival. The crowd outside wanted blood. No, they were demanding blood. Her blood. In addition, there were several more colorful ideas that the mob was passing around, each promoted with a single shout. For instance, one woman had screamed, "Let's mount their heads on pikes!" This was followed by a round of agreeable cheers. Then one clever scholar decided to build upon that first notion, crowing, "But first we'll drive the pikes up their butts!" The crowd thought that was brilliant. And another lad decided to add, "We'll gradually lower them down on top of the pikes, so it's nice and slow!" That really got them going and they attacked the door harder, seeing as they were now united with a single goal in mind.

Winter found all of this quite disturbing, but the most troubling was a particular voice she heard chanting over and over somewhere in the midst of the din, "Bare butts! Bare butts! Bare butts!" She crinkled her nose in disgust, and turned away to stride toward Breunor and Clarial, who were standing alone and speaking in hushed tones. The knight's arm was around her friend's shoulder and they appeared to be consoling each other, as sweethearts do.

When did this happen? Winter was momentarily perplexed, but quickly became distracted by a guard holding her halberd with its haft planted on the stone floor. He was holding it as if he was the weapon's proper owner.

"Now, now. This won't do at all," said Winter to herself as she swiftly approached the armoured laif. His already pinched features tightened when he noticed Winter stalking directly toward him. One might have believed he had shat in her ale by the sour expression on her face.

Dust swirled around her cloak as she came to an abrupt halt before the guard. "That belongs to me," Winter snarled, her eyes cleaving the laif's face in half. Before he could make a response, a pair of guards brusquely interrupted the scene.

"Go back with your companions," a guard with an extraordinarily high forehead advised sternly, gripping her left elbow.

Winter pulled away from the laif's probing fingers. "Happily!" she said, looking the guard directly in the face. "As soon as I receive what is mine."

"All in due time," Ringuil interrupted from the front dais, leaning on a rough-hewn staff that climbed to her shoulders.

Taking a step back, Winter disengaged from the guards and their obnoxious dissidence. "Where's Netty?" she demanded, this time the question pointed at someone who should have answers. Breunor and Clarial drew up beside her and the three began to stride toward the dais.

"That's close enough," Ringuil raised a hand, a devious smile drawing across her old lips.

The three companions halted and found themselves in the center of the great hall. Winter lifted her eyes to the ceiling and saw a painted circular pattern depicting a murder of crows swirling above their position.

"With knowledge comes sorrow," the Mudarfael began apologetically, needing to raise her voice to be heard over the mob outside. With a half-hearted gesture, Ringuil indicated that the guards descend upon their guests. Entirely outflanked and outmaneuvered, the tactician within Winter advised her to surrender. It was clearly the sole viable option when such a scenario overtakes one. Unless one wished to die, of course.

The guards removed the prisoners weapons and latched shackles to their wrists, securing the chains to the floor where a large eye anchor sprouted from the stonework. *So that's what that's there for,* Winter chuckled to herself. She lifted her eyes to the crows on the ceiling and shook her head ruefully in defeat.

"What is this about?" demanded Breunor, giving the chain a yank.

"Also in due time," replied Ringuil placidly.

Winter walked as far as the shackles would allow. "We don't have time—or *due* time for this!" She gave the chain a violent pull. "Take these chains off of us immediately!"

"I don't think so."

"Now!"

Ringuil shook her head and her scowl pulled her wrinkles into jowls. "As long as we keep you apart from Netty, from the girl who has been selected to carry out the Utvarae's perfect justice, then there will be no interference."

"Start making sense!" commanded Winter.

"Ah," the matron replied, the word croaking out from her throat. "You aren't aware of just who you are escorting? But I believe your knightly friend knows. Don't you, Sir Breunor? The knight who abandoned his illustrious post in Camelot to dedicate his life to slaying kapreta. Such a petty existence, fueled by a thirst for revenge that will never be quenched," Ringuil closed her eyes and shook her head.

Clarial shot an accusing look at Breunor. "I thought you said you'd never been here before?" she whispered.

The knight appeared just as surprised as Clarial. "I wasn't lying."

Ringuil continued, ignoring the exchange, "Sir Breunor is well aware that the Utvarae, or Abowraith, as you mortals like to call it, has marked the girl and intends to use her as its next vessel. You see," the halflaif continued, directing her next words at Clarial and Winter, "the kingdom made no response to the massacre at Knotwithstadt, a peaceful village that somehow managed to exist in perfect harmony with human and laif. How they did such a thing, I do not know. It's worth noting just how remarkable that fact is. But when such an act is committed, then surely there must be repercussions. And that, my dear ones, is when the ancient magics in Fenrirfang arise and provide their own version of justice."

Violently Breunor turned his face from the dais. "There will be justice for the Church's crimes!" he spat.

"Prove it!" Ringuil trembled as if she were about to explode. "There is no proof that your king has even heard that the people of Knotwithstadt were slaughtered in their beds! Women and children alike! All sleeping! Dreaming!"

"Why do you think—" the knight's bitter rebuttal was cut short by a regiment of knights entering from where the matron had emerged. Leading the group of armoured laives was a thin, gaunt hollow-looking laif who had Netty by the hand. The pair ascended the stairs to Ringuil while the knight escort remained below the platform.

The pale laif dropped Netty's hand and creeped behind the matron, speaking just loud enough for Winter to barely hear what he said.

"The knights you sent into the forest to retrieve them have yet to return, my Mudarfael," the laif, who Winter surmised was some sort of advisor, continued much louder and spoke with his eyes locked onto Winter's. "But we trust that we should have them well in hand shortly. The gargoyle has only one operational wing and the werewolf is muzzled."

"Excellent," exclaimed Ringuil. She hunched her shoulders in glee and bent down to Netty. "Soon you will achieve your destiny, little one."

Breunor stuttered in disbelief. "Wha-wha-what have you done?!" he wrenched his manacles again, this time drawing blood.

"Were you not listening?" Ringuil clicked her tongue and spoke as if she were talking to an amputee that had just discovered he no longer had his sword hand. "Tonight the Utvarae will claim a fresh body," the matron hovered a hand over Netty's head. "And all those responsible will pay for what they have done to my fellow laives! To my fellow immortals who should have been spared the inconvenience of death!"

"Why do you think Percival came to Camelot?!" Breunor shouted defiantly. "Arthur released Percival and his brother from the killing fields to exact vengeance! The king's vengeance! Our *perfect* vengeance! And now you've gone and mucked it all up!" he paused to breathe for a moment, his shoulders rising and falling violently. The knight's eyes were pinned to something on the ground, then suddenly he looked up murderously. "Our spies secured a list of the guilty. Do you think this "Utvarae" has such accurate descriptions?"

The news clearly took Ringuil by surprise. Her jaw dropped and she clasped a vein-covered hand to her collarbone in stark wonder. The matron struggled to dispel this new development with a flimsy wave of her hand. "No matter," she said with a pinch of uncertainty, looking above the three. "The werewolf no longer has his fangs and the gargoyle cannot perform the act it was designed for."

Winter smelled bullshit. "How could you possibly suppress Sir Percival from transforming into a beast?"

Ringuil chuckled. "It's remarkable how the most beautiful and striking things—in the natural world and in the *unnatural*—often promote the most danger. Even the most visually desirable *objects* can become the bane of the most powerful king, queen, or *armoured knight*."

Winter rolled her eyes in recollection. *That gorgeous tourney helm!* She wanted to slap her own forehead, but recalled the metal restraints on her wrists which would inflict a much more painful strike than desired.

"Judging by your expression, my dear," began Ringuil, lowering her gaze onto Winter. "You have deduced that it was the helm which we provided. You see, it has been imbued with a magic that only I possess the verbal key to unlock. Your knight will remain merely a man, unable to shift into another skin until the helm is removed...by me," she paused. "But it seems that we grossly underestimated his basic prowess," she glared at the advisor next to her and continued, "the way he managed to use that useless lance we gave him to remove Sir Gularion's face, was well...it was quite impressive. Terrible, indeed, but impressive."

Winter could perfectly recreate in her mind the way Percival's lance shivered and broke right at the fringe of impact, directly on Gularion's faceplate. The laif knight's helm spun upward exposing his face for only a fraction of a moment, but it was all Percival needed. With violent precision, he had punched the hard pommel of the lance into Gularion's teeth. There had been no resounding crash, as Gularion had completely missed Percival's shield. The only sound was the sickening meaty slap of the knight's jaw being shorn from his immortal face. *Not even a lampyr at the top of their game would be able to piece that puzzle back together.* The knight's death had been instant, thus the extreme outcry from the laives.

*Speaking of outcry...*The frothing crowds had abruptly ceased their intolerable racket and the atmosphere in the church felt very strange. It was as if a fine stiletto had sliced every throat beyond the cathedral door.

And that was when the *real* banging on the door began. These resounding demands were not like the clamoring of the disgruntled laives before. No, this was banging intended to take the door down, and it was wracked with overwhelming rancor that could be felt inside the cathedral.

Immediately Winter knew who was knocking at the gates.

"Not one of you is getting out alive," she whispered, a smile creasing her lips.

IT'S REMARKABLE THE AMOUNT OF VIOLENCE a mere two beings can inflict upon a decent sized contingent of defenders within a relatively open space. Once again, the tactician within Winter rose up to admire the skill, no, the artistry being displayed by a flightless gargoyle and a fully armoured knight (whose vision, it must be noted, was grossly inhibited by the helm he sported).

After the second enraged thud against the door, splinters had been sent flying along with a good two thirds of the guards. The knights by the dais remained steadfast, swords drawn and peeking over their kite shields, prepared for a most wicked onslaught.

The door burst into particles after the third concentrated slam, and Winter spun in her shackles in time to watch all the surety in the universe drain from the Mudarfael's wretched old face.

As he ran by, Winter observed the precise moment that Percival's eyes found Netty, his footfalls suddenly falling with greater purpose than when he had first emerged from the wreckage. Relic set himself against the remaining guard nearest the threshold, and the ones that did not drop to their knees in surrender were provided a swift death.

Winter kept her eyes focused on the thieving guardsman that still held her halberd. She pointed desperately at him. "Relic! Get him! Get him!" she screamed. She tried to follow the guard as he made a panicked retreat, but the chains that bound her brought her up short with an aggravating tug. The thief-guard's eyes were terror-stricken and his body language showed indecisiveness. He clearly wanted to aid the laives that he grew up with and trained with and served with his entire immortal life. But now there was this woman screaming at him, directing the whirling beast's attention to his doorstep. If the gargoyle had heard her pleas, he made no indication of such, so if it was luck or he was obliging her, she could not tell for certain. What she did know was that Relic was fast upon the thief, leaving dead and dying corpses and weeping laives in his wake.

The guard raised the halberd like a staff between his two hands in an attempt to block the gargoyle's overhead stroke. But the gargoyle was not interested in sparring, which was clearly all this laif had ever been privy to. Relic feinted the blow and deftly maneuvered his blade beneath the halberd. If Winter had blinked, she would have missed the sword punching under the guard's ribcage, but she would definitely not have missed the torrents of blood rushing from the immortal's eviscerated organs as the gargoyle withdrew. One thing led to another and Relic wrenched the halberd from the dying laif before driving the sharp point of his armoured kneecap into the crescent of his foe's nose.

"You did hear me!" shouted Winter in relief as she watched the gargoyle toss the halberd within grasping distance of her on his way toward the dais.

Retrieving the halberd, Winter gained purchase with her fingertips on the spear-tipped blade. Glancing at Breunor and Clarial, she saw they were staring, frozen by what was transpiring at the forefront of the cathedral.

"You won't kill me," Ringuil croaked, quaking and clutching her cane with both hands as if she were on the stern of a ship, resisting a gale. Winter had no pity for the old woman. The matron continued, trying her best to maintain some semblance of composure as she beheld the physical embodiment of vengeance standing before her. "Only I can utter the words that will release you from the helm's embrace," she reminded the werewolf.

Percival's arm and sword were drenched in matching crimson, and as he stood, a puddle began to form under him. The slight tilt in the building's foundation caused the blood to spill over the rim of the dais and drip onto the cold floor. The matron was alone, save for Winter with her companions, all the others were either dead or had fled.

Inclining his head in order to look directly at the matron through the meager eye slits, Percival spoke with venom. "Free me."

"I would advise that your next words should contain the incantation," offered Relic, placidly cleaning his sword while keeping an eye on the dark hallway the laif knights had retreated into.

Ringuil fussed with something underneath her layers of winter garments, and when she looked up at the faceless knight, she appeared to have aged centuries. Perhaps something about the werewolf's eyes triggered something deep within the recesses of her mind, for a look of catharsis suddenly bloomed over her features, and the tone of the old woman's voice shifted confidently, "I *know* what you are, we have—"

This time Winter made the mistake of blinking.

A red slit gradually thickened just above the matron's collarbone, the tendons connecting her ancient chin severed, and Winter watched as Netty wiped the spatter of blood that had struck her face when Percival lashed out. The knight finished the strike by deftly terminating his blade into its scabbard, then without pause, clasped the little girl by the hand and led her away from the crumbling husk of a halflaif.

STARTS WITH BACON

"I knew it!" Winter announced, thrusting an accusatory finger at Percival as they rushed deeper into the forest surrounding the village.

"Make your emboldened speeches later, Winter!" said Clarial, speaking without looking back at her friend. "You heard what Lenebra said, we need to get far away as fast as possible!"

"Yeah, yeah..." Winter rolled her eyes, abruptly ducking a branch weighed low by the mounds of snow piled atop it. In daylight she would have spotted such an obstacle a mile away, but the creeping darkness was beginning to make travel more difficult and tedious than was welcome.

After rushing from the cathedral earlier, they had made for the grandstand where their supplies and belongings had been left behind in the confusion. When they had arrived, the lists were vacant as were the bleachers, platforms, and grandstands. Where such raucous displays of life were on display mere hours ago, an ominous silence now permeated. The air was thick and invasive, and even their mists of breath seemed to appear denser in the torchlight.

To their great disappointment, they discovered that their belongings were not where they had last left them. Thankfully, Sir Lenebra appeared from the darkness to inform them that the twins had absconded with their belongings amidst the fray. The Opossum Knight then went on to explain how fanatical some of the laives of Malupraevo were when it came to ancient curses and the like. She explained that it would be in their best interest to quickly hide in the forest, and promised that she and her men would retrieve their belongings. There was little time for debate, yet both Relic and Sir Breunor took a moment to hastily issue warnings of specific violence if Lenebra proved a false knight.

"It is actually I who is in debt to you," said Lenebra, her eyes furtively darting all around, "now that Sir Gularion is dead, I actually have a chance at winning the tourney!" The flickering torchlight gave the knight's elongated smile a rather sinister appearance as she held the party in her gaze. "Well, perhaps not this year, you know...because, well, you went and killed the matriarch of the host village, and well..." She trailed off, not needing to conclude her statement.

The party gave her the heartiest thanks they could conjure before departing for the nearest treeline, though

Relic paused to make a gesture as he passed that made it very clear he would be watching her.

Lenebra proved to be a knight of her word and soon reunited them with their stolen gear and supplies, along with a warning. "Get as far away as you can as fast as possible. I doubt anyone will be foolish enough to give chase, but you just never know when it comes to revenge." With that, the Trobarkljova knights and squires bid the party farewell. One squire offered a flaming torch as a parting gift, but Relic stepped forward to decline the offer. The gargoyle could see equally well in the darkness as in the light, and such an item would only serve as a beacon for their foes.

The party rushed through the forest, following behind their grounded gargoyle, with just a few specks of passing moonlight to guide their steps. Arriving in a clearing allowed them to fan out, which Winter found to be a nice change as she was growing a bit irritated by Clarial clomping down on her heels every dozen paces or so.

"Hold a moment, Relic," Breunor requested, and the winged knight obliged with a reluctant turn. "I feel we are growing closer and closer to the next ward," Breunor said, "I do not want to cross it completely unaware."

In the darkness Winter could barely make out the gargoyle's visage, but she imagined that his forehead crinkled in disbelief. "You wish to halt for the night?" he asked.

"Aye," said Breunor, placing his hands on his hips and sucking in the frigid night air. "I think we should settle in for the night. This clearing should give you ample view from the treeto—" the knight cut himself off, forgetting that their scout was now confined to the earth like the everyone else. At least, confined until they came across a lampyr that could fix such a wound, which would probably not be anytime in the foreseeable future.

Relic did not show any signs of offense at the statement, but simply surveyed the other faces to gauge their feelings about the idea. Though with the pervading darkness, it was all but impossible to share any looks of either agreement or disagreement.

The gargoyle heaved his shoulders and released a heavy sigh. "Alright, I will try to find a good place to keep watch. Morning will not be arriving any time soon, so sleep with your weapons close."

Winter fumbled for some time, clawing through her pack in search of her heavy blanket. After clearing a spot for herself, she settled in for the night. Unfortunately, the ale she had slugged back all afternoon was ready to remind her of its existence once again. As soon as she had closed her eyes for the night, her bladder began to announce that it was overfull and in need of a purge. Removing herself from her encasement of blankets and fabrics was quite the exercise, and she felt it was possible that she may have soiled herself just a bit on her exit.

Fortunately, the moon was at its apex and was blasting the clearing with helpful rays, assisting Winter with finding the perfect tree nearby. She suddenly realized something was amiss when she noticed Relic's silhouette sitting bolt upright on a branch, followed by the distant crunching of snow growing closer and closer. The steps were really just plodding along, there was not much urgency in the solitary footfalls, but still, an approaching creature at this hour was cause for at least a small degree of alarm.

She sighed in exasperation at the compromising pose she found herself in. *Of course, it would be my luck to die like this.* The pressure in her bladder was hardly relieved and stopping midstream was out of the question. *I have literally been caught with my pants down.*

"Percival!" Breunor hissed a warning across the glade.

The werewolf knight was already awake, his calm voice carried from the thicket. "I know," he said.

Come on, come on! Winter urged her body to finish its business.

Whatever was lurking in the forest had not slowed its methodical pace. Relic leapt from his perch and rolled in the powdery snow, making for the intruder. He tapped Percival on his pauldron to alert him to his presence, and the pair set off together into the darkness. Breunor and Clarial, weapons drawn, formed a barricade around Netty, ready for an ambush from any angle. And Winter was still squatting against an elm, trying to avoid getting pee on her garments.

A stone's throw from the encampment, the gargoyle made a startled noise which sounded like a shout of surprise or possibly a laugh. Winter could not be sure, but she did not hear any ensuing struggle following that break of silence.

Soon three figures emerged into the clearing, two walking upright as men, and the third was a creature that at first appeared to be an overly muscular doe. Standing up to secure her belt, Winter soon realized who the intruder was.

Aw, really? She widened her jaw in irritation, popping her eardrums. *How did that beast track us down?*

It was as if the creature could read Winter's thoughts, it suddenly shot her a toothy grin as Breunor patted its haunches.

"Seems like he really took a liking to you, Percival," the knight said, a tinge of awe in his voice, his eyes admiring the laifhorse that Percival had ridden in the tourney.

The beast had somehow managed to track him all the way from the lists to their current location. *Which is amazing,* Winter thought, *but if that dumb animal can find us in the pitch of night, then perhaps we are not nearly as safe as we think.*

A SOLITARY PATCH OF MORNING SUNLIGHT managed to pierce the canopy and press itself unabated directly against Winter's closed eyelids. *For everything we hold sacred!* Winter complained to herself and rolled over to her other side. When she finally pried her eyes open, eyelashes crisp with tiny ice crystals, the pressure in her bladder immediately made itself known.

A muffled shout of terror woke Winter completely, bolting her upright. Looking around the clearing, she felt that the early morning shadows deadened the sounds in the surrounding trees and she was unable to find the source of the scream. *Did I imagine it?*

Coiling the blanket around her, Winter made for the tree she had used the previous night as a garderobe, but a discontinuity in the elm's silhouette made her stop short. A slight ringing in her ears began, perhaps brought upon by the inordinately quiet moment and the stark reality of what was pinned against the tree. Wintery mist swirled from the blood pooling on the ground below the body as well as from various points of exposed flesh. Winter looked more closely to find the spear portion of her halberd buried in the throat of a thin-framed laif, his boots dangling several inches from the scarlet snow. He was quite dead, freshly dead it seemed, as the blood was still spilling in rivulets from his corpse.

Winter recognized the laif fixed to the tree. "Lamben," she whispered.

Beyond the newly decorated elm, Winter caught the glimmer of armour against the wintery backdrop. Another shout echoed from the distance, and Winter thrust her blanket aside and tried in vain to remove her halberd from the laif's trachea. The weapon had been lodged into the tree with such tremendous force that she reckoned they would need to hew the tree down in order to retrieve it. The sounds of struggle seemed to originate from where she had seen the glint of steel, so abandoning her attempts at reclaiming her halberd, but quickly scooping up an abandoned sword on the ground, likely dropped by Lamben upon his abrupt conclusion, she rushed to see what was transpiring.

As she moved into the trees, she marveled that she was the only one in their camp who seemed to have noticed anything. Upon approach, she saw one of the knights from the village church standing over the pitiful form of a female laif on the ground. But as the distance waned, Winter recognized the elaborate helm adorning the knight's head and recalled that Percival had taken a mantle from one of the dead littering the cathedral. A clump of bundled fabric stood next to Percival, just to his left, holding the warrior's hand. *Netty.*

"The spell should wear off," Melfina promised, staring up with glassy eyes at the werewolf barred by magic. "I do not know how soon...it could be days or weeks? The Mudarfael did not have ample time to create the incantation. I believe its effects will not be felt for much longer."

The laif's elbows trembled as she tried to remain propped up on the frigid ground. "You do not understand! If the utvarae does not complete its task, the daemon will turn its unfaltering wrath upon the surrounding people. *My people!*" Her eyes darted between Netty and Percival in a pleading manner.

Melfina's appeal resonated with Winter and caused her to inhale much louder than she intended. Instantly she regretted making her appearance known as all three faces turned to look at her. Percival's hand twitched to his hip but relaxed as he recognized the approaching woman.

"So you see?" Melfina continued, "we do not wish harm on this little girl," a tear trickled out from under the laif's eyelid. "But we have no choice. Can't you see?"

"There is always a choice." Percival's voice rang out from under the steel. Behind him snow began to fall in great clumps as vultures alighted on the boughs. "If you cannot remove this," he said, tapping a finger to his armoured temple, "then we have no use for—"

Winter stepped in, though she immediately cursed herself for doing so. "Go on your way," she commanded, feeling Percival's withering gaze upon her, "I'm sure your brother is impatiently awaiting your return." Winter lied, hoping to encourage the laif to take a swift retreat.

"My brother!" Melfina sputtered, her eyelashes fluttering as if dust had been flung at her. "We had split up...he lives?" she asked, peering up at Winter with hope in her eyes.

"Oh, yeah," Winter affirmed. "I saw him tearing a path through the snow back toward your village." She fluttered a hand vaguely toward the beyond.

"But I felt within my breast that he had expired..." Melfina began to wipe the tears from her face and gave Percival a speculative glance before standing. "You shan't ever see me again," she promised, then whirled away, taking off in the direction that Winter had indicated.

Netty, Percival, and Winter stood in silence watching the desperate laif until she was well out of sight. "What is silver shadesgill?" Netty asked.

"Why do you ask?" inquired Winter, turning back for the camp.

"Mel said that if we had a bucket of silver shadesgill nectar, we could pour it on top of Sir Percival's head and that would break the spell."

"Ah." *Good luck with that one.*

WHEN THEY RETURNED, they were greeted by an unoccupied space. Only their supplies strewn about marked where they had slept. And, of course, the dreadful laifhorse that had ingratiated itself into their company was standing about expectantly with its tail swishing eagerly.

"Where is everyone else?" Winter stated the obvious question.

"Did you not hear the commotion?" Percival responded with another question.

Winter raised her eyebrows and pursed her lips in surprise.

The knight continued, "As soon as the sun crested the horizon, we were set upon by five or six laives."

"Do they *want* to die?"

"Quite the opposite. Apparently."

Melfina's words came back to Winter. She could hardly blame the laives at this point. *We are all striving for survival, one way or another. Even, it seems, those blessed with immortality.* "As soon as the others return, we should make for Knotwithstadt as quickly as possible," Winter advised as she began to bundle her belongings. "And would you mind removing my…" Winter trailed off, gesturing at her halberd which was still protruding from Lamben's neck.

Percival placed a hand on the haft of the halberd. "Do you have that wineskin?"

"Why?"

"I believe we have our means to pass the next ward," he explained, inclining his head at the dead laif.

*Such a pragmatic werewolf…*Winter found the skin and passed it to the knight. When enough blood had been procured, Percival simply tugged the weapon free, and reverently offered the weapon to her.

"Thank you," she said, accepting the halberd with both hands.

"It is a powerful tool."

RELIC SOON RETURNED TO THE CLEARING, clearly frustrated. Breunor and Clarial were fast on his heels, both appearing equally vexed. "They all got away," Breunor announced.

"Well, not all of them," Winter quipped, thumbing at the husk now splayed at the foot of the elm like a discarded doll.

Ignoring the statement, the gargoyle glanced around and sniffed the air. "We must move now!" he shouted, extending his remaining wing, the stump of his other wing reciprocating and twitching with meager life.

RUNNING THROUGH THE FOREST was remarkably less cumbersome now that they had employed their very own packhorse. After only a few minutes of coaxing, Percival had remarkably managed to persuade the proud beast into bearing their burdens. It was the first time Winter had seen the werewolf employ tactics that were not rooted in intimidation.

Returning to their single file formation, the group ran along a few cavernous bluffs and traversed stag trails worn by centuries of use. Their fast pace made it exceedingly difficult for Winter to hold a conversation with Clarial, one which she desperately desired to have.

The sun was nearing full peak by the time they stopped. The laifhorse, *Travis*, as he had been named by Netty, without protest, was now encumbered with their mantles atop the supplies, as the party had doffed their duds as the day progressed. Breunor finally called for a halt as they neared the mouth of a cave hunched along a clearing. The knight looked around in mild confusion and rubbed his miraculously groomed beard. "I thought for sure we'd be crossing the marshland by now..." he mumbled to himself.

Winter seized the opportunity to satisfy her intense urge for gossip. Placing a firm hand on Clarial's shoulder, she spun the runner around and escorted her far from any prying ears.

"I'm just going to cut right into the thick of this," said Winter, leaning her halberd against a snow mounded statue, its features entirely shrouded in the white powder. "Just when did you and the kapreta slayer begin this..." she trailed off, seductively bobbing her eyebrows.

Clarial tucked her chin and recoiled, glancing at the others. "For being the sharpest person I know, Winter, you can sometimes be... quite the opposite of sharp."

"Dull?"

"No, you're far from dull," Clarial corrected, "you're just not quite as sharp sometimes...anyhow, yes, Breunor and I *fancy* one another."

"When did all that start?"

"It started with the bacon."

"Ah, it starts with bacon and it leads to the makin'!'" Winter instantly regretted every syllable of the botched quip that had just left her mouth.

Clarial pinched the bridge of her nose in grave disappointment. "Creator's clothes, Winter! That was—"

"I know, I know. Let's move on."

"Please, let's."

Anxious to move on, Winter quickly reached to retrieve her halberd, knocking loose the small pile of snow around the stonework features of the statue it had rested upon. The detail was remarkable, easily recognizable as a round-faced child screaming in abject horror.

"Impressive work," Winter admitted, tightening her lips and nodding in admiration of the work.

"I'll say," Clarial agreed.

"Though a tad bit disturbing."

"And realistic."

"The precision alone..."

"Winter..."

"Yes?"

The others took notice as well. A sudden hush seemed to increase the gravity around them, pulling their eyes toward the mouth of the cave fifty paces distant.

"Do not look to the cavern!" Relic screamed in near hysteria, the first time Winter had heard the gargoyle abandon his composure. "We are in a gorgon coven, friends!"

~ 17 ~

GHOSTS

Gorgons, wraiths, and fanatical laives! Winter cursed to herself as she panted, running as fast as her body would allow. "How far are we from Knotwithstadt?!" she shouted to the others.

"I don't know!" replied Breunor, swallowing air with a great gulp, "maybe two more days or so?!" he added.

Being pursued by gorgons had definitely not made the list of activities Winter wanted to experience before the end of her life. "Are they still following us?!"

"I'm not looking back to check!"

"Keep running!" Relic advised from behind Winter. As the gargoyle could not be affected by petrification, he was the only one at liberty to determine when they could stop running. Clearly, if Relic was still urging everyone to continue their cross-country sprint, he likely had very good reason.

That reason probably being that there are gorgons following us beyond their lair! "Why?!" Winter shouted in dismay. For some reason she wished for confirmation of her fears. Her imagination could sometimes run away with itself and she found herself picturing all kinds of increasingly bizarre scenarios behind them.

"Because there are gorgons chasing us!"

And there it is.

Clarial and Travis were leading the pack, clearly neither was running at full speed, as both could easily have left the rest behind. Breunor was directly behind them, Winter and Percival following, running neck and neck with Netty clinging to the werewolf, arms tightly wrapped around his collar.

"How close to the ward are we?" Clarial shouted.

"Uh," Breunor slowed in contemplation.

"Don't slow down!" she commanded.

The knight immediately renewed his pace. "It's pretty close, I think!"

"You think?"

"It's close!"

I don't think we're going to get out of this one. "What's in this ward?" inquired Winter, drenched in sweat.

"Gorgons!" came Breunor's pained reply.

Wait. What.

"I'm sorry, I think you misspoke!" Clarial shouted, requesting clarity.

"No!" he replied, "it's protected by gorgons!"

"Well, that hardly seems fair!"

With an enraged grunt, as if he had just made the worst decision of his life, Relic yelled, "Keep running and do not look back!"

Winter somehow mustered the energy to arch an eyebrow. "That's nothing new!"

She could hear the gargoyle's pace slowing. "It has been a pleasure," he said softly.

Oh no, Relic.

"Relic! No!" Breunor yelled, the others joining with a chorus of dissent that Winter knew was falling upon deaf ears.

"Take this!" Winter threw her halberd behind her.

A solid slapping noise pierced the air, and Winter could tell that Relic had caught the mighty weapon.

"My thanks."

His voice was falling far behind them, and Winter wished with all she had that she could look back and see the moment when a lone gargoyle faced off against a horde of gorgons. *That is a sight that would have definitely made the list.*

BREUNOR RAISED A HAND, calling for a stop. "Clarial, Trevor," he called, heaving great gasps of air. Clarial glanced back at the knight and clicked her tongue at the laifhorse running next to her.

His face a cardinal red, Breunor frantically turned back to Winter and Percival, his eyes squeezed tight. "The wine skin!" he prodded.

Winter pointed at Travis. "It's on the horse!" she made her way toward the laifhorse, but Clarial was already there, feverishly rummaging through their gear.

Turning to look at Percival, Winter's eyes widened with horror as she saw the little girl craning her head backward. "Netty, no!" she screamed. Time seemed to stand still for the span of a breath, yet miraculously, the child did not turn to stone before them. Guessing that the coast was clear, Winter hazarded a furtive glance backwards as well.

Empty!

The path that lay behind was lined with ancient trees barren of leaves, but heavily waylaid with snow, and their reaching boughs grasped at nothing but air. A wintery draft swirled the powdery surface snow, accenting just how blank the canvas actually was. Not even the sound of desperate combat could be heard, which Winter supposed was just as good as it was bad.

She turned back to the ward just in time to catch the distasteful portion of the ritual. Breunor was slugging back the wine skin, sucking down Lamben's blood as if it was a sweet red wine. The memory of the laif twins performing their revolting ritual at the last ward flashed into Winter's mind for a moment, and she suddenly felt a heaping amount of pity for the knight. *Filthy creatures...and now he's drinking that disgusting laif's essence...sick!* Winter shook her head violently, wishing for the images to tumble out of her ears.

Taking a deep breath, his shoulders rising and falling in resignation, Breunor swept his dagger across his palm and began to sew his blood onto the papery white ground. Winter could not decide if his tremors were from fear or pain, but she hoped, above all, that the knight's liturgy would prevent a surge of magicked gorgons from making an unwelcome appearance. Pausing in his traipse across the ward, Breunor abruptly slashed his other palm, dousing the area with more of his blood.

"I see what he's doing," Winter said to Percival, who nodded in agreement. *He's not taking any chances this time.*

The copious amount of blood seemed to appease whatever magic inhabited the ward, and the entire party moved across without any incident. They moved at first with great care, taking slow and exaggerated steps. Once Breunor wagered they were safe, he shouted for them to get moving and set a quick pace, though less frantic than before.

"One moment!" Winter cried, stalling their momentum. She turned back to the crimson soaked patch of ground and looked beyond to where she imagined Relic was in a struggle to survive. Though she could not see their friend embroiled in his battle, she offered prayers of victory and wished (though with very little hope) that she would see him again. Now that they had crossed the ward, they were safe from the gorgons' pursuit, but it also meant that Relic would be barred from reaching them. With his gift of flight rescinded by that razor tipped bola, the gargoyle would no longer be able to soar over the wards.

"Farewell, Relic," whispered Winter to the skies.

And farewell, my lovely little halberd.

BREUNOR ELECTED TO TAKE FIRST WATCH for the night, and of course Netty could not allow him to stay up all alone. After all, she was not at all tired, and probably could go another three days without sleep.

The others had fallen asleep long before, and their rhythmic breathing filled the silence between the sentinels. Every once in a while, Percival would seemingly wake to clear his throat, and the helm made it sound like a pebble falling down a well, skipping along the walls.

Breunor turned his attention from the quiet winterscape to the girl propped up on a boulder next to him. "Tell me, Netty, I'm dying to know how you managed to escape from the church? Perhaps a similar strategy could be employed with our current...predicament."

The little halflaif's nose crinkled. "I acted like the snake Gaius threw on my lap once."

"Gaius?"

"My older brother," she said solemnly, "I loved him."

Breunor inclined his head. "I'm sure you did, Netty," he continued, "But what do you mean by 'acted as a snake?' Did you slither your way through a crack in a balustrade? Did you bite someone?"

"The fat churchman put me on his lap and the look in his eye made me feel weird. Once the orphan marm closed the door to his office, he began to pet my head. Like you would pet a dog or a cat, but he kept looking at me, and getting weirder and weirder."

"Creator's wings of vengeance," Breunor mumbled through the fingers that masked his gaping mouth.

"And when he leaned down and tried to cover my mouth with his..." she frowned, looking at Breunor from the corner of her eyes. "I threw up on him."

Breunor barked a laugh into the stillness, causing Winter to mutter a string of curses. "That's a brilliant strategy, little one," he admitted, patting Netty on the back. "Not one that I wager will help us defeat our foes though..."

"And then I jumped from his window and ran away," Netty finished. "The abowraith probably won't stop chasing us even if we spew on it."

Breunor nodded in agreement and sheared a strip of dried meat with his front teeth. Admiring the two halves for a moment, he leaned over to offer Netty the bigger one.

"But," Netty paused, "it does speak to me. When everything grows quiet. Since Relic left, the voice has gotten louder. It was afraid of him."

"What?" Breunor looked as if the meat had spoiled in his mouth.

"Oh, yes. Ever since that night you and Percival rescued me from it."

"And what has *it* said most recently?"

"It waits for me to bury my family's remains."

Breunor resumed his chewing. "How very accommodating," he remarked dryly, working his jaw.

"Percival won't allow it to take me," Netty reassured the knight. "Even with his muzzle."

"You know, before Percival became the wardog he is now...and don't you tell him that I told you this, but he and your mother spent some time working together."

"I know. It's why he cares for me so much."

"I imagine that's part of it, little one."

"He told me that some debts can never be repaid, but that doesn't mean you have to stop trying to pay them."

Breunor cast his eyes to the moon. "Percival said that?"

"Yeah, something like that," Netty said, then a glimmer of mischief entered her eyes. "You *like* her don't you?"

The sudden change in subject took the knight by surprise. He inhaled a breath and hesitated for a moment, mouth still wide, and he quickly decided to redirect the conversation. "Ah," he said, squinting one eye at his companion, "when you are older, we can discuss such topics."

"Well, I think she's very pretty."

"In an alternate timeline, perhaps I may be so lucky."

"What does that mean?" Netty asked, wrinkling her nose.

"My path does not include others."

"That dead old lady said that all you do is hunt kapreta now. Is that why you can't be with Clarial?"

Hunching his shoulders, Breunor grimaced. "Can you keep it down!" he hissed.

"Sorry," she whispered. She sat silently for a moment, before attempting her own topic shift. "Can you tell me why you live like you do?"

"It's a very long story…" Breunor stood and began to scratch the back of his head. Netty looked around, exaggeratingly sweeping her face over the landscape, below and above. She wanted to hear the tale very badly, and she hoped her pantomime would stir the knight into telling his story.

"Alright!" Breunor relented, "I get it, we have nothing better to do. Put away that hopeful gaze."

Netty adjusted her seat, settling in for a good yarn.

"I'm not very good at story time," the knight admitted, "well, not since…" he trailed off, the light in his eyes dimming.

"Breunor?"

The knight recoiled as if someone had splashed icy water in his face. "I'm back, yes, hello there."

Netty felt a ripple of pity as she regarded the blank expression on the man before her. "Maybe you can tell me some other time, Sir Breunor?"

"Yes, of course," he said, appearing dazed and speaking to the ghosts in his mind as he sauntered off, "some other time."

"IS THAT WHAT I THINK IT IS?" Winter asked loudly, inquiring of anyone that was listening to her and looking at what she was looking at.

"Yep," Breunor replied, his voice dull and sounding nearly as hollow as Percival's in the current state of things. Since sunrise, the bearded knight had exhibited a diminished amount of vigor and had appeared quite sullen.

A solitary tree stood out in the swamp, a truly massive tree, and it appeared as if its base had been tunneled through to allow for carriages to pass.

"Aspweavers?" Winter guessed.

"Yep." Breunor's tone had not altered.

"Seems a rather foolish place for it, don't you think? Out in the middle of a boggy swamp?" Winter squinted her eyes trying to imagine the landscape without its covering of snow and ice. Aspweavers were completely horrid monsters of nightmares. Possessing a spider's head sitting atop a serpent's body, they spun their webs high inside hollow trees, waiting for any unsuspecting passerby to walk underneath. The victims are quickly snatched and supplanted into the web, or, if one is so lucky, they are immediately consumed.

After a listless scan of their surroundings and an uncomfortable silence, Breunor finally replied, "No. In the heat of summer the swamp's stench attracts musk trolls and other creatures that enjoy the scent of death and decay. You'd be surprised just how stupid animals can be," he said harshly.

The tone in the knight's concluding statement seemed to be pointed at someone, but Winter was unsure who it was meant for and what he meant by it so she carried on, ignoring the possible barb. "They go dormant in winter, don't they? And they don't stray far from their putrid lair?" she asked with uncertainty.

"Huh, no," Breunor scoffed. "They are active year-round and during lean times, they *will* stray."

"How far?"

"I'm not sure, but I don't think we will need to worry about that," he said, pointing toward the tree.

At that moment a stag and a doe were ambling toward the aspweaver infestation. Winter found herself wanting to shout a warning, but at the same time wanting to see what would happen. In the end, she simply mumbled, "Poor babies..."

A startled squeal erupted from the doe as she was immediately set upon by an aspweaver. Apparently the cold weather had made it more difficult for the creature to gain purchase on its prey, and the predator faltered, only managing to latch one pincher into the deer's flesh. Winter was spellbound by the activity, and she could barely squelch a cheer when the stag, without hesitation, reared back and charged, burying its mantle of prongs into several sets of the aspweaver's eyes. The unexpected attack forced the aspweaver to retract its mandibles and release the doe, and she readily bounced a few paces away, seemingly grateful for the second shot at life.

"How nice!" remarked Winter as she watched the pair bound away. "Did you guys see that?" She looked to her companions and immediately discovered that she was the only that had stopped to watch the spectacle. Rushing to catch up, she reflected on their journey. The trek over the swamp had been easy thus far, and soon they would be crossing over into the Crescent Marshes. That morning, Breunor had informed them that Knotwithstadt was only a half day's march from the marshes. He had made the dry announcement right after he and Clarial exchanged some hushed, bitter sounding words.

"Something got lodged in his craw," was all Clarial had offered to Winter as an explanation for their leader's drastic change in demeanor, of course following with, "And I don't want to talk about it."

I'm not going to pry, Winter decided while taking in the simple surroundings. No more trees barring paths, or hills to embarrassingly misjudge as mounds of snow and end up toppling face first into a pile of powder. The swamp was as flat as ironed vellum, and nearly as bleached. Once in awhile her footfall would crack the ice, (which made a very satisfying sound) but even then, the water below was not deep enough to swallow her up were she to take an unexpected plunge. She had to applaud Breunor, it was truly a brilliant decision to ford the frozen swamps and marshes during this season.

"Hey, Clarial."

"Yes, Winter?"

"What's the first thing you're going to do when you get back?"

"Back to what? The capital or the killing fields?"

A smile lit Winter's face. "The capital of course, you silly goblin."

Clarial peered suspiciously at her friend and muttered *"Silly goblin?"* before straightening her chest armour with a firm tug. She cleared her throat and continued, "I plan on continuing my holiday of doing nothing at all. I'll put my feet up and drink whatever is left in your spirit closet, then I'll go out and fetch some more whenever that's all dry."

"Good plan," Winter conceded, "I dare you to punch Bill Markman in the face," she added mischievously.

"What the...what?" Clarial sputtered.

"I know, I know, just saying his name gives me a visceral reaction. I can feel the hives developing in my windpipe!"

The runner had never been one to back down from a good dare. "If we survive this—"

"Whoa, whoa, whoa," Winter cut her off. "*When* we survive," she corrected.

Accepting the amendment with an unenthusiastic chuckle, Clarial continued, *"When* we survive this journey, then yes, I will punch Bill Markman in the face." She pressed one finger to her lips, focusing on something far in the distance. "Does he have to see it coming," she said, grinning, "or can I surprise him?"

"Ohhh!" Winter raised her shoulders impishly, and breathed some warm air into her hands, "That's an excellent question."

A judgmental *tisk* came from Travis at that moment, the laifhorse emitting a grunt filled with dissent.

Winter whirled around. "Shut your whore mouth, Travis!" she spat.

The laifhorse responded by studiously gazing away from the woman, pretending that he did not notice her presence. Returning to her conversation, Winter drew Lamben's sword at her hip and began to playfully test its balance. "I think you should do it whenever you feel the moment is right. Who knows? Maybe as soon as you walk into the palace, he'll be standing there holding some asinine conversation with an underling, and you can just blast him right in the mouth," she said gleefully, holding the blade to her eyes, gazing over the crossguard.

Clarial laughed. "And you just know that I would not be interrupting anything important."

"Oh, most assuredly not!" Winter grinned, "you would be doing the underling a favor."

"Little blighter would owe me."

BEHIND HER, WINTER AND CLARIAL were laughing and carrying on about something, and it made Netty wish to be a part of their world.

The adult world. The moment drifted away, and a feeling of melancholy took it its place when the little girl remembered that she would be an adult for well over one thousand years. Maybe more. And she would see everyone she was walking with right now pass away. She would outlive the entire lot.

She looked up at Percival walking next to her in his magicked headgear, and found she missed his consistently grave countenance, crosshatched in scars. Even with the ever-present helm, she noticed there was a shift whenever he spoke to her. It was like a glimmer of something happy that he seemed to reserve just for her, hidden behind that husk of ferocity and malice. She watched as the knight once again tugged the helm just below his chin, checking to see if the spell had worn off yet. She thought it was a small blessing, perhaps, that the predicament had befallen him in the winter as opposed to the summer. A fixed face helm like that would be unbearable under the sun! The knight would likely bake in such conditions! When he finally removed the helm, there would be nothing but the remnants of a burnt cookie where his head should be.

Netty giggled darkly at the thought. Percival, hearing the sound, leveled his gaze in her direction. Though he did not voice a query, Netty knew he was curious. "I miss seeing your face," she said brightly, and imagined a grin spreading underneath his helm.

"Which one?" Percival asked.

The question gave Netty pause and she chewed on an answer for a spell, her lips swishing back and forth. "Both," she finally replied with a firm nod.

"Huh." The knight faced forward, satisfied with the answer.

Netty's gaze did not waver from the man walking beside her.

"Percival."

He looked down at her between the helm's meager eye slit.

"What happened to Sir Breunor?" she inquired meekly. Percival inclined his head in a manner that requested more detail from her. "Why does he not want a family?" she clarified.

Netty could tell that her question made the knight uncomfortable. He looked at Breunor walking alone before them, and turned his head away from her, giving the helm another hopeful yank. It was to no avail, the helm remained fixed in place. A growl emanated from the opening under the knight's grizzled jawline, and he turned back to the halflaif.

"His family took ill," Percival finally said, his tone somber. "A wife and daughter. Both died, and after that, he abandoned his service to the crown and dedicated himself to eradicating a perilous scourge."

"Why kapreta?"

Percival shrugged in response. "That I do not know."

~ 18 ~

BLOOD'S COPPERY TANG

A silvery fog greeted the travelers as they woke on the frozen marsh. The night had been particularly cold, colder than the previous nights, and Breunor advised that they sleep in a pile as opposed to pairing up like they had in the past. Winter viewed his idea as wisdom, but Clarial saw it as a slight against her. The two had been sharing body heat and blankets, surviving the winter nights together, and now Breunor seemed to suddenly be putting distance between himself and Clarial.

"Have you spoken to him since yesterday?" inquired Winter, bundling their blankets, preparing to load them atop Travis' back.

Clarial did not look up as she angrily furled the fabric. "No," she spat, looking up at Winter and throwing an invading lock of hair aside. "But it's fine, really." Her tone was unconvincing.

She really does care for this tortured soul.

"Alright, but if there is anything that I can say or do—"

Clarial cut her off. "No! Please just stay out of this one, Winter."

I understand. "As you wish." While Winter loved getting involved in such intrigue, she decided to leave this one alone. Life for Clarial out west at the forefront of the killing fields probably had left little time for romance. And Breunor was handsome, in a tormented artist sort of way, though Winter did not fancy him in the least. Clarial had never seemed the sort to settle down. *Age has a way of catching up with all of us, I suppose.*

"Let's move!" Breunor urged loudly, his voice piercing the dense fog. "The gorgons may no longer give chase, but there are hundreds of other horrors that could rise to the surface." Through the icy mist Winter saw the knight gaze over his left shoulder. "We should be there before night-fall."

They set off at a jogging pace, aiming to make as much headway as possible before the daytime predators rose. Even though it was wintertime, Breunor stated that he did not want to take any chances. Winter elected to jog at the forefront beside Breunor for a time. She had questions that needed answers, but as soon as she opened her mouth, she heard Clarial loudly and gratuitously clearing her throat from behind. Winter shot her friend a look that she hoped said, *Don't worry,* but Clarial's face still rippled with uncertainty.

"Sir Breunor," Winter huffed, enunciating the name as clearly as she could at their hectic pace. The knight grunted indistinguishably in reply, merely acknowledging her presence. Previously, Breunor had always seemed to hold a bit of mischief behind his eyes, but that glimmer had dissolved.

Winter continued, sweeping her eyes over the austere visage next to her. "These kapreta that you seek and hunt—ah, fack!" A cracking sound from below interrupted her statement; her left boot had found a thin patch of ice causing her to stumble for a breath. "As I was saying, these kapreta that you kill, I assume they hibernate during the cold months?"

"You would be correct."

Winter peered at the knight from the corner of her eyes, expecting him to go on. He did not, so she continued her inquiry, filling the silence. "So we should not see any resistance from their type when we reach Knotwith-stadt?"

What could be perceived as a chuckle cracked from the back of Breunor's throat. "Lake Patreka is warm year-round," Breunor's face was suddenly etched with resolve. "The surrounding area does not endure winter's chill."

The revelation made Winter slow her pace briefly, the concept latching onto her mind. "But wait," she said, hastening to catch up. "We won't be facing *that* many kapreta, will we? Surely there are worse lakes?"

"Aside from Lake Humiel? No, Patreka is an ideal breeding ground."

"Do you visit often?"

"Only when the feeling to try out some new techniques overtakes me, but it's basically a lost cause to eradicate them from this lake. Won't stop me from trying, though."

Strangely enough, this topic seemed to have a warming effect on the knight, and Winter believed that she even caught the hint of a smile cresting his lips with his last statement.

"Let me ask you something," said Breunor, abruptly changing the subject. "You were wondering why Arthur did not send a missive warning you that Percival and Lamorak were being dispatched."

Winter could clearly recall her statement and the emotions around it. "Yes, and?" she replied.

"What difference would it make?"

"What do you mean?"

"It's not like anyone can stop him... or his brother, for that matter. There is a good reason Arthur has kept those two close by his side for all these years," Breunor gave Winter a hard look. "If Rebekah's daughter had not surfaced, the brothers would have long finished their task and been back to the killing fields by now."

Winter thought, her eyes narrowing. "All I was requesting was a heads up," she explained, looking back at Percival. "Then I would have known to steer clear."

"I'm sure Arthur has his reasons," remarked Breunor, ending the conversation.

A simpleton's answer for difficult speculation. "Of that, I have no doubt," muttered Winter, less than impressed, and slowed her gait to allow Breunor to resume vanguard.

Two or three hours later, the terrain remained the same: open, placid, white, flat, and *boring.* At least this boredom was welcome after the unfortunate excitement of earlier. Winter would be glad to be bored for the remainder of their excursion if it meant she would not lose another friend.

From the front, Breunor made a now familiar gesture, raising a closed fist to signal a halt. "This is the final ward," he declared solemnly. Removing the wine skin, he raised it as if toasting the air. He kept a space between his lips and the wine skin's spout, and Winter witnessed the liquid cascading down in a solitary vein, sparkling in the sunlight, as it invaded the knight's gullet. When he brought it down, Winter noted that the skin was still fat, inspiring the hope of a return trip.

"Wait! Breunor!"

Winter's sudden outburst startled the knight. Wincing as he reached for his blade, Breunor glared at the surroundings. Percival and Clarial reacted in the same way, regarding the empty environment with malice, hands to weapons. Even Travis, feeding on the tension in the air, began to tear at the ground, splashing boggy water all over and sending dormant plants flying over the snow.

"Oh. No, no, no," Winter said sheepishly, waving her arms as if to dissipate their anxiety. "I only wish to try the ceremony this time." She fluttered her fingers as she reached for the wine skin, recalling the lifeless laif below the elm produced a brief pause, yet still, she continued to reach.

Breunor hesitated, barring the passing of the wine skin. "Are you sure?" he asked, gradually relinquished the pouch to the equally hesitant woman.

"I am," she weakly reassured him, eyeing the leather object as if for the first time. "How much should I drink?"

"Just a mouthful," Breunor advised, "and don't spit it out! The ward's magic will take offense."

Winter assumed that he was exaggerating, believing the knight simply did not want her to waste any more of the precious fluid. But she also understood that stranger things were reality, and so treated the information as truth. She gave the knight a dubious nod, and lifted the wineskin to her lips.

"Don't touch the spout!" warned Breunor.

Winter lowered the skin by a few inches and fixed Breunor with a skeptical look. "I'm drinking blood, Breunor," she said, "you're really concerned about hygiene at this moment?"

"Fair point."

With that, Winter resumed her pose. Sealing her lips over the spout, she imagined sharing hearty ales at the Bloody Fork, seated with friends near the roaring hearth. Far from kapreta, curses, and frozen bogs. Far from abowraiths, frostbite, and dead friends. She hardly noticed the coppery tang of the blood as it passed over her tongue. *Surprisingly smooth.* "Not even a clot," she stated, handing the skin back to Breunor. Her face pinched with mild disgust, she worked her jaw and exposed her offended tongue to the cold air, causing muffled giggling to spill out from Netty.

"Do you feel that tingling in your gut?" inquired Breunor.

"No, I don't feel—" an unsettling feeling suddenly began to overtake her innards. "Wait, yes, there it is," *I wouldn't describe it as a tingle.* She slowly blinked, choking back the queasiness. "What do I do now, sir knight?"

"Perfect, excellent!" Breunor looked relieved. "That means the magic has taken hold. All you need to do now is drag a blade over your flesh and sprinkle it on the ground as you have seen me do."

Drawing Lamben's sword, Winter looked at the weapon and felt a moment of irony pass over her. *This feels oddly poetic.*

"Across the palms is what I find is easiest," said the knight encouragingly, holding aloft a bandaged hand with a blotchy scarlet stain across its center.

Winter bobbed her head in agreement.

"And remember, whatever you do, ignore any urges to spit."

Winter continued to nod.

"Tuck them away," he emphasized.

Winter stopped nodding, and leveling Breunor with an unimpressed expression, slashed her left hand. She was proud of the fact that she did not even wince. *But, oh my, did that sting!* She began to do her best impression of a peasant feeding a team of ducks, sprinkling bread to their hungry little beaks. Only she was not sprinkling delicious baked goods, but the blood of a laif that had been murdered by a twice cursed werewolf. Well, he only had collected the two as far as she knew. But does the initial curse of being a werewolf count as a curse, or is that just a base level curse? Maybe you don't count that. *Why am I thinking about the curse collection that Percival is amassing?* Winter had absentmindedly been distracting herself as she painted the marsh with her blood.

"That's good enough!" shouted Breunor from the fringe of the crimson stained snow.

Winter turned around and felt a wave of fatigue pass over as she surveyed the amount of gore she had just expelled.

The party stepped over the red ground, crossing toward Winter. Clarial looked as though she admired her friend's courage, yet at the same time was disturbed by what she had just witnessed.

"Good work, lady," Clarial said as she passed the gaping Winter, giving her friend a reassuring pat on the shoulder. "You better eat something, eh? You look pale as a ghost."

JUST WHEN I THOUGHT NONE OF THE OTHER WARDS would be nearly as entertaining as the first... Winter reflected as she wrapped her wounded hand.

"You sure you don't want to sit for a spell?" Clarial probed, gazing at her friend's pale visage.

"No," Winter replied with as much enthusiasm as she could muster. "But if you have any more of that salty dried meat, it would be greatly appreciated." *Wish I had my halberd back,* she thought as she accepted a small bundle of meat strips. *It acted as an excellent walking staff, among other more noble purposes.*

As the afternoon continued, the sun rose to its full peak, the part of the day scholars speculated a marked knight would attain the apex of his strength. Winter had often wondered about that theory. *What if the knight started his duties at twilight and worked through the night? Would he then gain his power halfway through the night, or does the sun actually bestow this theoretical power and the grave shift knight would be shit out of luck?* Her mind wandered around, chewing on a variety of things while her strength gradually returned to her appendages. Her festival of thought was abruptly dismantled when Travis began to bark...or shriek. She could not quite identify what the sound was, but it was certainly a warning of some nature.

Breunor was the first to drop to the ground and the others followed suit. Though they were drawing nearer to the treeline as they traversed, growing closer to

Knotwithstadt every hour, they were still out in the open and susceptible to all manner of attack.

Winter pressed her spine as far as she could into her stomach, hearing the links of her armour grinding into the snow. *I hope we don't run out of oil,* she thought as she scanned their surroundings. *This armour will be nothing but clacking rust by the time we get back. Oh, wait, what—* "—is that?!" she finished aloud.

Percival and Breunor's heads were already pointing in the direction Winter had indicated and Clarial quickly joined the watch, carefully rotating her shoulders while lying prone. Looking to her left, Winter saw even Travis had lowered himself to the ground; the laifhorse managing to make himself much flatter than she believed any horse was able.

"Don't move!" Breunor hissed.

Netty was to Percival's right, completely covered with the knight's mantle, remaining still and quiet. Percival, on the other hand, had his head bobbing up and down in a ridiculous manner, but Winter could deduce what he was attempting. Moments later, her guess was proven correct as the knight began to earnestly shove the helm at its chin, trying in vain to pry it free and rid himself of the cursed item once and for all.

Crouched just beyond the thicket, Winter saw what appeared to be a hovel sized bird nest tipped upside down. It was an expertly crafted dome of logs, sticks, and branches that would be obscured by brush and brambles during the warmer seasons, but the winter's bare flora did not provide any sort of practical concealment now. The hovel was not what alarmed the Lord Commander. The dwelling was surrounded by a fence comprised of pikes, all cocked at varying angles from the turf. And what prevented the pikes from standing perpendicular were the many decapitated heads adorning the tops of the posts. The heads were from a variety of races and monsters, some of which had decomposed into skulls.

As recognition bloomed into her mind, Breunor almost simultaneously voiced just what it was beyond the boundary of the marsh. "A bleeding carnal shrike this far north?!" he asked, slumping his shoulders in defeat.

"I thought they hibernate over the winter?" whispered Clarial hopefully.

The knight slowly blinked as he racked the annals of his mind.

"They do!" Winter confirmed, boldly rising to her feet and dusting the snow from her armour. Some of the repelled flakes clung annoyingly to her leather gloves and she began to wag her hands in the air as she continued, "I'm going to take a closer look at that skull menagerie over there. It's not every day that a girl gets this close to something like this!"

Breunor rotated up onto his right pauldron. "I would strongly advise—" he began.

"I'm coming with you!" Clarial interjected, springing to her feet.

Travis emitted an ominous burping growl that did not inspire confidence, but remained firmly rooted to the ground.

Approaching the carnal shrike's lair with Clarial beside her, Winter was completely focused on what was ahead. The surrounding forest was hauntingly silent, the nearest denizens instinctively giving this den of carnage a wide berth.

"Did you see Breunor's face?" inquired Clarial in hushed tones.

Winter smirked, "I did not..."

"I don't believe this hazard was on his map," Clarial noted, tapping her temple, "It must be a new arrival."

The women crouched, skulking like assassins and making their bodies sink further than the lowest of the pikes. It was likely that the monster was firmly locked in repose, but as they were already taking an exceedingly unnecessary chance by traipsing so close, they thought it best to not draw any attention to themselves.

Noticing a few of the pikes were bereft of ornament, Winter began to scan the posts for anything humanoid. "Let me know if you spot a human skull," Winter advised Clarial.

In Winter's limited understanding of carnal shrikes, she knew that the monster collected only one head from any particular race. There had never been any reports of duplicate trophies on display. But even if the women were to spy anything resembling a human skull, it did not mean they should abandon caution.

The first head they passed was a musk troll, its fur-lined jaw slackened to a grotesque depth as gravity continued its incessant tugging. After that was a plain old badger, its maw locked in a defiant snarl that aptly defined the species. *This shrike does not seem to leave any stone unturned,* Winter thought as she gazed up at a pike with a dainty frog head pinned to the very tip. The slippery critter's tongue fell languidly from its mouth, and the shrike had meticulously swirled the sticky flesh around the pike's blade in a grim display of aesthetics. Most of the heads seemed fairly fresh with only a few withered to complete bone. The chill in the air thankfully dimmed the aroma of rotting flesh, but the stink still pervaded in measured doses.

"I think I see a man's head!" announced Clarial, slapping Winter's chest with the back of her hand.

"Where?"

"Just past the flying squirrel."

Flying squirrel? Winter's view of the squirrel was momentarily obscured by the long snout of a decapitated horse, but after a few paces, she caught sight of what Clarial was talking about. "Oh, yeah, you're right," Winter conceded. "Good eyes."

Trudging forward faster while remaining crouched, they huddled beneath the human head and gazed up at it.

"Somebody you know?" Winter asked, biting down on her knuckle.

Clarial's eyes swept over the dead man's visage. "Nope," she shook her head. "But he doesn't look that old. I mean, the age of the man, not the age of the skull."

"I know what you meant."

"You think he was a knight errant?" Clarial speculated.

"Probably," Winter agreed. "He leaves behind a grieving widow and fourteen kids."

"And two cats."

"He looks like he liked cats."

"Definitely a cat person."

Winter pursed her lips and twitched her head to the side. "Did you notice that this fence of death lacks a gate?" she asked.

"No shit, Winter," Clarial looked at her friend curiously. "Carnal shrikes fly."

Ahhh, of course! Winter wanted to smack herself in the forehead. It seemed that these consecutive cold nights were starting to freeze more than her fingers and toes.

Adjacent to the errant knight was the head of a slender faced female laif. Her prominent cheekbones and cleft chin proudly displayed her race's exquisite bone structure. Unlike most of the other displays, this piece's eyes were closed as if in slumber.

"She looks so peaceful," Winter murmured.

Clarial's eyes flicked from the man and focused on the laif. "You think she's a survivor of Knotwithstadt?" she asked, her voice tinged with sadness.

Winter's chin sunk in consternation. "I really hope not."

"Can you imagine escaping such a massacre only to end up as a monster's memento?"

Dragging one hand over her face, Winter tried to wipe away the horrid ideas careening through her mind. "One can only hope to escape such a fate," she quietly offered to her friend. Breathing a pained sigh, Winter's shoulders sunk low after the exhale, as if a bit of her spirit had escaped into the chilled air.

"We should carry on," said a voice from behind, startling both women. With hands clasped to their weapon's pommels, they whirled around to find Breunor raising both hands in surrender. "Easy now," he said calmly, lifting both eyebrows. "We are merely an hour shy of Knotwithstadt, so I think it best that we keep moving," he paused, his open palms closing to point to the path ahead, "Almost there."

~ 19 ~

DESTINY UNRAVELING

The harsh winter weather gradually lost its grip on the forest the closer they drew to Knotwithstadt. While there were no flowers in bloom, the group could see the actual ground for the first time in ages. As the warmth enveloped them, they stopped and began to shed their mantles and extra layers, adding them to the pile atop Travis's slender back. Surprisingly, the laifhorse accepted the burden without any complaint. Ever since they had passed the carnal shrike's home, the laifhorse had withdrawn and grown much less animated. The opposite, however, could be said for Sir Breunor who seemed to be brightening more and more, doffing his layers of warm clothes along with the sullen attitude he had been sporting.

"I could use a bath," Clarial said to Winter as she wrestled her heavy coat off. "I wonder if there is a part of the lake that is safe?"

"I wouldn't count on it," Winter replied. "And yes, you definitely need a bath."

"Ha, ha," Clarial did not sound amused. "Speak for yourself, twit."

"Lake Patreka teems with kapreta, so I would not count on it for much of anything," Breunor interjected, draping his mantle on Travis.

"Well, that's why we brought you!" Clarial said with a playful laugh, "see if you can go about clearing us a tidy patch of water, sir knight."

Breunor's eyelids fluttered in surprise for a moment, then the knight softened, and with a stately bow formally replied, "I will see what I can do, my lady."

Clarial haughtily raised her chin and looked down upon the man. "See that you do."

Netty giggled at their weirdness, drawing their attention to her.

"Ah," Breunor said loftily, striding toward the halflaif and bending down with both hands on his thighs. "Doth the lady wish to add to the request?"

Shaking her head, her giggles became uncontrollable chortles. *He's so funny!* "I just want to go home."

The bearded knight brought himself to one knee in front of her. "Very well, m'lady," he said, his voice taking on a serious tone. "You said the wraith is going to wait until we bury your family before it tries to take you?"

Netty nodded somberly, and immediately felt the forest hush around her. Winter and Clarial appeared at her eye level, gazing at her with looks of both sadness and admiration.

"We are going to see this through," vowed Winter, more serious than Netty had ever seen her. "And we will handle whatever befalls us after."

THE FOREST WAS IN A SILENT SPRING, or at least that's what Netty's father had called it when there was winter everywhere else except around their village. There were "no blossoms blossoming, or birds birding," he would say to her as they beheld the barren treetops, walking hand in hand.

That was the time of peace, Netty thought, finding herself growing sadder and sadder as they drew closer to her home. *Maybe not really sad,* she thought, *I don't know how to describe how I feel...*

She felt dry pine needles crunch under her foot, then—

"RUN! BACK! RUN!"

She saw Percival standing still while the others turned to run. He was doubled over wrenching on the helm, twisting it as hard as he could to no avail. She could hear him growling in anguish, trying to free himself from the curse.

One of the women, she wasn't sure if it was Clarial or Winter, tried desperately to pull Netty away. She resisted, twisting free of their clasping hands, and bolted for cover to a hiding hole she and her brother had discovered the summer before. It was not far at all.

"The wraith lied!" Breunor's agonized voice carried to the entire group. Netty watched the knight indecisively turn back and forth between retreat and Percival, his feet stuttering every urgent step. Clarial and Winter had cleared Travis of his burdens and mounted the terrified laifhorse while shouting for Breunor to run.

"Breunor! Escape with us!" pleaded Clarial, tears pouring down her face, "Escape with me!" She held a hand toward the knight as Travis cantered in a frantic circle, tearing up clumps of earth.

Standing within arm's reach of Clarial, grim resolve took hold of the knight and he gave the laifhorse a spurring slap on the rump. "I can't!" he shouted, his voice carrying over Travis' shrieks. "Go! Get away from here! Travis, fly!"

Clarial screamed inarticulately at Breunor as he rushed to Percival's side. Netty watched the women abandon them, leaning low in the saddle as the magnificent beast carried them out of sight within the span of a breath.

Netty's eyes slowly crept back to the horrors bearing down on them. The horrors that sent hardened warriors to flight and made even the unshakeable Sir Percival look desperate for the first time ever.

A tide of monsters was charging through the barren trees straight toward the group.

At first, Netty believed them to be the same kapreta that had swallowed her village last year, but she soon realized she was mistaken. For hanging above the tide, sailing forth as a beacon of untamed power, was the abowraith. The horde's pace did not slacken, and Netty speculated that they were now well within bowshot.

Her eyes flicked back to the knights just in time to see Breunor place a calming hand on Percival's pauldron, and the werewolf relenting the fevered tugging on his helmet. The knights stood tall and turned together to face the impending onslaught.

A solitary tear trickled down Netty's face. She was sure her heroes were about to fall.

Coming closer, the abowraith did not appear as spectral as the halflaif recalled, its form now had more substance. Its abyssal jaw snapped open and an unnatural voice issued from its depths. "I WANT THEM ALIVE." The order reverberated through the entire forest, causing the young stalks of the plants surrounding Netty in her hidey hole to tremble in response.

With that, the wraith's skull swiveled and immediately locked onto Netty in the place she had stupidly believed was safe. Waving a few skeletal fingers in her direction, the wraith commanded a contingent to retrieve its prey. A handful of faewolves broke away and streamed directly toward her.

"Percival!" she could not help but shout.

The knight turned in the direction of her voice.

He thought I got away...

As the faewolves ripped her from her hiding place, she strained for one last glimpse of Percival. The knight rushed headlong into a mass of monsters before being swallowed into the horde.

WHERE THEY TOOK HER, SHE DID NOT KNOW. Upon retrieving her, the faewolves had raised her high above their heads toward the abowraith. It swung its gaze over to her and she immediately fell asleep and could remember nothing else. At least, all she could remember of what had happened in real life. Her dreams were a much different story.

It had all felt so real. She could even smell the dirt under her fingernails and the lavender scent of her mother's hair. She could feel the tickly scruff of her father's beard when he swept her up into his arms and twirled her a few times before setting her down. She ran into the sunlight, joining her brother on his exploration of the surrounding groves. The village was as bustling as she remembered, and it glimmered with gold all around its trim.

She knew it was a dream and would end, but she brushed aside the warning coming from the back of her mind, following closely behind her brother as he entered into the trees. *Just a few more hours...a few more hours is all I want...*

Ducking the familiar branches and peering into the cavernous haunts, Gaius would turn and wave for her to follow. A smile creased his face every time he turned, and the light in his eyes was just as bright as she remembered.

"I want to show you something, Nutty!" he exclaimed, drawing to the edge of a canyon that she knew did not exist in the real world. *Nutty,* she had always disliked the nickname, but this time she welcomed it. "Hurry up!" Gaius laughed and offered a hand. She reached for it, and the warmth of his grip felt real. *A few more hours...*

"Look!" Gaius shouted in delight, raising his other hand in praise of the desolation that filled the massive ravine below them. A ravine that was entirely out of place. *There should be a pond here...*

"Look!" he urged again, hysteria latching onto his voice.

Netty became uncomfortable as her brother released his hand from hers and planted it behind her head, forcing her to look closer. "Look!" he commanded. The force of his hand brought her to her knees and when she tried to turn her head away, he only shoved harder. Her eyes strained trying to avoid looking at the sea of corpses in the canyon. It was filled with a sea of dead that she recognized from her village. Dead eyes and empty sockets focused on her, and the dead began groping at one another, tearing and rending, seething and clawing in their attempt to reach her. She could feel their overwhelming despair and their need for vengeance.

"This is your destiny!" Gaius sounded crazed. Releasing his hold on her, he jabbed the nape of her neck causing her to lurch forward and nearly topple into the pit. Her eyes darted all around, searching and fearful that she would see her mother and father in the dreadful mess below. She clamped her eyes tight, and stars graced her eyelids when her brother's boot jolted her from behind, sending her over the craggy edge.

She scrabbled at the dirt as she slid on her belly, rotating in a semicircle to avoid falling headfirst. Her momentum carried her too far too fast, and her feet dropped over the ledge, but her fingernails slowed the descent, and soon she was dangling with very little purchase.

"Gaius! Help me!" she cried.

The face that peered down at her was still her brother's, but instead of his smiling visage, it was the face she had beheld on the day her family had been murdered. Her last memory of him. Starting just below his left eyelid, cheek to collarbone, his flesh was shorn off. He had been slowed by a coward's arrow, doing his duty as a big brother and protecting his little sister. And when the gates had been flung open and the kapreta surged into their dwelling, his wound proved too much for him to keep up.

"No, sister!" The light in his eyes was gone. "You must help us!" With that, he carefully placed the heel of his boot on her knuckles and began to grind.

She fell and fell and just as she sensed the dead would take her with their decaying flesh and twisting maggots, she awoke with a gasp. *Where am I?!* Wherever she was, it was not overly cold but the ground was painfully solid. Her hands were bound with silvery thread and her feet were stuck together. Wriggling with all her might in the dim space, she hoisted herself up onto her knees and felt a razor sharp prick on the meat of her palm. A slice of light entered the enclosure, and she shuffled toward it to behold her new wound.

"A sliver?" she mumbled curiously, as she regarded the fragment of wood lodged in her hand. Tracing the faint illumination across the ground and up onto a wall, Netty realized she was encased in a large wooden box. A draft crept up her neck, entering from the thin beam of light, and when she tried to get closer, she was drawn up short. Her hands were tethered to one corner of the space.

Getting within inches of the opening, she noticed waves undulating the front wall. *This wall is made of cloth!*

The discovery yielded immediate confirmation as the fabric was violently flung aside, revealing a frightening picture that restricted the air from entering her lungs. Netty fell back in horror, crumpling awkwardly on her bound feet before slumping to her side. *This can't really be happening,* she told herself, closing her eyes. *I must be dreaming again!*

The noise of jeering growls and inhuman shrieks carried on, despite her attempts to wake herself. Her eyelids cracked open to see a mangled faewolf being removed from a muddy pit. Standing in the middle of the ditch was Sir Percival alongside Sir Breunor, both wearing tattered tunics. *He's still wearing that helmet!*

Above the ring was a host of monsters laughing and throwing debris at the soiled, disgraced knights. Breunor's face was puffy and purpled, his eyes mere slits. Weaponless and shifting around with their backs to one another, the men awaited their fate.

"WHO IS NEXT?" boomed a massive ogre, his tusks arching from his mouth all the way to the base of his horns. He dramatically leaned left and right, scanning the monsters for the next challenger. A pair of victus raised their claws together and pointed at one another, nodding like hopeful fools.

The ogre noticed them from the corner of his eye. "ONE AT A TIME FOR NOW," his voice rumbled through the air. The rat-faced creatures lowered their arms dejectedly, and one patted the other on the shoulder consolingly.

"WE'LL SEE HOW MUCH LONGER THE WEAKER ONE LASTS, BUT UNTIL THEN, THE UTVARAE WILL DECIDE."

Netty assumed that "the weaker one" must mean Breunor, who was struggling to remain standing. Propping herself upright, she inched to the mouth of her cage and dangled her legs off the edge to get a better view of the disgraceful theatre.

She lifted her head to the forest and noticed the trees were untouched by the season. *Then we are still close to home,* she thought, yet the realization did not bring comfort.

* * *

"THIS MAY BE YOUR WORST IDEA TO DATE," Clarial told Winter as she hopped clear of Travis. The tears that streaked her face had dried in several rivulets and curved back over her ears.

"Yeah, yeah," Winter batted the air dismissively. "Just lead Travis somewhere out of sight," she said, walking toward the carnal shrike's disturbing barrier.

Clarial stowed the laifhorse behind a particularly dense copse of hemlock and hastened across the snow to hike beside Winter. "Was it just today that we were here?" she inquired, flagged with emotional exhaustion.

"I know, right?" Winter walked along the fence line, scanning the pikes as if she were selecting an outfit for the day. "The days seem to run together. Seems like it was only yesterday we spied that pair of adorable owlbats snuggled up on that branch, right before twilight..." Winter spoke wistfully, "spring must almost be here."

"That wasn't yesterday," Clarial argued, twitching in confusion. "Wait, when did you see owlbats? And what are you looking for?" She took hold of her friend's vambrace to steal her attention. "Tell me what you're planning!"

"Calm down, calm down." Winter meticulously pried Clarial's fingers off one at a time. "What does a carnal shrike do?"

"Oh, for a coward's life," moaned Clarial, exasperated. "It collects heads."

Winter nodded, peering up at Clarial with bobbing eye-brows.

"Nevermind!" Clarial relented, "I give up! Just lead on."

"Don't mind if I do." She led Clarial around the pikes, inspecting each one swiftly. She frowned and furrowed her brow at the creatures with the most pronounced snouts while briskly passing those with flatter faces. A particular horse-like skull held her attention for several moments. She traced an "X" between its ears and eyes, paced back several steps then released an aggravated huff and continued on to the next pike. When they reached the point where they had begun, Winter folded her arms in satisfaction.

The silence became too much for Clarial at this point. "We aren't abandoning them, are we?" she begged, unsure of what Winter was plotting.

"Most assuredly not!" Winter cocked her head, mea-suring a gap in the pikes. "Follow me, and when I tell you to run...you run."

* * *

BREUNOR HAD BEEN FAVORING HIS LEFT HIP ever since the curtain had been drawn back. Netty figured that he must have taken a pretty bad blow to it earlier in the con-test.

The ogre commander loudly informed the horde that pairs would now be permitted to enter the pit. This news was greeted by an exultant wave of howls, shouts, and growls that made Netty draw back and cover her ears, wincing from the sharp pitches that she was not used to hearing.

"THE CLOSING CEREMONY WILL NEED MORE TIME TO BE PREPARED!" the ogre announced above the commotion.

Just prior to this proclamation, the knights had faced a smallish beta ogre who had really long limbs, which he used to connect several hits to Breunor's already damaged face. Percival had quickly acted as a shield for his fellow knight, absorbing several strikes while loyally preventing Breunor from sustaining a killing blow. The match, however, did not last very long at all. Percival brought it to an abrupt end when he caught the beta's leg halfway through a kick, and slammed his elbow down on the monster's femur, snapping it so completely that the bone was visible.

Netty's gaze darted between the pit below where Breunor spoke to Percival, gesturing to his hip, and above, where a throng of monsters had rushed the ogre and were making frantic demands to be the next combatants.

"WHERE ARE THOSE VICTUS WHO VOLUNTEERED EARLIER?" the ogre bellowed, scanning the crowd as it swarmed around him. Netty caught sight of the pair far off to the side, slinking away from the ecstatic monsters. Victus looked very similar to faewolves from a distance, though their posture was a bit more hunched and they took after rats rather than wolves. This particular pair did not seem interested in the contest any longer, lowering their heads and ducking away. *Seeing that ogre's leg snap like a matchstick stole a bit of the venom from their fangs!* Netty guessed. When the big ogre's eyes finally found them, she could see that he also recognized that the victus no longer had any interest in fighting.

"FINE, FINE!" The brute shook his head, turning his attention away from the cowering rodents. "YOU THERE! YOU'LL DO!" He pointed at a pair of furry lizardmen who immediately rejoiced at their selection. A cluster of four hobs mistakenly thought that the ogre had selected them, and made for the pit.

"NO, NOT YOU!" The ogre slapped his forehead in exasperation. "SOMEONE STOP THEM! I SAID ONLY TWO AT A TIME!" It was too late, the hobs were now squaring themselves at the knights, sizing them up. "OH, WELL NEVERMIND."

The lizardmen indignantly shook their fists at the hobs and kicked clumps of dirt down at them with their taloned feet.

Netty did not like this one bit. The hobs were slinking around, stepping sideways in a circular path, crisscrossing one another and lunging at the knights in a clear display of menace. Percival held his ground while Breunor used the walls of the pit to get himself back to his feet. He had used the lull to regain his breath, but when he finally stood upright, it was obvious that he was not anywhere near his full strength.

Steadying himself by placing a hand on Percival's shoulder, Breunor's lips moved but Netty could not make out the words. When Percival wavered at his friend's touch, Netty felt herself shrink. *He is weakened!* She cupped her mouth in shock. The knight who she believed could survive wading through a sea of wyrms, emerge from an aelder griffin's eyrie without a scratch, and single-handedly lay siege to an ogre battlement, was displaying mortality. Netty's world began to topple and tumble, flipping upside down and shaking her by the ankles. She tossed her head from side to side, trying to clear away the plague of doubt manifesting in her mind.

"He will prevail!" Netty shouted to the monsters, who did not react in the slightest to her sudden outburst. *He will!* She tried her hardest to convince herself it was the truth.

The hobs were continuing to circle, and Netty could see exactly what the horrid creatures were up to from her high vantage point. When one would swing wide, almost brushing the dirt wall, another would flank from the opposite side. They were trying to draw Percival far enough from Breunor so they could latch onto the wounded knight and make a sport of ending him. Netty remembered the hobs from the ward, and these ones were different. They intelligently communicated with one another and seemed to be much more alert to their surroundings. The ones from the ward had acted as if they were almost under a spell, acting in unison without even looking at one another. The ones now squaring off against her friends were focused and wild...and *scary*.

And it happened so fast, all at once. Netty did not even have time to cry out. Percival approached one of the hobs to his left, while another quickly swung around the opposite side, far out of the knight's reach. Percival staggered when he took a defensive step and the hob before him used the wall as a springboard, bounding from it like a loosed dart. The monster latched onto Percival's helmet and began tearing at the knight's shoulders and neck, while the remaining hobs surged toward Breunor. The knight was badly hurt and defended himself the best he could, but he was vastly outnumbered. Landing a backhand slap to the first hob proved effective for that foe, but the other two hobs leapt around their stunned mate and rapidly overtook Breunor. One jumped high while the other sprung low, toppling the knight...*too easily*.

Seeing how quickly Breunor fell, Netty was horrified. *He doesn't have much life left in him!* She knew that Percival could not see from his periphery due to the helm, but prayed that the sounds of Breunor's screams would be enough for him to react. They were not.

The halflaif could not see how Breunor was faring, she could only watch helplessly as the hobs raised and lowered their claws, viciously striking over and over again. If Breunor was defending himself at all, she could not tell. He was, yet, screaming for his life. Screaming for help.

Screaming for Percival. That name was the only word Netty could clearly hear.

Percival had been embroiled in a battle of his own. The single hob proved to be a much more stubborn opponent than Netty believed it would be. She had taken for granted how battle-capable Percival was. The small monster was still tightly fastened to the knight's head, much like the magic helm that could not be dislodged.

Breunor's now strangled voice must have reached a pitch that Percival could perceive. Spurred by his friend's frantic call for aid, Percival hunched down and drove his head, the hob still connected, into the earthy wall of the pit with such tremendous force that the creature's mouth formed a howl but no sound escaped. With a violent twist, Percival removed the hob's left arm from his helmet, and also from the creature's shoulder socket. Once a space was made, Percival thrust his arm up and peeled the winded monster off, discarding it like a soiled vestment. Blood from the dismemberment was flung into the air as Percival whirled around and set his sights on his friend's bitter struggle.

One of the hobs took notice of the approaching knight, and nudged his companion while gargling a phrase that Netty wagered meant, "See to him while I finish this one." The hob nodded greedily and gave Breunor's shin a swipe before obediently withdrawing. Without breaking his stride, Percival met the rushing hob with one outstretched hand. The knight's head remained focused on

Breunor, not swerving even a fraction as he palmed the darting foe's head, freezing the monster in place. Before the creature could lash out or attempt to gain sturdy footing, Percival clenched the hand encasing the hob's head, crushing its skull. He flung the lifeless monster aside and continued forward. Drawing closer to Breunor, he gave his helm a few hopeful tugs yet again, but to no avail.

The hob looked back at Percival and sneered, its eyes falling on the remains of his kin. Standing up, it began to launch a hasty retreat to the wall. The hob knocked down by Breunor finally lifted its head from the ground, but catching sight of Percival, quickly dropped its head back down, feigning unconsciousness. Netty felt it was a wise decision.

Scrabbling at the wall, the panicked hob reached out for help, trying to escape its fate. The lizardmen reached down and took hold, hefting the dangling hob upward in a friendly display. The gesture, however, rapidly waxed sour as the scorned lizardmen brought the hob up onto safe ground, brushed its shoulders off, then pitched the hob back into the pit, like a corpse into a burning tomb.

Before the terrified creature struck the dirt, Percival snatched it from the air by its windpipe, and drove the hob several inches into the soil. Only the creature's hands and legs were visible, grotesquely jutting upward, twitching its final death tremors.

The hob that had been playing dead miraculously remained motionless as a set of beta ogres cleared the pit.

They tossed the supposed corpse up to the awaiting ogres around the rim. Percival seemed oblivious to the bustling activity behind him as he cradled his friend's head with one hand while vainly attempting to remove his helm with the other. Netty could see Breunor's lips moving as he thrust Percival's hand onto his injured hip, and she tried her best to discern what the knight was saying.

"Fail safe?" the phrase puzzled the girl.

"NEXT!" the ogre boomed, toggling his pointed finger between the overeager lizardmen.

BEFORE THE BUTCHERS

Squeezing between a miniscule opening in the shrike's palisade, Winter crouched as she approached the creature's refuge, her boots cracking in the icy snow. Clarial tailed closely behind, and Winter knew that her friend's head was swirling with questions.

Branches completely bereft of leaves, buds, and twigs were intertwined into a seemingly impregnable cage that did not permit light to enter or exit. Circling the barren courtyard, Winter kept herself an equal distance from the pikes and the structure, inspecting the exterior for some sort of opening. As she drew closer, it became more and more evident that there was no identifiable entrance into this treacherous dwelling place.

How am I supposed to summon this daemon? Winter thought, simultaneously cursing the icy layer atop the snow for being so loud. Halting mid-stride, she knelt and beckoned Clarial to her side.

"Do you have eyes on where we came in?" Winter whispered, hovering an inch from Clarial's ear.

"I do," Clarial nodded, twirling a finger in her ear. "And that tickled."

"Good," Winter focused her attention back to the lair. "I mean, *good* that you know where the exit is, not the tickling part. But keep a tab on the exit. It's very important."

Not one sound came from inside the nest. Nothing stirred and Winter wondered if there was even anything in there at all. Breunor had told her that carnal shrikes hibernate during the cold season, but even if the beast was not as dangerous in the snow, it was still supremely lethal in comparison to most anything else one may stumble upon in Fenrirfang. *No matter how brutal or perilous you believe yourself to be, this forest always has a way of proving you wrong.* As the thought began its first echo in Winter's mind, another voice suddenly invaded.

"What do you want from me, tactician?"

To say that Winter was startled would be an understatement. The voice was definitely not Clarial's and it certainly was not coming from one of the decapitated heads surrounding her.

Winter pulled Clarial's sleeve. "Did you hear that?" she demanded, feverishly looking all around.

"Hear what?" Clarial appeared oblivious, not bewildered.

"That voice!"

"No."

"I am not speaking to the runner."

"Ah! There it was again!" Winter stumbled back a step from Clarial and stared into the shrike's haunt with an unwavering gaze. The voice sounded oddly similar to Relic's. "You can't hear the talking, can you?"

"I don't hear anything but your dumb nonsense."

"Alright, so it seems the shrike is speaking directly to my mind."

"What is he saying?"

"Nothing yet, just asking why we're here."

"Well, let him know!"

"Yes, let him know."

"Gah!" Winter yelled, recoiling. "This is going to take some getting used to." She cleared her throat and clasped her fingers together above her stomach as if she were about to formally recite a hymn. "Now, Sir Carnal Shrike, can you read my thoughts, or should I speak as I am now?"

"Speak as you are now."

Winter peered at Clarial from under a furrowed brow. "You sure you can't hear that?" she mumbled, thumbing in the shrike's direction.

"No! I can't!" Clarial replied emphatically, shooing her like a particularly dim rodent. "Get on with it! Our friends are in peril!"

"Friends? You seek aid?"

"Oh, good job Clarial!" said Winter sarcastically. "Now the shrike knows why we came."

"You beseech me in error, tactician. I serve only my own desires."

"What if your desire, which I assume is amassing a collection of skulls..." Winter paused, smiling faintly as she regarded the pikes. "Coincides with our needs."

"You have my attention."

"I am not overly familiar with your kind, but I can say that this is quite an impressive display you have here."

"It is the finest in all of this realm."

"Yeah, it's pretty great," Winter said, shrugging, "but I see that you are still missing a few pieces."

She paused to allow the shrike to consider her words. Silence filled the space where Winter believed there would be a response.

"What's he saying now?" queried Clarial, invading the silence.

Winter shot Clarial a look filled with unease, "Nothing."

Clarial sucked air between her teeth and grimaced.

"What can you offer?"

Winter released a sigh of relief and met Clarial's eyes, "He just replied."

"Finally!" Clarial shook her head. "What did he say?"

"He wants to know what we can offer."

Glancing at her friend's bosoms, Winter smiled from one corner of her mouth.

Clarial blocked her armoured breasts with a vambrace. "Don't be gross!" she hissed.

"Come on, Clarial," Winter coaxed, the other corner of her lips rising in a devious grin. "He must get pretty lonely out here..."

"I do not repeat myself."

"Oh, sorry."

"You should be!" Clarial huffed.

"Not you, you shameless hussy," Winter said, disdainfully looking her friend up and down. "You should really try not being so selfish all the time," she added.

Clarial feigned offense, clutching the collar of her cuirass and sneering.

Clearing her throat once again, Winter returned to the task at hand and addressed the hidden beast. "I have it on good terms that a small army of varying monsters, all sentient, mind you, have gathered just north of here outside Knotwithstadt."

"So the remnants of your contingent are embroiled in battle, and you came to me?" The shrike's voice seemed to darken bitterly. *"Hoping that I would be enticed by such a proposition? I do not involve myself in the affairs of man or laif."*

"Is that so?" Winter replied, folding her arms

"It is."

"And do you know what brought us here?"

Silence.

Winter continued, "I could not help but notice that your delightful 'fence of death' is missing a particular breed of horse..."

"An eryonkonj?!" The voice broke from its calm, disinterested cadence.

"Uh..." Winter glanced at Clarial, "Maybe? What is that exactly?"

"A laif bred destrier."

"Clarial! Run!" Winter drew her blade. "Get to Travis and fly to the village!"

The unnervingly placid dwelling suddenly emitted a scream that matched the voice Winter had been hearing in her mind.

"This is it," Winter hissed, watching Clarial's heels strike the snow, advancing below her billowing mantle. The runner slowed for the span of a breath to squeeze through the meager gap in the fence. And that was the last Winter saw of her friend before shifting her gaze back to the carnal shrike's lair.

***

BREUNOR TRIED HIS BEST TO STAND, but Percival would not allow it. Though he was encased beneath the helm, shrouded from visibility, Breunor could sense the despair within his friend. *My wounds must be pretty grievous to cause that tremble in his voice,* he thought, looking up at his friend while reclining his head against the steep base of the pit wall. It was the perfect angle for watching Percival, reduced to a regular warrior's strength, face an endless wave of foes. The position also offered an excellent view of the bloodstained carriage secured at the apex of a hillock above the pit. A familiar halflaif girl looked down on them from inside the opened door, her feet dangling and a look of grave concern etched on her face.

A pair of danegusts vaulted into the pit, their drake-like heads fixed with a look of contempt. Their reptilian lips undulated in sneers, revealing rows of tapered fangs. The taller of the pair stepped out in front and began to make threatening gestures at Breunor. Guttural phrases emanated from deep within his chest cavity, and the closer Percival drew to his friend, the louder and more frantic the danegust became.

"Just let them finish me," Breunor begged, clutching at Percival's belt, faintly tugging the creased leather. "It will be their last mistake, old friend."

* * *

"MOVE AWAY FROM HIM!" the lizardman shouted at Percival. "He is no longer worthy! We won't harm him! Just move away so *we* can dance!"

Netty admired the monster's sentiment. *But why isn't Percival stepping away from Breunor? He clearly means him no harm.*

The lizardman was cursing at Percival while his companion calmly strode to the opposite side of the circular hollow and leaned an elbow against the soil wall, waiting patiently for the battle to commence. In stark contrast, the larger lizardman was waxing hotter and hotter. The line of spikes cresting his skull began to grow rigid, gradually rising to their full height.

"Face us!" the lizardman shrieked, lunging at Percival.

"Let him come to us," the placid lizardman suggested coolly, his voice like spun silk. "Save your voice for the victory speech."

The angry lizardman spun toward his companion. "I despise his ignorance! It spurns me so!" he dramatically confessed, slapping his snout in aggravation.

"I know, brother," the lizardman replied, "this man, however, is a killer who cannot help but fill as many graves as possible," he stated serenely, admiring the sinuous claws on his right hand. "He will come to us."

Relenting with a raspy growl, the lizardman joined his brother. "Alright, good," the calmer monster said, "conserve your strength." The angry lizardman released another huff and tugged the hem of his brigandine impatiently.

After a short time, the monster's words proved to be true. The exchange between Percival and Breunor was impossible to hear, but Netty could tell that they were arguing about something. Breunor's dark blue tunic was caked with mud and blood, though Netty could not tell how bad his wounds were. *I think he's standing at death's gate,* she thought, feeling her throat tightening and her lips quiver without permission. She tried her hardest to smile at Breunor, who was looking up at her with such pain in his eyes.

They locked onto one another for a few fleeting moments before shifting to watch Percival.

The unarmed knight walked toward the lizardmen, tugging at his helmet, each step beleaguered.

I hope this is just an act! He can't be this tired...that's just impossible.

The more passive lizardman, who Netty named "Clyde" in her head proved to be anything but passive in combat. Trailing from each lizardman's smallest finger was a picket of barbs that appeared sharp as daggers, concluding around the bend of their elbow. Clyde concealed the forefront of his maw with his arm, leading with the barbs pointed at Percival, and feinted a stagger step to his left before exploding directly into the knight's center. Any semblance of balance Percival had was completely overturned and the knight was flung from his feet. Upon impact, Clyde came to an abrupt halt, standing stalk still over his foe. A dark stain spread across Percival's chest, directly beneath the fresh tears in the fabric of his tunic.

Clyde remained where he stood, looking down on his stunned enemy as his brother surged forward and drove his plate-scaled knee into the side of Percival's helm. Anyone else would have been knocked out cold from the force, but Percival used the momentum against the lizardman. Rolling his face with the blow, he grasped the invading reptilian leg and hooked his arm around his foe's kneecap, effectively rendering the appendage immobile. With an unexpected lurch, the knight arched his spine against the wall of the pit and bolted to his feet, still clutching the lizardman's leg.

Netty felt a rush of triumph flow over her scalp. *Break him!* she vehemently urged.

With a heave, Percival drew his adversary in, using the force of his entire body to smite the lizardman with a full-bodied forearm strike. Man and lizard met the earth, though earth met the lizard first.

This small victory was short-lived. Clyde reacted congruently, launching himself toward the fight. Before Percival could deliver a killing strike, the knight's head received another crippling blow delivered from a lizardman's knee. This time he absorbed the full force and his lower half seemed to crumple. Clyde placed a hand against the dirt embankment and administered two fell stomps with his taloned feet, depriving the fallen knight of any remaining air in his lungs.

The decision to attempt a third stomp on Percival's bloodied chest proved to be in error. When the lizardman planted the buffet, the fresh blood was slick as waxed hardwood, throwing the monster's feet out from under him. "Shite!" he wailed, Percival rolling out from beneath him

Percival was now the only one standing. His hunched posture with one hand pressed to his chest betrayed his struggle to breathe while the meat of his other hand repeatedly struck the base of the helm, hoping to finally wrest it free.

The blow the knight had delivered to Clyde's brother was more ruinous than Netty had realized. The lizardman remained on his belly in the soil, unmoving, save for the reluctant rise and fall of his brigandine as he breathed.

Staggering a few steps to his left, Percival's head tilted as Clyde got to his feet. The lizardman winced when he planted his left leg, and violently shook his head, attempting to ward off the pain. Percival staggered to his right, then straightened to his full height, his shadow falling upon Breunor.

"You stupid man!" yelled Clyde, pointing a claw at Percival. "We are not going to harm the fallen man!" he dashed forward, closing the space between them in the blink of an eye. "You are the one we—" the lizardman's rant abruptly cut off. During his forward surge, his injured leg had snagged on a recessed patch of soil. Clyde stumbled, teetered, and tried to refocus his charge, but Percival was prepared. Using the lizardman's force against him, the knight grasped the nape of his neck and steered him toward his downed brother.

With a heated shove, Percival smashed Clyde's head into the wall, dazing the monster. Reaching down, the knight gripped the brother's lifeless wrist, and yanked the monster up like a stringed marionette, snapping sinew, the popping sound clearly reaching Netty's ears.

Clyde did not have time to react, still submerged in dazed confusion. Percival exploited the brother's barbed arm, using it as a makeshift blade, cruelly thrust the barbs into Clyde's throat, snuffing the light from the lizard's eyes.

Backpedaling as if he had just released a massive boulder, Percival faltered along his path back to Breunor. Believing this round to be complete, he knelt down to see how his friend fared.

Netty screamed. For the first time, Percival heard her, and he looked up. She waved frantically, desperately pointing toward the lizardmen. *He did not know I was here,* she realized.

A tide of renewed strength seemed to sweep through Percival. The knight surged to his feet, despite the dozens upon dozens of wounds adorning his body. Clyde's brother had awakened and was completely enraged by the death of his comrade. He rose furiously to his feet and whirled around. Dangling free from its socket, his right arm slapped listlessly at his side as he charged toward the knights.

"You die this day!" he shrieked, his voice nearly spent.

A simple sidestep was all it took. In a wave of limbs, Percival had the lizardman on the ground, his hand clamped like a vice to the back of the monster's spiked skull. The spikes flattening as the knight applied pressure, and in a swift movement, he removed his hand and replaced it with his knee. A gurgle escaped the lizardman's snout from the force of the violent transition. His claws scrabbled at the soil, trying to gain purchase before his ghost left his body.

"NEXT!" the towering ogre boomed, waving at a handful of beta ogres crowded next to him. At his faint command, the smaller ogres readily jumped into the pit and began plying their trade, removing the dead lizardmen with as much reverence as a butcher with dead stock.

THE NEXT SEVERAL ENGAGEMENTS ended with Percival striking a decisive killing blow, and as the battles continued, the monsters' collective morale began to deflate though it was obvious that Percival's strength was waning. His steps were slackening and he was much slower to rise, giving the combatants hope that they would prevail.

After Percival had caught sight of Netty, his stamina seemed to double, but this only prolonged the inevitable. *How much longer does he have?* Netty thought, her eyes beginning to overflow with sorrow.

The sun was hovering just above the treetops, and judging by the rage in the ogre commander's voice, the contest was lasting much longer than the abowraith had allotted on its timetable. "THIS NEEDS TO END NOW!" the commander roared, picking up his tremendous axe.

The beta ogres scrambled to retrieve three monsters that had showed great promise at the beginning of the match. Netty wasn't sure what they were exactly. They had scrunched up bat-like faces with long flowing hair, and they scurried like hobs, but were much smarter and stronger. But not strong and smart enough.

That helmet must be so stifling! Netty shook her head, watching the knight stagger and fall down next to Breunor. This had become his ritual after each victory. The two knights would exchange words for the span of several breaths as the tumult above produced the next set of monsters.

The giant ogre leader secured a helm, carefully lodging it between his horns before skimming a thumb across the blade of his axe. He reared his head back and proclaimed, "I WILL END THIS!" to the triumphant screams of every monster within the stronghold. Their collective voices sent a wave of fear into the young girl's core.

A thickening shadow blossomed from the horizon, drawing Netty's eyes above the feverish crowd. The languid flapping of the somber host felt familiar. And as the forms grew larger as their distance slimmed, Netty realized, with unfathomable despair, just what was coming.

The vultures are here, she silently sobbed, *to finally feast on their knight.*

~ 21 ~

FEEDING CARRION BIRDS

For just a moment, Winter thought that perhaps this entire adventure was all an elaborate ruse. What emerged from the shrike's lair looked strikingly similar to Relic. Elation was quickly replaced by terror when the beast turned to face her and spread its remarkably long wings. Wings longer than Relic's by several feet, Winter wagered, taking in the sight, trembling with her sword in hand.

"Which direction did the eryonkonj break for?"

Winter willed herself to think about anything else.

"Up my butt?!" The shrike appeared repulsed, shaking his head as if he'd been slapped across the beak. "No matter." He spoke out loud for the first time, his calm voice matching the one that had invaded Winter's head. "I can still smell your friend," he said. With that, the beast bent at the knees and surged upward, taking to the skies at a much more reluctant pace than Relic would have.

"Ah, so the cold weather does affect them," murmured Winter, struggling to resheath her blade. She continued to shudder even after the beast's departure. After steadying her breathing and allowing a moment to center herself, she was finally able to slide the sword back in its scabbard. "Hopefully by the time I make it to the village, everything will be sorted out..." Winter confessed to the head of a slack jawed nockbogle as she wormed her way through the palisade.

* * *

THE GARGANTUAN OGRE PLACED A HEAVY HAND on the rim of the pit and eased himself down slowly, one foot before the other, as if he were entering a swimming hole. Breunor ignored the ogre, focusing his tired eyes on a spectre sailing from the boughs behind the carriage, high above the colossus.

He was not the first to notice. The wall of the pit had reached the ogre commander's chest, and as he extended a hand to retrieve his axe from the rim, he turned his head in the direction of the apparition.

*It's the fucking chilly wizard...*Breunor thought, hatred brewing behind his eyes. Every sort of face, beaked, fanged, or hideous, began to solemnly turn in the direction of the abowraith as it descended onto the roof of Netty's carriage.

Percival's shoulders sagged almost imperceptibly, but Breunor noticed the slight movement.

* * *

WHY ARE THE MONSTERS STARING AT ME? Netty looked down at her garb self-consciously, checking to make sure she was not glowing or anything. She wished she could shrink down to the size of a dormouse to avoid the host of evil eyes glaring daggers at her.

The boards above her head creaked ominously as if someone was standing there. Dry dust from the planks overhead began cascading to the floor, betraying the person's location. After moving forward one single pace the person above her stood completely still.

The ogre commander's face held a look of devout reverence, eyes fixated on whatever was standing over her. With a pained realization, the little girl knew exactly who was standing above her.

She tried to look brave for Percival.

* * *

"NEXT TIME YOU SAY JUMP," said Clarial between clenched teeth, clinging to Travis as they hurtled through the icy forest, "just point me to the nearest bridge."

Travis' eye flicked back at her quizzically.

"Not you, Travis," she admitted, patting the laifhorse's neck. "I'm talking about that dirty thunderwench who decided that this was a good idea."

The laifhorse snorted in agreement and lowered his head, renewing his pace.

***

"PROCEED!" THE VOICE over Netty's head proclaimed, matching pitch with cracking glass.

The little girl was grateful that she could not see the hideous wraith from where she was shackled. For the first time in days, she no longer felt the evil's presence inside her head, but now it was almost within spitting distance. Neither option was comfortable and deciding which she liked better was akin to deciding which eye to cut out. *I just want this all to go away...I just want to go home!*

She inclined her head down toward the pit in time to see the ogre nod to its master before rotating to face Percival. The knight shifted his weight and collapsed to one knee in exhaustion. A sharp growl escaped from under the helm as he pushed off and made to stand, unarmed and grossly outmatched. The ogre towered over the knight, nearly double his height and more than three times his width. Every limb was like a tree trunk, a single arm equal to Percival's waist, and his neck looked hard as marble and thick as the side of a mountain.

Giving the heavily wounded knight a surveying glare, the ogre sneered and tossed his axe aside. Percival's head pivoted to the fallen weapon for the fraction of a moment while the rest of him remained completely passive. He was waiting for the giant to act first.

Breunor lay several paces behind Percival, staring up at the late afternoon sky, appearing to be at peace with his fate. His hands rested across his heaving bloodstained chest, fingers interlaced, ready for burial.

Percival shifted his weight to the opposite foot and toppled over once again.

The ogre released a booming laugh, raising his hands and dramatically pivoting around, receiving riotous adulation from the monsters hungry to see this knight fall for the last time.

"I MAY JUST TAKE MY TIME WITH THIS ONE," yelled the ogre, surveying his legion with a grin plastered to his jawline. "WHAT SAY YOU?" The question was answered with an immediate roar of approval. He turned his close-set eyes to the abowraith, awaiting encouragement. The monsters hushed for a moment, each one still as statues, expectantly awaiting permission. Netty could not see the abowraith's gesture, but the host erupted in a frenzy of flailing limbs and gnashing fangs, so she imagined it must have been a nod of agreement.

"ALRIGHT!" The ogre tilted his head, peering at Percival from behind a tusk. "TIME TO MEET DEATH, KNIGHT." He bounced on his heel and sprung forward with more agility than Netty wagered a monster of his size could display. Percival tried to duck the backhanded swipe but was too weak to move quickly enough. The knight was blasted far across the pit, crumpling against the cave wall and sliding down on unsteady feet. His knees buckled under the weight of his own body as he struggled to maintain his balance. He righted himself and stood before the ogre, butting his palm against his helm, which remained firmly fixed in place.

The simple gesture was indescribably disheartening to the little girl in the gore-stained carriage. As her emotions swirled around her, overwhelming and choking, a stream of dust rained down on her head. The abowraith was shifting its feet.

"HE IS ONLY FLESH AND BONE!" the ogre shouted, leveling an accusatory finger at Percival's forehead. "HE CAN HARDLY STAND! WHAT WAS SO DIFFICULT?!" He turned his back to the knight and without bothering to even look back, rotated his hips and struck out halfheartedly, landing another blow. "SEE?!" he roared, twirling like a clumsy showman.

Percival's right shoulder struck the soil first, carving a trench, his body coming to a rest an arm's length from Breunor. Without a glance, Breunor's lips moved as he spoke to his downed friend. Netty desperately wished she could hear their exchange, clenching her eyes tight and focusing on the knights.

Miraculously, Breunor's voice carried, and she heard him speaking distinctly. "We can end this," he stated plainly.

She opened her eyes as the knight tugged groggily at his hip and continued, "It's zero sum, but at least it will all be over with."

Percival strained to his hands and knees, and slowly brought his head up to Breunor. "This pit is not our grave," he insisted.

The ogre, who had been soaking in the buckets of praise from the spectators, unaware of the brief conversation, casually returned his focus to Percival.

"WHY DO YOU KEEP RISING, LITTLE MAN?!" the ogre taunted with hands on his hips. Staggering forward and ignoring the question, Percival gave his helm a few optimistic tugs as he moved closer to the ogre. He wisely remained just out of striking distance, which caused a brief flicker of hope to bloom in Netty. *He's alive enough to keep away!*

The ogre strode forward, closing the distance between himself and the quavering knight. Standing inches from Percival, his body eclipsed the knight, gazing down at him as one peers down a deep well.

Collapsing to a knee once again, Percival steadied himself with one arm. The ogre scanned the crowd, derisively arching an eyebrow and adjusting his helm. Using more energy than Netty thought the knight had, Percival lunged for the ogre's left foot, grasping onto the tendon that connected calf to heel. In a delirious state, he must have believed that he could activate his claws, and he pathetically began scrabbling at the ogre's solid flesh.

"THAT TICKLES!" the ogre rumbled, his laughter joined by cackles and guffaws that reverberated into the treetops. Flinching free from the knight's faint grip, the ogre soundly kicked Percival in the chest. The blow folded the knight immediately, and Netty could practically hear the knight's lungs crackling under his damaged ribcage as he sucked in meager amounts of air. Fresh blood poured from under the helm, mirroring the fresh tears pouring down the little girl's face. Her shudders were greeted with another spiral of dust from overhead.

"You're killing him!" Netty shrieked, her voice absorbed into the atmosphere. Not one creature acknowledged her pleas, not one eye lifted to the carriage. "You! Are! Killing! Him!" she staggered her screams, articulating the phrase. She rubbed her neck, and when she swallowed it felt like she had sand stuck in the back of her throat. Her violent outburst had been futile and had only hurt her windpipe. The ogre did not hear her. *Not like it would make any difference...*

The brute stooped down with one hand on his thigh and brought his head down to Percival's eye level. The knight was crawling and propped himself up with one elbow as he turned to meet the ogre's gaze. "HAD ENOUGH?" the ogre asked, shaking his head and feigning disappointment.

The knight raised a finger to respond, but his body shuddered with a cough, which produced more red liquid from under the helm. With the finger still raised, the knight lifted himself to his feet, tottering in defiance.

Snatching Percival by the tabard, crumpling the fabric in his enraged fist, the ogre lifted the knight off his feet. "I GROW BORED!" the commander bellowed as he raised the knight to his face. The thick spittle flung from his lips joined the dried scarlet stains adorning the knight's helmet. The grotesque patina made Netty squirm in discomfort.

Percival struggled to raise his arms, but they were completely spent and unresponsive.

"I CAN SMELL THE CURSE ON YOU!" the ogre jeered, tapping Percival's helm with the tip of his fingernail. "YOU STINK OF MANY CURSES! YOU STINK OF DEATH! AND YOU WILL CONTINUE TO STINK AS YOUR BODY ROTS AND FEEDS THE BUZZARDS AND WORMS!"

Dangling now, his body nearing lifelessness, Percival merely shrugged in reply. Slowly extending the knight outward with one arm, spanning his limb to its full length, the ogre drew his empty fist back to aim the killing blow. His tongue performed a lap around his lips as he closed one eye, summoning all his strength into one hand.

Percival did not turn away from the blow, though Netty did. The girl had no desire to be a witness to this tragedy.

With a focused strike, the ogre smote Percival directly in the faceplate, and Netty heard the meaty thump as the blow struck true. A second thud, following impossibly fast, drew her left eye open. Though the ogre had proved to be quite fast, there was no way he was *that* fast. Definitely not fast enough to strike in such rapid succession.

Her chest tingled and the blood in her limbs rapidly receded. Her eyelids fluttered in shock, her mind in utter disbelief at what she saw.

For rolling to a languid halt several feet from Breunor's boots, the cursed helm teetered on its round dome and settled in place. Her eyes flashed to her knight still rendered immobile by the ogre's vice like grip on his tunic. His hair was slick, drenched in blood and sweat, and clung to his face, neck, and shoulders. As the brute readied another blow, the knight spat and grinned maniacally at his foe. The ogre wavered for a moment, startled by the spark of life.

"Ha!" Netty screamed, unable to contain her elation. She shot forward as far as her tethers would allow, eagerly watching the fight. "Take them!"

Percival sustained a blow to the chin, but his head instantly snapped back to the ogre, the grin remaining. In one furious movement, his body exploded in a whirlwind of claws and fangs, consuming the brute's arm, exposing bone for the faintest second before it was scored into oblivion.

Wood particles rained down on Netty as the abowraith seemed to perform a frantic dance above her, stomping and stamping.

The entire host reeled back as they watched the best of their ranks succumb to the werewolf knight. Latching onto the ogre's shoulders, Percival slapped the helm from the giant's head. He leaned back with his claws sunk deep into the ogre's skull and released a howl into the darkening skies. Any monsters that had not already set to flight were now tearing the earth, fleeing as fast as their appendages would allow them.

The werewolf brought his head down and opened his jaws to their fullest extent, stretching the soft flesh at the corners of his maw. The wailing ogre swatted with his remaining arm at the beast perched atop his cranium, vainly attempting to rid himself of the monster. The werewolf deliberately encased the ogre's head from crown to eyes, his fanged snout passing between tusk and horn, and he slowly and steadily began to lock his jaw. As soon as the werewolf covered his enemy's eyes, the brute began to flail blindly with doubled effort and his screams reached a pitch that Netty did not believe was possible. A resounding snap followed by a string of crunches brought instant stillness from the commander, his arm falling motionless.

Percival leapt from his perch, leaving in his wake an ogre with blood seeping from between the splintered cracks traversing his skull. The ogre crumbled to his knees with a look of terror on his damp visage, and for a few moments his features softened as he began plucking his bottom lip in sheer disbelief. The defeated commander remained cowered on his knees as his ghost, like the host of others before, left him.

*****

BREUNOR LOOKED TO THE CARRIAGE and saw the sheer panic on the abowraith's previously calm demeanor as Percival began to do what Percival did best.

Feeding carrion birds...

The horde clawed and tore at one another in their panicked attempt to escape. No doubt a wave of terror passed through their ranks when Percival's helm had fallen off, but likely watching their leader's head transform into a bloody pyramid added a bit more pep to their steps.

From above, Breunor noticed a renewed panic emerging. The knight tried to arch his back to gain a better view of the sky, and catch a glimpse of what was transpiring, but the shooting pain throughout his body reminded him that he was probably teetering on death's threshold.

Percival was locked in a stance at the epicenter of the pit, staunchly gazing up at whatever was approaching.

"What is it?!" Breunor shouted, coming across more desperate than he had intended. The werewolf responded with a quick shake of his head. Apparently, he was also unsure of what was transpiring in the forest.

Suddenly the werewolf's chin retreated as his eyes narrowed. "Clarial and Travis?" he stated with marked confusion.

Clarial?!

"Are the monsters attacking her?!" demanded Breunor. This time he could not try to hide his desperation.

The werewolf shook his head fractionally once again, as if he were twitching an insect from his snout. Breunor tried to roll to his side but the pain coursing through every fiber of his being rendered him utterly invalid.

From the carriage, Netty shouted something that sounded like *"rat trick."*

Percival whirled around to the sound of the girl's voice, and Breunor could not help but smile, which also proved painful. The abowraith looked a frantic mess, desperately attempting to take flight, hovering in place. Wavering and clambering at the air, the spectre appeared as one trying to sprint on top of loose rugs.

Descending like an avenging angel, a familiar shape shot across the skies on course for the lingering abowraith.

Rat trick..."Relic!" Sudden realization took hold, and Breunor's body painfully stiffened in triumph. "Get it, you beautiful beast!"

~ 22 ~

FROM THE GALLOWS, TO
THE GRINDER

It was over before it really began. Netty did not see the cataclysm, but she felt the impact. She heard the wraith squeal a terrified "No! Please!" right before its end. And she also felt it in her head...her mind was at peace. The peace settled within her at the precise moment the wraith's existence was snuffed from this realm, and a serenity passed over her, cleansing her soul, not even leaving a grimy film behind. She was finally free.

***

WAIT! BREUNOR SWIPED AT THE BLOOD that had crusted over his right eyelid. "That's not Relic!" he shouted. From overhead, a pretty face crested the rim of the arena, eyes sweeping the pit before coming to rest on him.

"We need to go!" Clarial's face was etched with urgency. "Now! You lazy—" she choked on the words, coming up short as if she had been punched in the gut. "Your wounds..." she trailed off, looking up at Percival, who immediately understood her unspoken request.

Staring past the approaching werewolf, Breunor saw the beast he had believed to be Relic sever the head from the abowraith's cloth wrapped shoulders. "Be easy!" Breunor pleaded with Percival as the knight stooped down, placing an arm under the wounded knight's knees and the other behind his head. "What in the hekk is *that?!*" Breunor pointed up at the mysterious creature, resting his arm on Percival's furry shoulder as he was scooped up off the soil.

"It's a carnal shrike," admitted Clarial, her tone wavering between pride and guilt.

Sucking air between his teeth in sheer agony, Breunor coughed out a laugh, immediately regretting everything he had ever done to lead him to this point. "So that's what a shrike looks like..." he began. "Ow!" a searing burn permeated the shattered ribs behind his lungs as Percival attempted to gingerly place him on the grass outside of the pit.

"We really must go!" said Clarial, her eyes fixed on the decapitation taking place on roof of the carriage. "The shrike is after Travis, but thankfully he got distracted by the abowraith."

Percival stood above the broken knight. "That was indeed fortuitous," he growled before lowering down and retrieving Breunor again. "But where is Travis?" the werewolf asked, scanning the treeline.

"He took off," Clarial replied. Extending her arms, she reached toward Breunor, "I can take him."

"Do not go far for shelter," commanded Percival, his lip twitched in a fleeting sneer. "He cannot sustain any further trauma."

Clarial looked down at Breunor's nearly lifeless body in her arms. "He's lighter than I expected," she mumbled.

"Most of his blood resides in the pit."

"Oh..." With nothing left to say, the runner backpedaled away from Percival and slowly turned with one foot after the other, keeping her charge as still as possible.

As they passed under the darkened shroud of the forest, the last glimpse Sir Breunor caught before he slipped from consciousness was the exquisite cut of Clarial's chin. *What a stunning creature...*

***

THE STRUGGLE ABOVE HER HEAD HAD FINALLY CEASED. Netty spent equal time peering between the slats overhead, trying to catch a glimpse of their old gargoyle friend, and gazing down at her knight.

Finding a decent sized hole where a knot had been knocked loose, she squinted up at Relic, her concentration only broken by the sound of claws dragging on the wooden floor in front of her.

The claws belonged to Percival, and he had arrived much, much faster than she could have anticipated. He had a very angry look on his werewolf face.

"We must go," he demanded, briskly rising to his feet and snapping his head toward where Relic had been.

After believing that she would never have another chance to see him while he was alive, Netty wanted nothing more than to wrap her arms around Percival. He had seemed so utterly defeated in the fighting pit, his mortality on display for all to see.

She was confused by his sense of urgency. "But the abowraith is dead, and Relic won't—"

"That's not Relic," stated Percival brusquely, still surveying the ceiling.

"But!" Netty wanted to protest, though deep in the recesses of her mind, she realized that there was validity in Percival's admission. She shook her head, "Then who is that?" she asked, watching Percival dart to the floor behind her and tear apart the anchor that tethered her.

As if on cue, the beast she had believed to be Relic descended and hovered less than a dozen feet from the carriage's door. The head of the abowraith was clutched in its talons, the wraith's eye sockets empty of the evil kindling flames they had once held. In the twilight gasping behind the beast, Netty could now tell that was definitely not Relic.

Percival immediately pushed Netty behind him and conjured the most savage roar she had ever heard.

The relic imposter backed away a few feet, settled its gaze on the werewolf defender, and gave an oddly reassuring nod. Then the creature took to the skies, setting off in the direction from whence it came.

Once the final danger had withdrawn, the werewolf seemed to deflate, returning to human form. Fur retreated, shedding in clumps, and once Percival was *Percival* again, Netty took his hands in hers as he slumped to his knees. Blood trailed from the left corner of his mouth to the bottom of his earlobe, and his jawline, ordinarily straight as an arrow, was rounded and swollen just below it.

"What was that?" she asked, feeling her question was inadequate.

"That?" Percival weakly looked to the opening, his eyes moving the opposite direction of his body as it collapsed. "That was a carnal shrike," he said, before finally succumbing to overwhelming exhaustion.

* * *

CLARIAL REMAINED AWAKE THROUGHOUT THE NIGHT. Her nerves were stretched thin from watching Breunor's chest heave in odd increments. She was never certain when the last would be and found herself holding her own breath in solidarity.

Rushing through the forest with Breunor in her arms, fortune had smiled a blistering ray of light down upon her in the climbing shadows. Amongst a dense copse of evergreens, she had happened on an ancient bristlecone tree that offered a closet-sized cave. Believing it would be obvious for the carnal shrike to spot, yet she knew she needed to stop jostling the dying knight. Cares quickly began to drain, and with an internal shrug, she pressed inside the natural shelter and prayed that she was not crawling into some horrid creature's trap. Her prayers, as usual, were answered. This time, however, silence was the most welcome response she hoped to receive.

Dawn came and went, and the knight was still hanging on to life. After yet another rattling heave, the knight seemed to come to some lucidity, placing a wandering hand to his left hip.

Clarial blinked back the dry film over her eyes, and reached for his hand, "It can wait until later," she whispered, "just go back to sleep."

Breunor's hand held a surprising amount of strength, and his eyebrows twitched as he tried to pry open his blood plastered eyelids. "He kept telling me to save it for the kapreta...like we'd be getting out," he said deliriously, waking from his mild coma.

What? Clarial squeezed the knight's open palm, furling it into a loose fist before reverently laying it back on his chest as he returned to sleep.

"Like we'd be getting out..." Breunor repeated, his lips barely moving when forming the words. His eyebrows stopped twitching and his body became still once again.

Arching an inquisitive eyebrow, Clarial decided to investigate what the knight was reaching for. *Perhaps a deep wound,* she predicted, tenderly probing the area with her fingertips. Her left pinky brushed something under the fabrics that felt like a bulbous tumor or a bone jutting from flesh. Clarial inhaled a shocked breath and pulled away from the discontinuity.

"How much time do you have left?" she softly asked the knight, gingerly plucking the hem of his tunic up and reaching a hand inside to get a better feel of whatever new challenge they would be facing. *A bandage?* She felt a tight cloth dressing wrapped around the knight's thigh. *When did they have the time to perform aid?* Her fingers glanced lightly over the bandage, tracing a path to where she thought the fracture or tumor had been.

"What the—" she withdrew her fingers, squinting one eye in disbelief. *That's not natural...*her fingers returned to the tightly wrapped orb. She jostled it ever so slightly, confirming that it was not attached to his flesh.

"A bomb," she said in disbelief, reeling her arm back from under the tunic and scooching away from the knight. "You idiot."

She remained pressed to the inside of the tight cavern, afraid to leave Breunor, but also cautious of the newly discovered explosive danger. Relenting to her exhaustion, she drifted off wrapped in the warmth of the early afternoon sun.

Approaching footsteps snapped her head from off her chest. *How long was I asleep?!* She reached for her dagger, still in its scabbard.

"Oh, no...Breunor!" said a child's voice in clear distress.

Clarial recognized the voice and breathed a sigh of relief, removing her hand from the hilt of her weapon. Rushing footsteps ushered Netty into view, and the little girl fell to her knees as soon as she entered the shelter.

"Is he...dead?" She looked up at Clarial, tears streaming down her cheeks.

Clarial went to her hands and knees and drew beside Breunor. "No," she replied, gazing down at the knight. "He's been sleeping soundly all night and all morning. We do need to get some fresh water for his wounds," she paused, moving her eyes to Percival, who, although looking quite haggard, was still upright. "What of the shrike?" she asked him.

The knight shook his head. "He abandoned us."

"That's for the best."

Netty turned back to Percival. "Fresh water can be found in the lake near my village..." she trailed off with marked unease.

Clarial understood the girl's apprehension and speculated that there would surely be a plethora of wells inside Knotwithstadt, but the perils below the surface of Lake Patreka mirrored the ones in the village. The host of kapreta that swelled in the lake now also teemed within the village after the barrier gate had been released during the massacre. "If only we had a lampyr with us," Clarial said in a breathy tone, pursing her lips in disappointment.

"'If only' many things," Percival said, crouching down to their level, "I am going to the village. I will return."

Netty moved to accompany him, but the knight placed a hand to her shoulder. "Stay with Clarial and Sir Breunor," he instructed, forbidding her from joining. "Keep watch while Clarial gets some rest."

AS SOON AS PERCIVAL LEFT, Clarial reclined on her side with her back hugging the circular wall of the cavern. After a few steady breaths, the woman was asleep. The tension had left her face and she looked peaceful for the first time all day.

Netty had slept beside Percival in the carriage the night before, and felt more awake and alert than she had in a long time. Her mind wandered, thinking of her village and wondering what Percival would find. *Would the kapreta still be running rampant? Would he be able to reseal the gate? Will Breunor live?* Her face softened as she looked over the knight. *And where are Winter and Travis?*

Growing restless, Netty left the cave and walked under the trees mottling this patch of the forest. She remembered this area but did not recall that particular tree with the wide mouth. *If Gaius were alive, he would have transformed it into a fortress...Oh, the games we would have played...*her eyes began to fog with tears, and the trees began to tumble in her submerged view. Suddenly, she straightened up and swiped her nose with her wrist. "No more of that!" she scolded herself.

Netty found a good climbing tree near their shelter and perched on a sturdy branch with her feet dangling, languidly making circular patterns with her toes focused to the ground.

When Percival returned, she looked to the trunk of the tree to climb down but rapidly realized her knight was not alone.

"Winter!" she exclaimed, excitedly scrambling along the bough.

The woman walking beside Percival smiled up at the girl. "Did you find my village?" Netty asked, dangling from a lower branch before dropping to the ground.

"We did," Winter answered, kneeling to greet the girl in an embrace.

"I missed you," Netty proclaimed, wrapping her arms around the woman.

"I missed you too, little lady." Winter rested her chin on Netty's head and combed her fingers through the little girl's impossibly straight hair. "But we need to figure a few things out before you can return home." She swiveled her chin toward the old bristlecone tree. "It seems our kapreta expert is a bit incapacitated at the moment..."

HOME

"Better a decent plan today than a perfect one tomorrow, I suppose," said Winter, a long strand of wheat grass clenched between her teeth.

Breunor was momentarily awake, but there was no telling when he would slip out of consciousness once again. Earlier he had given them brief instructions regarding the bomb, which Clarial now held, but he had abruptly passed out halfway through his explanation.

"You just pull the pin," Breunor instructed, picking up where he had left off before his inconvenient foray into oblivion. "And whatever magical concoctions are inside mix into one another, and then you have about 10 fleeting moments before it blows up." He struggled to sit up and winced. "I could really use a drink of water, if you have some?"

Both women shook their heads. "Well, if I don't succumb to my wounds," Breunor continued, dabbing a finger on his tongue. "Then I will die of thirst. Both options sound rather lovely." The knight glanced disappointedly at his dry finger and rolled his eyes, seemingly in irony, except they did not return as they should have, and his body relaxed as he fell unconscious.

Leaving Breunor in Clarial's capable hands, Winter searched for Sir Percival, finding him leaning against a tree a mere stone's throw from the village. Unsurprised to see her, he simply pointed a finger toward a pair of kapreta fighting over a bone, possibly a human femur, and scratched his chin with an irritated sigh.

As they feared, the kapreta were still alive and well within Knotwithstadt.

"ALRIGHT," WINTER STOOD and wiped her hands on her tunic. "Everyone knows what to do, right?" she asked, glancing at Clarial and Percival. Ducking out of the shady hollow, she turned to Netty. "Keep your eyes on Sir Breunor," she asked the girl, her voice hardening, "if he passes..." she trailed off, looking over the girl's head at some distant fragment in the forest. "No one wants to die alone."

"ARE YOU HAPPY?" CLARIAL ASKED, lying motionless beside Winter about forty feet from the village border.

"Specifically?" Winter queried, cocking one eyebrow at her friend.

"This is where your boredom has gotten us."

Winter could not hold back the giggle. "I don't know about you, but I feel like I have really grown since we set off." She spoke in a serious tone, but ruined it by finishing the statement with another giggle.

Clarial shook her head. "You're the worst."

"Yes," Winter agreed, "but I am also ready. Are you?"

Producing Breunor's ball shaped explosive from her hip, Clarial admired it as if it would reveal her future. "I am," she responded. "Just waiting for our mutt to take care of his end of the bargain."

He should be arriving any moment now, Winter thought, rising up on one elbow to survey the area. "Here doggy, here doggy," she called, puckering her lips and kissing the air while pretending she held a treat in her hand.

Clarial laughed uneasily as she looked around, fervently hoping that Percival had not crept up on them. "But seriously, Winter," she began, drawing her friend's attention. Pointing at the dozens of kapreta wandering around the village, she continued, "What do you think was going through the holy knights heads before they made their assault on this village? In a way, we are about to mirror them. Except we're retaking it from monsters...but still, these creatures have no idea what's about to happen to them."

"Eh," Winter's lip curled into a sneer. "Forget 'em."

At that moment, Percival strode toward the village filled with the unsuspecting kapreta. He turned his head for a single beat and winked at the women while continuing forward.

"Was that the signal?" Clarial inquired, perplexed by the knight's cheeky display.

"I'm fairly certain that was it, but I'm moving regardless! Let's go!"

Surging to her feet, Winter watched through the trees as Percival become a werewolf, scattering some of the lesser kapreta immediately while a few of the more stout stood their ground. Arms outstretched, Percival stopped and released a roar, sending a wave of panic into the denizens of Knotwithstadt.

They only get one warning. Winter admired the modicum of chivalry the knight managed to maintain even while wearing his monster skin.

For several exaggerated breaths, the werewolf stood and glowered at the lingering kapreta who did not have the good sense to retreat for the safety of the lake beyond the village. A mere one third remained, the rest had peeled off and streamed through the rear gate.

Without another sound, Percival rushed into the village and swept through the meager resistance with relative ease. It was rather thrilling to watch, if one was taken with bloody dismemberment...and also held a strong sense of justice. Though Clarial might argue that the kapreta had only done what they were designed to do, Winter viewed the wretched creatures as obstacles. Plus, her inner tactician couldn't help but cheer the werewolf on. *He's like the Creator's sickle. A real thing of beauty!* Winter admired the werewolf's craftsmanship as he seemingly focused his attention on ripping the jaw from a kapreta with one hand, completely ignoring the venom, and with the other hand, he palmed the head of another foe, stopping it short before it could mount his back.

It's like he was designed to fight armies...

The kapreta swirling around him converging in a concerted effort were repelled at once, the few survivors sent reeling.

Followed behind in the wake of carnage, Winter instinctively eased her sword an inch from its scabbard, but found she did not need to remove it in order to ease the passing of any kapreta. They were all dead. *Very dead.* The werewolf was thorough and had left no survivors.

"He certainly has excellent herding instincts," joked Clarial, rushing toward the fleeing monsters that were hastily funneling through the gate. None stood in opposition any longer and Percival arched his back and howled. Clarial split from Winter, setting off for the stairs leading to the sentinel towers, leaving Winter to continue toward the massive gate.

As the last kapreta poured out of the village, Percival paused and latched his claws to the substantial gate door. With a tremendous heave, the werewolf sealed the giant door behind him on his way out.

Excellent! Winter smiled in triumph as she closed in on the gate's locking mechanism, located just to the right of the doors. She backpedaled a few paces, sweeping the scenery for any stragglers, and turned back satisfied that she and Clarial were all that remained.

Using two hands, she gripped the lever and pulled with all her weight, testing to see just how much strength she would need to exert. *Well, this is not moving at all.* She placed a foot up against the wall and activated every muscle in her shoulders and back, wrenching with every ounce of her being. The mechanism still did not budge an inch. Hands on her hips, she moved back a few paces, tracing the mechanism to its termination along the gate's hinges. Opposite from where she was standing an identical mechanism was still locked in place.

"I'm going to need a second set of hands, I reckon," Winter drawled.

All was quiet, save for the splashing and frothing of the waters beyond the gate. The plan had gone perfectly thus far, and Winter was glad that they had not needed to use the bomb. She backed up and fixed her eyes on Clarial's position at the left guard post, overlooking the lake.

"Hey Clarial!" she shouted. At the same moment her friend was tugging the pin free from the explosive device. "Oh, shit!"

Clarial locked eyes with Winter, and with a shrug, tossed the bomb over her shoulder. Counting down from ten, Winter feverishly climbed the ladder leading to the right tower opposite Clarial. 8, 7, 6...she placed her hands on the flagstone surface and burst forward, leaning over the parapet, 3, 2... She glanced over at Clarial to find her mirroring the pose, staring down expectantly.

And nothing.

Winter raised her palms in bewilderment. "Did you pull the pin thing all the way—" she was unable to finish the question as a resounding blast erupted from below, billowing any loose fabric on her person. A mist of lake water showered the air, muck and mud plastering everything within the detonation's radius. The nearby kapreta were either obliterated or flat on their backs from the sheer force of the concussive blast. A wave shot out from the freshly made crater and headed toward the center of the lake, curling upon itself as it rolled away from the explosion. In its wake, the scorched water fizzed and bubbled as a cauldron over a fire.

Winter was leaning as far as possible over the parapet. "That was..."

"Amazing!" Clarial yelled, watching a handful of fish flop around on the shores.

"I was about to say 'unnecessary,' but 'amazing' will suffice," Winter shouted, dull chimes humming in her ears. "But I need your help down below."

Clarial gave a nod, twirling a finger into her left ear, apparently suffering from the same irritating ailment as Winter.

The mechanism was leaps and bounds easier to move once Clarial had released its mate on the opposite side. The women simultaneously nudged the levers into the locked position, effectively preventing another kapreta invasion for the foreseeable future.

"This should make things much easier for Netty now," said Winter, rubbing her hands together, removing the crumbly rust on her palms.

"Yep," Clarial agreed, matching stride with Winter. "It's astounding what one can accomplish when one travels with a werewolf."

"And bombs."

RETURNING TO THE OLD BRISTLECONE, the women found Breunor wide-awake and upright. The knight's warrior constitution was finally kicking in, and some of the lesser wounds had already receded into scars.

"How was it?" he asked, eyes sparkling with delight. He was clearly referring to the explosion, no doubt the sound had carried all the way to the tree.

Clarial was the first to reply, "Glorious!" she announced, lowering herself down to his level and raising a flask of cool water to his mouth.

"Is my village safe again?" inquired Netty, already guessing the answer.

Winter nodded at the girl, dispelling any lingering doubts in the halflaif's mind. "Right now, we need to see about getting these wounds dressed," she said, pointing in Breunor's direction. "But we'll need to go to your village anyhow, so..."

Netty picked up where Winter trailed off. "I can finally go home."

BREUNOR WAS PIGGYBACKED TO CLARIAL, and she would intermittently render loud complaints that his beard was tickling her neck.

You like it, you little wench. Winter narrowed her eyes at her friend. *Don't pretend you don't.*

Percival was waiting for them in his human form in front of the first home inside the village. He was dripping with clear water from head to foot, all remnants of blood and ichor cleansed from his flesh. "Are you ready to do what you came for?" he asked Netty, a hint of wet fur musk lingering in the air around him.

"Yes," replied Netty.

"Let us, then." Percival looked to Clarial, "I believe you are more than capable of tending this knight's injuries?"

Clarial was already lowering Breunor down under the waterspout in front of the house. "Leave it to me, sir knight."

Winter, Percival, and Netty walked forward into the relatively undamaged village. Save for a few homes that had been burnt into piles of ash and the various skeletons scattered all throughout, the village appeared oddly habitable.

"How will you know which bones belong to your mother?" Winter asked. She had held that question pent up inside her for the duration of the journey, waiting for the appropriate moment to pry. She also wondered why Netty had never mentioned burying her father and brother, but she wagered that they had probably been consumed by kapreta, and chose not to ask.

Shadows passed over their heads as Netty replied, peering up. "She will be easy to spot."

Winter also looked to the sky. *If you say so...* "Your buzzards are right on time, Perc."

"As they are wont," came Percival's unexpected agreement. Winter reeled for a moment at the sound of his voice. Her dumb quips were usually met with solemn silence and cold glares.

An ornate fountain decorated the village's central square, and as Winter admired the detail of the leaping fish around its base, Netty released a gut-wrenching sob. "Mother!" she cried, sprinting toward an empty patch of ground ornamented with hundreds of arrows jutting up from the soil. The multi-colored fletchings were a strangely welcoming accent to the somber affair. Percival and Winter doubled their pace to keep up, but did not match her speed, allowing space for the reunion.

Netty's knees and shins became scraped and bloodied by the arrows she carelessly waded through with complete abandon, but Winter was utterly unprepared for what she saw next. A warrior-sized skeleton, its face turned to Netty as if they were conversing, was pinned to the ground under the sea of arrows. Netty was curled on the ground beside her mother's bones, and her lips moved in whispers between gasps. *She was right,* Winter thought, fighting back the emotions slowly wrapping around her trachea, *Rebekah always was easy to spot.*

THE CEREMONY WAS SILENT AND BRIEF. They buried Sir Rebekah where she had fallen, and Winter promised to fund a proper ornament for the location as soon as she returned to Camelot. For now, a heavy rock was placed in its stead with a claw-inscribed emblem, courtesy of Sir Percival, that read, "Sir Rebekah—Mother before Warrior until the end."

THE SILENCE CONTINUED as they left the village. They had scoured a few of the empty homes for supplies and goods before setting off, and the only words exchanged had been the necessary ones.

"What is that for?" Winter overheard Percival ask Netty as they took the first steps of their journey. The halflaif was fervently stuffing a long scarf into her satchel, one end dragging behind. Emblazoned upon the fabric were small symbols that took Winter a moment to recognize—*Cats.*

"It's for Relic," revealed Netty, burying the final segment of the scarf. "If we bump into him on the way back."

"HOPEFULLY WE'LL STUMBLE UPON TRAVIS, maybe?" said Clarial to no one in particular, breaking the lull. She wore an elegant laif gown that she had procured from one of the abandoned homes, which was not great for travel, but worked to turn Breunor's head once or twice.

"I suppose anything is possible," Winter acknowledged, sifting through her satchel for her pipe.

A sizzling crescendo cut through the air and was followed by a sickening puckering noise. From Winter's periphery she saw Clarial stumble then double over with a gasp. "No! No!" Clarial screamed, placing both hands to her left knee, desperately yanking on the arrow that was buried to the bone. Percival scooped the wounded woman up and ran for cover. Winter did the same with Netty, trailing behind the encumbered knight.

Breunor reached for Clarial. "Look at me! Look at me!" he shouted. "You're going to be fine!"

Percival set her down behind a boulder, but before he could advise her to leave the arrow alone, Clarial reached down and pulled it free with a full-bodied wrench. Unexpectedly, blood did not spray as it should have.

"Oh, my," Clarial whispered, realization bloomed on her face before she even looked at the wound. Winter placed Netty down and hastened to her friend's side, applying pressure to the already hardened wound, covering it from sight.

"You have to be joking...basilisk venom..." murmured Clarial, staring at the arrowhead in disbelief.

Winter could feel Clarial's skin turning to stone, steadily spreading across her flesh. She likely only had mere minutes before she would be overcome.

"Stand!" Clarial sputtered, a look of resolve flashing in her eyes. "Stand me up!" she demanded, placing a hand on Winter's shoulder. Once she was steady on her feet, she placed a hand to Winter's scar. "What sort of pose should I make? I'll be here for all eternity, lady. I may as well leave an impression."

Winter began to weep, her gut feeling as though it had been kicked by a destrier.

"Remember..." began Clarial, stroking Winter's cheek with her thumb, "Remember when that knight shat himself at that weird laif tournament?"

The mournful convulsions became strangled laughs, which proved more painful than the stomach twisting sobs, and Winter finally met her dying friend's eyes. Clarial looked down at Breunor, her flesh creeping to gray just under her clavicle. "Perhaps you can make finding a cure for petrification your new obsession?" she said wistfully, the slightest smirk accenting her face. Breunor tried to reply but was too overcome with grief.

She turned back to Winter. "Now, what sort of pose should I—" she began, but it was too late. The curse flowed past her lips and began overtaking her eyes, which held a look of staunch determination to the very end.

"I love you," Winter said to Clarial's eyes just before the stone swept over them. *You harlot*, she concluded in her mind. The fingers that had been stroking Winter's cheek were hard stone, but she stayed there for a few more moments, lingering in her friend's final touch.

Breunor screamed in rage and tore at the earth while Netty silently cried into Winter's tunic. Percival, however, was too focused on the unknown enemy to display any sort of emotion, and he scanned the area with hard eyes.

"That is a one for one, I believe," chirped a familiar voice. "Judging by the sounds of your marked distress, I'd say your friend has become a rather lovely statue?"

Melfina! Winter removed herself from Clarial's cold fingers, and silently stooped down to retrieve the tainted arrow.

"I see that your dog has finally wrested free from his muzzle, but rest assured a hasty rebuff would be fruitless. He would not be able to catch us, even with a strong wind at his back." Melfina continued to drawl, "but I would say that we are now even. Agreed?" The laif paused to allow the party to reply, and when none came, she continued, "We are going to take our leave now. My brother can rest well knowing that his sister has seen to his vengeance."

~ 24 ~

FAREWELLS AND PROMISES

Even if Breunor had wanted to move, which he did not, his body restricted any such action. Winter suggested that they stay in the village until his wounds healed. There were plenty of vacant estates available, after all, and each had their pick.

Netty wanted to show them her own house, though Winter was pretty sure she already knew which one it was. The little girl confirmed her suspicions, raising a finger at a pretty cottage with a colossus of a tree sprouting from the inside that carried far into the sky...and a front lawn decorated in a field of arrows. When asked if she wanted to stay there, she had simply swished her head back and forth and strode off. Percival gave Winter a look that seemed to say, *"I'm not going in there either,"* and Winter had nodded sagely in agreement.

After spending a week in Knotwithstadt, Winter remembered that she still had more than two months to get back for her induction ceremony. *This journey feels like it's been much longer...*she mused while lying in a child's bed, much too small for her frame. This room had walls that were naturally tapered and completely comprised inside the heartwood of a huge oak. Many of the houses in the village were built around the trees, slowly becoming one unit over time. Winter recalled what Melfina had loftily stated about laif culture, *"Laives do not need to tear down in order to build up,"* or some other nonsense along those lines.

"A pox on her crotch and her children's crotches," Winter spat. She forcefully willed herself back to the present for fear of another wretched bout of uncontrollable sobs. The gagging and sputtering spells were becoming unbearable. And it did not take much for her to break down, she felt as if every fiber of her being was frayed.

Staring at one knot on the ceiling, which oddly resembled the stately profile of Sir Bors, Winter miraculously quelled the storm brewing within her guts.

"Speaking of knights..." said Winter, swinging her feet over the meager bed frame. "Let's see how Sir Breunor is faring this fine day." With a firm tug on her borrowed laif tunic, Winter ducked through the threshold and set off for the village's athenaeum. Now that the knight was back on his feet, he had dedicated his time to the study of all things petrification.

She found the knight where he could usually be found; his nose deep in some scroll or bound book that revealed secrets and mysteries that more often than not had little or nothing to do with reverting people back from stone.

"Is today the day?" asked Winter cheerfully, lifting a delicate roll of vellum and gently blowing the dust from it.

Breunor returned the woman's optimism with salt. "Every day is a day," he huffed, not looking up from the tome he perused, his eyes darting from paragraph to paragraph. The usually fastidious knight's beard had grown unruly and his raiment was stained with an unhealthy mix of fluids. His odor was quite apparent before Winter had even set foot in the solar. After the third day of his obsessive behavior, Winter and Netty had brought a change of clothing for the knight, but she noted despondently that the pile remained untouched.

"Are you aware that 'Tyrants despise laughter'?" Breunor burst out with disdain. "At least that's what this, this, this...ridiculous blathering stooge has to say!" He held the book in the air, bending the spine back, and throttling it in heated frustration. "Useless!" he shouted and pitched the book aside, discarding the swath of knowledge as one would a soiled undergarment.

Winter was glad that Breunor was strong enough to display such fits of rage. He had been a bit touch-and-go right after the fighting pits, and hopefully this meant that he was able to begin the trek home. At the same time, she was rooting for him to find an antidote, and was disappointed each time the collection failed to reveal anything substantial.

"Well," began Winter, intertwining her fingers below her stomach, "when you are ready to set off for home, please let me know." She carefully continued to speak in the same pleasant tone she had presented him with earlier.

"Yes, yes." The unkempt knight dismissed her with a wave and retrieved the next volume on his stack.

Might as well see what Netty and her faithful companion are up to, Winter thought, walking out into the sunlight. She brushed a few cobwebs from her sleeve and took a deep breath, graciously accepting the morning air. This library, like all the others she had ever encountered, was extraordinarily musty. *And boring.*

When Percival was not scouring the forest, he could be found close to Netty. The pairs' waking hours spent together had been relegated to disciplined training and instruction. The tiltyard was still functioning, and Percival ensured that they made use of it while awaiting Breunor's recovery.

"Any sign of Travis?" Winter called to Percival. The knight had a buckler strapped to his wrist and was sustaining a series of blows from his knight-in-training.

Percival lifted a hand, pausing Netty's onslaught for the moment. "No," he stated evenly, as he had each time she had asked about their missing companion.

Winter did not believe him.

She had started out despising the laifhorse, finding him incredibly creepy, but the creature had grown on her over time and she found herself missing him.

Netty looked curiously at Winter, her wooden practice sword resting against her shoulder. "Is there anything else?" she asked, clearly impatient to continue her exercise.

"Do you have any idea when you would like to set off for Camelot?" inquired Winter, mindful of using the word "home."

Netty and Percival exchanged a look and both shrugged. "Tomorrow?" they said in unison.

"Really?" Winter tried to contain her excitement. "Because I think Breunor is well enough for—"

Percival cut her off. "He has been well enough to return, physically...but," the knight paused, tapping the side of his head. "I think the man is struggling *up here* at the moment," he concluded.

"You know him better than I," said Winter.

"Yes," Percival agreed, adjusting the buckler, "and if we do not intervene, he will be in his bubble until he has read every scribble on every parchment, maybe twice or thrice, or until he is satisfied. And that day may never come."

"It's for the best," added Netty, her feet starting to dance.

With a bow, Winter began walking backwards. "I will not delay you any longer..." she twirled a hand at the pair, encouraging the bout to commence.

Percival nodded at Winter and pantomimed dropping a visor over his face, squaring his shoulders at his protégé. He raised the buckler as she brought her blunted blade down in a perfectly executed arc that sent tremors up into his collarbone.

Winter crested the hill overlooking the tiltyard, and from the distance she heard Percival remark, "Well done!" after another resounding thud reached her ears.

THE FOLLOWING MORNING the party departed the village an hour before daybreak. Winter and Netty said their good-byes to the town, promising that they would spread word that it was safe to be inhabited once again. Knotwithstadt would most assuredly have thanked them for their service if it were capable.

Winter had planned a detour toward Clarial to offer her friend one last farewell, but when she made her plans known, the others seemed uninterested.

"I vowed that the next time I see her," disclosed Breunor. "I will have a cure in my hands."

Fair enough, Winter thought, unsurprised by the sullen knight's sentiment. She bid them not to wait on her and promised to catch up. Breaking into a swift jog, she headed for the boulder marking her friend's upright grave. It was not very far from the village at all, and she instantly spotted the massive rock nestled at the center of a shallow dale though it appeared different than what she remembered. *I don't recall going down an embankment,* she mused, *then again, we were fleeing for our lives at the time.*

Another unfamiliar structure greeted her as she drew closer to Clarial. Residing beside her friend's feet was a sizable black lump swelling from the earth, sporting colors and textures that did not match the surrounding flora. When Winter's heel crunched unexpectedly on a dry twig, the lump pitched its head up and hissed. On the end of the long stalk of a neck, ivory fangs and red eyes warned the woman that another step would not be encouraged.

Holding completely still, her boot awkwardly hovering an inch from the ground, Winter held an arm out to balance herself. Slowly and tentatively, she lowered her foot down onto the earth, and continued to stay still, attempting to match Clarial's amount of movement.

The beast relaxed, Winter realized that what she had believed to be horns sprouting from the creature's head were actually ears.

"Travis?!" she sputtered in disbelief. "Where have you been?"

The laifhorse gazed warily at the woman, then flicked his eyes to Clarial's frozen form.

"Ah."

Travis huffed and settled his head back down, demonstrating the pose of a laifhorse in mourning. As Winter approached, she saw that Travis' snout was slick with tears, and the look he gave her seemed to convey rather clearly, *"She was my person."*

"I know," said Winter to the animal.

Stepping forward into Clarial's waiting fingers, reliving their final pose, she spoke again. "We leave for Camelot today, Clarial," she said, fighting back the lump gathering in her throat. "Next you see me, I will have one less hand. I'm not too broken up about it, but I think I should warn you, nonetheless. I don't want you to freak out or anything when you see that I am not the same as you remember me."

Winter placed her hand to Clarial's stone cheek, stroking the cold surface. "And also, I think Breunor is fast upon finding a cure for your current ailment," she revealed, smiling at the statue. "So fingers crossed...I'll cross all of mine for you. And I'll be sure to punch Will Markman square in the jaw for you..." she paused to compose herself, rising on tiptoes to press her forehead to Clarial's. "You just hold tight, Clarial." No longer able to find words, she raised the arrow that had done the damage. *Should you never return to this life again, I want you to know that I will never forget what was done to you. And won't forget who it was that did this.*

Winter swiped at the tears on her cheeks. "Come along, Travis," she said, turning on a heel. But she knew that he would not be following her.

WATCH THE SKIES

*O*ne week, Winter thought as she lounged in her solar, feet propped up and aimed at the roiling hearth. *One more week, then I will be in charge of overseeing a right mess of a constabulary.* The chair across from her, where Clarial had sat on the night she returned, was vacant, but a glass of amber liquor rested before it, untouched.

"One for you," she had murmured as she poured, "and one for me." She missed her friend beyond words. It was odd, Winter considered, when Clarial was away at the killing fields fulfilling her runner's duties, she would often come to mind, but did not *miss* her. Not with this much drowning pain.

Tilting her glass at the empty chair, she then took a sip of her drink, reflecting on the weeks leading up to this calm silence. It all began with the mystery, the brutally murdered church officers and knights, that set her off on this journey that she had no idea would change her and rattle her so much. The liquor burned her throat as it raced downward, but dissolved into a welcome warmth in her core. Her mind jumped to that strange, smelly old man in the prison.

"Hold the girl away from the wraith's gaze. It will feed upon your despair," she whispered. Rudder's phrase suddenly hatched in her mind. She squinted into the flames and uncrossed her feet, placing the left atop the right, alleviating the slight tingle in her toes. *Perhaps there's more value in that old man than he exudes...*she lifted the glass to her lips and threw back the last sample.

The quiet and the calm was usually unsettling to her, but today, right now, it was perfect. She stood and gave Clarial's ghost a nod then set off for another pour.

Netty was asleep in the master chamber. Winter had given Percival a solemn promise to take care of the girl. A return to Knotwithstadt would not be in the cards for the time being, so she would be staying in Winter's quarters within the palace for now, then they would be off for the estate granted by her new station soon. Netty's eyes had brightened when Winter described where they would be living. Just the two of them, and a handful of servants, within a manor set atop a sprawling landscape where she would be able to keep horses and dogs and cats, or whatever her little heart desired. *Maybe if a particular laifhorse ever returns...*

Not now, maybe someday Sir Percival would settle down somewhere, but right now, his lot in life is far from anything resembling tranquility. *He has his list to work through,* and before they parted, Winter told him she would turn a blind eye to his business, but in the future, before laying waste to churchmen, offer a heads up. He had simply nodded in reply. And once his task is complete, he would be returning his neck to the king's leash far west in the killing fields.

On their morose return trip, she had to internalize and squelch a dozen or more dog references, and now some of them were just bubbling up without permission. She had said one aloud to Breunor, a jest about a treaty, emphasizing the "treat" in treaty, but the knight had only smirked from one corner of his mouth and batted a gracious eyelash. He recognized the humor, but his spirit was not in any shape to laugh.

In secret, Winter duplicated a key to the royal library and gave it to Breunor, along with a signed sigil, so he may further his studies. She had almost forgotten to mention this to Kay when she gave him a report of her journey. As long as the acting steward was aware that Breunor was granted discreet access to the library, then the knight would avoid any sort of prosecution.

Sir Kay had advised against spreading word that Knotwithstadt was a safe place. Right now, overseeing a mass migration through the forest would take up more resources than they could afford to spare. Winter understood his rationale and decided to leave it up to him to decide when the right time would be.

After splashing another couple mouthfuls into her glass, Winter decided to check on Netty. Winter's shadow spread across the floor and transcended the raised bed frame, darkening the blankets. Where a small lump in the gratuitously large bed had been was now flat as if no one had ever been nestled there. A moment of panic overtook Winter, but a slight movement behind the window drapes a few steps from the bed cooled the rising anxiety.

"What are you looking at?" Winter asked the shape behind the curtains.

Netty knelt on the cushioned window seat, gazing upward at the night sky poked with millions of shiny pinholes. "I'm not looking *at* anything," she replied, unwavering, "I'm looking *for* someone."

Winter immediately understood. "Looking for Relic, eh?" she asked, parting the curtains so she could join the search.

"Yes," Netty said. Her face was so close to the window that the reply left a small circle of fog on the glass. "Do you think he made it out alive?"

Probably not. "Anything's possible."

"I hope so," Netty scratched at a smudge on one of the panes. "Even though I don't think he liked me very much."

Winter was taken aback by the admission. "Why would you say that?" she asked, a bit dismayed. "He sacrificed himself for you."

"I don't know if it was a personal thing or not," said Netty, shaking her head. "I just don't think he likes children."

"Ah."

"When he babysat me in Breunor's home, the way he looked at me, it seemed like I made his skin crawl."

Without knowing what to say, "Well, you and Relic are magical beings, so maybe there was some sort of interference going on that we don't really understand right now," offered Winter, following a bird as it descended onto a clay shingled rooftop.

"No," Netty said convincingly, "I don't think he likes kids."

"Well, I suppose you would know better than me," Winter took a step back, "I'm going back to the hearth, you're more than welcome to join me."

"I think I will," Netty finally turned to meet Winter's eyes. "It's silly of me to watch the skies anyways. After all, Relic only has one wing."

EPILOGUE

"Hey Netty!" Winter, dressed in her formal sheriff garb, nudged the halflaif in the ribs. "Use your new hearing trick to tell me what that handsome gentleman just said about me."

Netty crinkled her forehead. "How do you know he's talking about you?" she asked, raising her voice above the din in the pub.

"Because he keeps glancing my way, and each time he does there's the glimmer of a smile."

"I don't know if I can—"

"Just try! Please?"

Netty acquiesced with a sigh, placing her elbows on the gnarled tabletop and pressing her palms to her temples, focusing on her target.

"What's he saying?!"

"Shhh!"

Using her teeth, Winter gave the wrap on her right hand an experimental tug, still feeling tender after carrying out her promise to Clarial. She smirked recalling the utter shock on Kay's face when she interrupted whatever dumb conversation they were embroiled in with a knockout punch to that smug asshole Will Markman's jaw. Her left hand, however, was noticeably absent, as was customary for those salaried by public funds.

"Uh," Netty coughed, "he said..."

"Go on."

"You were right. He was talking about you."

Winter brightened, straightening her spine and projecting a seductive smile toward the handsome stranger.

The halflaif cleared her throat and continued, articulating the phrase carefully, "He said that you are, 'good from afar, but far from good.'"

Winter's posture wilted. *Of course!*

"Sorry," offered Netty, her head retreating into her collar.

"I know I'm not gorgeous, or pretty, or beautiful, or striking, or elegant, or alluring, or exquisite, or gorgeous..."

"You said gorgeous twice," Netty commented quietly.

Winter ignored the girl and continued her list, "...or splendid, or fair, or jaw-dropping, or—"

A male voice interrupted from behind their booth, "Excuse me, miss."

Percival, seated across from Winter and Netty, appeared confused, but not concerned by the stranger. Winter swiveled her head and gave the man a once over. The portly man seemed familiar, but she was unable to place him.

"I don't know if you remember me," he began, focusing a milky eye on her. "But I do believe that I owe you this." As the man extended a down-turned fist toward her, Winter suddenly recalled the drover who had sold her the sheep when they had first set out for Breunor's hovel.

"Twiggy returned so fast, I thought that maybe you did not even leave the city."

Thirteen rather moist gold coins trickled into her hand.

"Thank you ever so much," said Winter between clenched teeth.

The drover nodded at her and at each of her companions in turn before he rocked on his heels and shuffled away.

Percival abruptly straightened up, his spine flush to the backrest. "I will return," he stated, cocking his head to the side. He removed himself from the booth without disturbing the table, and set off for the back door.

* * *

"WHERE HAVE YOU BEEN, BROTHER?" a hooded knight inquired, slivers of torchlight reflecting off the armour under his mantle.

"It is none of your concern," replied Percival.

"I see," the knight removed his hood and smiled, eyeing the gathering clouds. "Well, the list has been dwindling in your absence, and now we have only four names to check off." Knowing his brother was not likely to respond, Lamorak continued, "Would you like to split the remaining four?"

"Sounds agreeable."

"Good. Glad to see that you'll be pulling your weight again," said Lamorak, "I'll be making for the Bloody

Fork..." he trailed off, looking back at Percival as he strode away. "Looks like rain."

ACKNOWLEDGMENTS

Thank you for picking this up and reading it.
Means the world to me.

Thanks to Ryan Krebs, Tom Kent, and Scott Telle for
their wise words and sage advice.
This book wouldn't be what it is without you.

To Jonathan Myers and Nicholas Burrell
for the hours spent working with me in the DMaD
Universe.

Thank you to my family and friends for their tireless
encouragement. A wink and a nod to Anne Hooper for
buying nearly a dozen copies of Beyond the Spire for
Christmas distribution purposes.

Gratitude to my wife. My love for you will never fade.

And Mikey, I dedicated this book to you because it reminded me of those many afternoons spent playing with
our action figures, concocting tales and waging quests.
This story garnered much of its inspiration from those
days long gone. I often wonder, when we sat down to
play our last game together, all those years ago, did we
know it would be the last? I love you little brother.

ABOUT THE AUTHOR

M. Warren Askins resides in the
Northeastern United States with his family.

Scan the following code to
check out his list of current works.

www.ingramcontent.com/pod-product-compliance
Lightning Source LLC
Chambersburg PA
CBHW011550190726
48287CB00010B/2826